Jackaby

WILLIAM RITTER

ALGONQUIN 2014

For Jack, who makes me want to create impossible things,
and for Kat, who convinces me I can and insists that I do.

Published by
Algonquin Young Readers
an imprint of Algonquin Books of Chapel Hill
Post Office Box 2225
Chapel Hill, North Carolina 27515-2225

a division of
Workman Publishing
225 Varick Street
New York, New York 10014

Printed in the United States of America.
Published simultaneously in Canada by Thomas Allen & Son Limited.
Design by Joel Tippie.

LIBRARY OF CONGRESS CATALOGING-IN-PUBLICATION DATA
Ritter, William.
  Jackaby / William Ritter.–First edition.
    pages cm
    Summary: Newly arrived in 1892 New England, Abigail Rook becomes
  assistant to R. F. Jackaby, an investigator of the unexplained with the ability
  to see supernatural beings, and she helps him delve into a case of serial
  murder which, Jackaby is convinced, is due to a nonhuman creature.
  ISBN 978-1-61620-353-5 (alk. paper)
  [1. Mystery and detective stories. 2. Serial killers–Fiction. 3. Murder–
  Fiction. 4. Supernatural–Fiction. 5. Imaginary creatures–Fiction.
  6. New England–History–19th century–Fiction.] I. Title.
  PZ7.R516Jac 2014
  [Fic]–dc23   2014014706

10 9 8 7 6 5 4 3 2 1
First Edition

Jackaby

Chapter One

It was late January, and New England wore a fresh coat of snow as I stepped along the gangplank to the shore. The city of New Fiddleham glistened in the fading dusk, lamplight playing across the icy buildings that lined the waterfront, turning their brickwork to twinkling diamonds in the dark. In the inky black of the Atlantic, the reflected glow of the gaslights danced and bobbed. I made my way forward, carrying everything that traveled with me in a single suitcase. The solid ground beneath my feet felt odd after so many weeks at sea, and looming buildings rose up around me on all sides. I would come to know this city well, but in that cold winter of 1892, every glowing window and dark alley was strange, full of untold dangers and enticing mysteries.

It was not an old city—not by the standards of those I had seen along my travels—but it bore itself with all the robust pomp and granite certainty of any European harbor town. I had been to mountain villages in the Ukraine, burgs in Poland and Germany, and estates in my native England, but still I found it hard not to be intimidated by the thrum and pulse of the busy American port. Even as the last of the evening light faded from the sky, the dock was still alive with shadowy figures, hurrying about their business.

A storekeeper was latching the shutters as he closed up shop for the night. Sailors on leave sauntered down the harbor, looking for wild diversions on which to spend their hard-earned money—and women with low necklines looked eager to help them spend it faster. In one man I saw my father, confident and successful, probably strolling home late, once again, having devoted the evening to important work rather than his waiting family.

A young woman across the dock pulled her winter coat tightly around herself and ducked her chin down as the crowd of sailors passed. Her shoulders might have shaken, just a little, but she kept to her path without letting the men's boisterous laughter keep her from her course. In her I saw myself, a fellow lost girl, headstrong and headed anywhere but home.

A chilly breeze swept over the pier, and crept under the worn hem of my dress and through the seams of my thick coat. I had to throw up a hand to hold the old tweed cap on my head before it blew away. It was a boy's fashion—my father called it a newsboy—but I had grown comfortable in it in the past months. For once I found myself wishing I had opted for the redundant underskirts my mother always insisted were so important to a lady's proper dress. The cut of my simple green walking gown was excellent for movement, but the fabric did nothing to hold back the icy chill.

I turned my wooly collar up against the snow and pressed forward. In my pockets jingled a handful of coins left over from my work abroad. They would buy me nothing but sympathy, I knew, and only if I bargained very well. Their foreign faces told a story, though, and I was happy for their tinkling company as I trudged through the crunching powder toward an inn.

A gentleman in a long brown coat with a scarf wound up nearly to his eyebrows held the door for me as I stepped inside. I dusted the fresh flakes from my hair as I hung my hat and coat beside the door, tucking my suitcase beneath them. The place smelled of oak and firewood and beer, and the heat of a healthy fire brought a stinging life to my cheeks. A half-dozen patrons sat scattered about three or four round, plain, wooden tables.

In the far corner stood a box piano, its bench unoccupied. I knew a few melodies by heart, having taken lessons all through grammar school—Mother had insisted that a lady should play an instrument. She would have fainted at the notion that I might someday put her fine culture and training to such vulgar use, especially unescorted in this strange, American tavern. I quickly turned my thoughts away from my mother's overbearing prudence before I might accidentally see reason in it. I put on my most charming smile, instead, and approached the barman. He raised a bushy eyebrow as I neared, which sent a ripple of wrinkles to the dome of his bald head.

"Good afternoon, sir," I said, drawing up to the bar. "My name is Abigail Rook. I'm just off a boat, and I find myself a bit short on cash, at present. I wonder if I could just set up a hat on your piano and play a few—"

The bartender interrupted. "It's out of service. Has been for weeks."

I must have shown my dismay, because he looked sympathetic as I turned to go. "Hold on, then." He poured a frothy pint and slid it across the bar to me with a nod and a kindly wink. "Have a seat for a while, miss, and wait out the snow."

I hid my surprise behind a grateful smile, and took a stool at the bar beside the broken piano. I glanced around at the other patrons, hearing my mother's voice in my head again, warning me that I must look like *that sort of girl,* and worse, that the drunken degenerates who frequented these places would fix their eyes on me like wolves on a lost sheep. The drunken degenerates did not seem to notice me in the least, actually. Most of them looked quite pleasant, if a bit tired after a long day, and two of them were playing a polite game of chess toward the back of the room. Holding the pint of ale still felt strange, as though I ought to be looking nervously over my shoulder for the headmaster to appear. It was not my first drink, but I was unaccustomed to being treated as an adult.

I peered at my own reflection in a frosty window. It had been scarcely a year since I had put the shores of England behind me, but the rugged young woman looking back from the glass was barely recognizable. The salty sea air had stolen some of the softness from my cheeks, and my complexion was tan—at least tan by English standards. My hair was not braided neatly and tied with ribbons, as my mother had always preferred it, but pinned up in a quick, simple bun that might have been a little too matronly if the wind had not shaken loose a few curving wisps to hang free about my collar. The girl who had fled the dormitories was gone, replaced by this unfamiliar woman.

I forced my attention past the reflection to the flurries of white flakes somersaulting in the lamplight beyond. As I nursed the bitter drink, I became gradually aware of a body standing behind me. I turned slowly and nearly spilled the pint.

It was the eyes, I think, that startled me the most, opened wide and staring with intense inquisition. It was the eyes—and the fact that he stood not half a pace from my stool, leaning ever so slightly in, so that our noses nearly bumped as I turned to face him.

His hair was black, or very dark brown, and nearly wild, having only enough civility to point itself in a tousled heap backward, save a few errant strands that danced about his temples. He had hard cheekbones and deep circles under pale, cloud gray eyes. His eyes looked like they could be a hundred lifetimes old, but he bore an otherwise young countenance and had a fervent energy about him.

I pulled back a bit to take him in. He was thin and angular, and his thick brown coat must have been as heavy as he was. It fell past his knees and sagged with the weight of several visibly overstuffed pockets. His lapel was bordered by a long, wooly scarf, which hung almost as long as the coat, and which I recognized as the one I had passed coming in. He must have doubled back to follow me.

"Hello?" I managed to say, when I had regained balance atop my stool. "Can I help–?"

"You're recently from the Ukraine." It was not a question. His voice was calm and even, but something more . . . amused? He continued, his gray eyes dancing as though exploring each thought several seconds before his mouth could voice it. "You've traveled by way of Germany, and then a great distance in a sizable ship . . . made largely of iron, I'd wager."

He cocked his head to one side as he looked at me, only never quite square in the eyes, always just off, as though fascinated by my hairline or shoulders. I had learned how to navigate unwanted attention from boys in school, but this was something else entirely. He managed to seem both engrossed and entirely uninterested in me all at once. It was more than somewhat unsettling, but I found myself as intrigued as I was flustered.

With delayed but dawning comprehension, I gave him a smile and said, "Ah, you're off the *Lady Charlotte* as well, are you? Sorry, did we meet on deck?"

The man looked briefly, genuinely baffled, and found my eyes at last. "Lady who? What are you talking about?"

"The *Lady Charlotte*," I repeated. "The merchant carrier from Bremerhaven. You weren't a passenger?"

"I've never met the lady. She sounds dreadful."

The odd, thin man resumed examining my person, apparently far more impressed by my hair and the seams of my jacket than by my conversation.

"Well, if we didn't sail together, how did you ever–ah, you must have snuck a peek at my luggage labels." I tried to remain casual, but leaned away as the man drew closer still, inspecting me. The oak countertop dug into my back uncomfortably. He smelled faintly of cloves and cinnamon.

"I did nothing of the sort. That would be an impolite invasion of privacy," the man stated flatly as he picked a bit of lint from my sleeve, tasted it, and tucked it somewhere inside his baggy coat.

"I've got it," I announced. "You're a detective, aren't you?" The man's eyes stopped darting and locked with mine again. I knew I was onto him this time. "Yes, you're like whatshisname, aren't you? The one who consults for Scotland Yard in those stories, right? So, what was it? Let me guess, you smelled salt water on my coat, and I've got some peculiar shade of clay caked on my dress, or something like that? What was it?"

The man considered for a moment before responding. "Yes," he said at last. "Something like that."

He smiled weakly, and then whirled on his heels and away, tossing his scarf around and around his head as he made for the exit. He crammed a knit hat over his ears and flung the door open, steeling himself against the whirling frost that rushed in around him. As the door slowly closed, I caught one last glimpse of cloudy gray eyes just between the wooly edges of his scarf and hat.

And then the man was gone.

Following the curious encounter, I asked the barman if he knew anything about the stranger. The man chuckled and rolled his eyes. "I've heard lots of things, and one or two of them might even be true. Just about everyone's got a story about that one. Isn't that right, boys?" A few of the locals laughed, and began to recall fragments of stories I couldn't follow.

"Remember that thing with the cat and the turnips?"

"Or the crazy fire at the mayor's house?"

"My cousin swears by him, but he also swears by sea monsters and mermaids."

For the two older gentlemen on either side of the chessboard, my query sparked to life an apparently forgotten argument, one that burst quickly into an outright quarrel about superstitions and naivete. Before long, each had attracted supporters from the surrounding tables, some insisting the man was a charlatan, others praising him as a godsend. From the midst of the confusing squabble I was at least able to catch the strange man's name. He was Mr. R. F. Jackaby.

Chapter Two

By the following morning I had managed to put Mr. Jackaby out of my thoughts. The bed in my little room had been warm and comfortable, and had cost only an hour's worth of cleaning dishes and sweeping floors– although the innkeeper had made it very clear that this was not to be a lasting arrangement. I threw open the drapes to let the morning light pour in. If I planned to continue my bold adventure without reducing myself to living beneath a bridge and eating from rubbish bins–or worse, writing to my parents for help–I would need a proper job.

I hefted my suitcase to the bed and opened it with a click. The garments within were pressed up to either side, as though embarrassed to be seen with one another. To one end, fine fabrics with delicate, embroidered hems and layers of lace began immediately to expand, stretching in the morning light as the compressed fabric breathed again. Opposite the gentle pastels and impractical frippery sat a few dust-brown denim work trousers and tragically sensible shirts. A handful of undergarments and handkerchiefs meekly navigated the space between, keeping quietly to themselves.

I stared at the luggage and sighed. These were my options. One by one I had worn through everything in between, until I was faced with these choices, which seemed to reflect my lot in life. I could costume myself as a ruddy boy or as a ridiculous cupcake. I plucked a plain camisole and drawers from the center of the suitcase and then pulled the top closed in disgust, stuffing the fancy dresses back down against their muffled protests. The simple green walking dress I had worn for my arrival hung over the bedpost, and I held it up in the sunlight. Its hem was tired, still a bit damp from the previous night's snow, and growing frayed from use. I pulled it on anyway and wound my way back downstairs. I would look for a job first, and new clothes after.

By the light of day, New Fiddleham felt fresh and full of promise. The air was still crisp as I embarked on my trek into town, but the cold was a little less invasive than it had been during the night. I felt the tingle of excitement and hope tickle along my spine as I hefted my suitcase up the cobbled streets. This time, I resolved, I would find conventional employment. My previous and only real prior job experience had come from foolishly following an advertisement with bold, capitalized words like EXCITING OPPORTUNITY, and CHANCE OF A LIFETIME, and, probably most effective in capturing my naive attention, DINOSAURS.

Yes, dinosaurs. My father's work in anthropology and paleontology had instilled in me a thirst for discovery—a thirst he seemed determined I should never quench. Throughout my childhood, the closest I had come to seeing my father's work had been during our trips to the museum. I had been eager to study, excelled in school, and had anticipated higher education with excitement—until I found out that the very same week my classes were to begin, my father would be leaving to head the most important dig of his career. I had begged him to let me go to university, and been giddy when he finally convinced my mother—but now the thought of suffering through dusty textbooks while he was uncovering real history made me restless. I wanted to be in the thick of it, like my father. I pleaded with him to let me come along, but he refused. He told me that the field was no place for a young lady to run around. What I ought to do, he insisted, was finish my schooling and find a good husband with a reliable job.

So, that was that. The week before my semester was to begin, I plucked the EXCITING OPPORTUNITY advertisement from a post, absconded with the money my parents had set aside for tuition, and joined an expedition bound for the Carpathian Mountains. I had been afraid that they wouldn't take a girl. I picked up a few trousers in a second-hand shop—all of them too big for me, but I rolled the cuffs and found a belt. I practiced speaking in a lower voice and stuffed my long, brown hair into my grandfather's old cap—it was just the sort all the newsboys wore, and I was sure it would complete my disguise. The end result was astounding. I had managed to completely transform myself into . . . a silly, obvious girl wearing boys' clothing. As it turned out, the leader of the dig was far too occupied with managing the barely funded and poorly orchestrated affair to care if I was even human, let alone female. He was just happy for a pair of hands willing to work for the daily rations.

The following months could be described as an "exciting opportunity" only if one's definition of excitement included spending months eating the same tasteless meals, sleeping in uncomfortable cots, and shoveling rocky dirt day in and day out on a fruitless search. With no recovered fossils and no more funding, the expedition collapsed, and I was left to find my own way back from the eastern European border.

"Stop your dreaming and settle!" seemed to be the prevailing message of the lesson I'd spent several months and a full term's tuition to learn. It was on the tails of that abysmal failure that I found myself at a German seaport, looking for passage back to England. My German was terrible—nearly nonexistent. I was halfway through negotiating the price of

a bunk on a large merchant carrier called the *Lady Charlotte* when I finally understood that the captain was not sailing to England at all, but would be briefly making port in France before crossing the wide Atlantic bound for America.

Most jarring of all was my realization that the prospect of sailing across the ocean to the States was much less frightening to me than that of returning home. I don't know whether I was more afraid of confronting my parents, having stolen away with the tuition money, or of confronting the end of my adventure, which felt as though it had never really even had a middle.

I purchased three items that afternoon: a postcard, a stamp, and a ticket on the *Lady Charlotte*. My parents most likely received the post about the same time I was watching the shores of Europe drift behind me, and the vast, misty blue ocean expand before me. I was not so naive and hopeful as I had been when my voyage began, but the world was growing larger by the day. The postcard was brief, and read simply:

Dearest Mother and Father,

Hoping you are well. As you had previously cautioned, a professional dig site proved to be no place for a young lady to run around. Currently in seek of a better location to do so.

Regards,

A. Rook

Now that I was here in New Fiddleham, I was not ready to abandon my foray into adventure, but I would compromise by taking a conventional job to sustain it.

My first prospective stop was a general goods store. A bell chimed as I entered, and the shopkeeper, a thin, older woman, looked up from a flat loaded high with flour sacks. "Good morning, dearie! Be right with you!" She heaved one of the heavy bags to a shelf behind her, but it caught the corner of the rack and threw her off balance. The parcel hit the floor and burst in a billowing, white cloud. "Oh bother! Would you wait, just a moment?" she said apologetically.

"Of course. Please—let me help you with those," I said, setting my suitcase beside the door and stepping in. The woman accepted my offer happily, and I began lifting bags to the shelf while she fetched a broom and dustpan.

"I haven't seen you in here before," she observed, sweeping up the mess.

"I only just made port," I confirmed.

"I'd say London, by the accent?"

"A few counties southwest, actually. A little town in Hampshire. Have you been to England?"

The woman had never left the States, but she was happy to hear my tale. We chatted pleasantly, and I made quick work of the heavy bags. When I had stuffed the last one into the shelf, she pushed the empty flat into the next room, disappearing behind racks of dry goods. She was still away when the chime rang and a bushy-bearded man with rosy cheeks stepped in.

"I'll have a tin of Old Bart's, thanks."

I realized I was still behind the counter, and looked around quickly for the shopkeeper. "Oh, I'm not–I don't . . ."

"It's pipe tobacco, darling. It's just behind you, there–the one with the yellow label."

I pulled down a tin with a robust sailor printed on the front and laid it on the counter. "The shopkeeper will be back out in a moment, sir," I said.

"Oh, you're doing just fine." The man smiled and began counting out coins.

The old woman finally reappeared, brushing her hands off on her apron. "Oh, good morning, Mr. Stapleton!" she called, pleasantly. "Tin of Bart's?"

I slipped out from behind the counter and let the woman conduct the transaction. "I like your new girl," said Mr. Stapleton before he left. He gave me another friendly smile as he opened the door. "Don't worry, darling, you'll get the hang of it. Just keep that pretty chin up." And then he was off, the door jingling shut behind him.

"What was that about, then?" asked the shopkeeper.

"Just a misunderstanding."

"Oh, well. I can't thank you enough for the help, young lady," she said, clicking shut the cash register. "Now, what was it you needed?"

"Well, actually–if you have any other work–that is, if you might be hiring . . ."

She gave me a pitying smile. "Sorry, dear. You might try

the post office—they get pretty busy over there—but I've got all the help I need."

I looked briefly to the shelves behind her, sagging slightly under the weight of the merchandise, and wiped a bead of sweat from my forehead. "You're quite sure you couldn't use just a little help?"

She sent me on my way with a wrapped piece of fudge for being such a good girl, which did nothing for my self-confidence as a mature adult. I picked up my suitcase and, following Mr. Stapleton's advice, did my best to keep my pretty chin up as I plodded farther into town.

I met more polite but unavailing storekeepers and office managers as I explored the frosted streets of New Fiddle-ham. It was a remarkable city, though difficult to wrap my head around geographically. It felt as though no two roads ran parallel for more than a few blocks. Each avenue seemed to have been built to accommodate necessity, rather than according to any city-wide orchestration. Gradually I began to recognize the town's loosely defined quarters: a cluster of showy commercial buildings here; a block of practical, nondescript office buildings there; and the industrial district, where the buildings grew into wide factories and sprouted smokestacks. Residential neighborhoods overflowed in the gaps between.

Every street was bursting with character, with broad structures elbowing one another on either side for dominance of the neighborhood. The roads were dotted with street vendors peddling their wares in spite of the snow, kids racing up the sloping hills to slide back down on soap-box sleds, and the press of people marching every which way, their footsteps and carriage wheels beating out the constant pulse of city life.

I had been at my task for hours when I finally found myself in the New Fiddleham post office. In spite of the shop-keeper's suggestion, I found no better luck there. As I turned to go, however, something caught my eye. On a public post-ing board, peppered with lost pets and rooms to let, hung a simple sheet of creased paper with the words –SSISTANT WANTE– just visible between a sketch of a runaway collie and notice of a room to let on Walnut Street.

I carefully freed the advertisement, which read as follows:

INVESTIGATIVE SERVICES

ASSISTANT WANTED

$8 PER WEEK

MUST BE LITERATE AND POSSESS A

KEEN INTELLECT AND OPEN MIND

STRONG STOMACH PREFERRED

INQUIRE AT 926 AUGUR LANE

DO NOT STARE AT THE FROG.

Peculiar though the notice was, I felt I met the require-ments soundly—and eight dollars per week would keep me fed and out of the snow. I got directions from the postman and walked the short mile or so to the address.

The little building was nestled among much taller, wider structures in the business district. On either side, men in stiff suits hurried along the frosty walk. As they passed number 926, they seemed to walk all the more quickly and find things in the opposite direction in which to take a sudden interest, like schoolboys carefully avoiding an embarrassing younger sibling at recess.

From a curled, wrought-iron pole above the door hung a sign that announced: 926—INVESTIGATIVE SERVICES in large letters and PRIVATE DETECTION & CONSULTATIONS: UNEXPLAINED PHENOMENA OUR SPECIALTY in smaller ones.

Three stories tall with, perhaps, room for a small attic, the building was busy with gables and ornate trim. With no apparent consideration for either form or function, the architect seemed to have included columns, arches, and carved festoons wherever space was available in whatever style was handy. Balustrades and cornice windows peeked out from a variety of angles, some of which seemed uncertain to which floor they belonged. Despite all of the mismatched chaos of its design, the building coalesced into something that seemed, somehow, *right*. No two elements of the property belonged together, but taken as a whole, not a thing stood out of place.

The door was brilliant red and humbly adorned with a knocker the size and shape of a horseshoe. I stepped up and rapped three times, then waited. I strained my ears for the telltale sounds of footsteps approaching or a chair shifting in the interior. After several long moments, I tried the handle, and the door swung open.

"Hello?" I called, gingerly stepping in. The entryway opened into what might have been intended as a waiting room of sorts. A wooden bench faced a desk, which was occupied only by stacks of books and loose papers. I set my suitcase to the side and stepped in farther. On the right side of the room, a long bookshelf housed several leather-bound volumes and strange, assorted artifacts including an animal skull, a small stone statue of a fat, nude figure, and a nestlike bundle of sticks and string. At the end of the shelf sat a glass box with dirt, leaves, and a little pool of water inside it.

I leaned down and peered into the glass, looking for an inhabitant. It took several seconds before I recognized the shape of a lumpy, gray-green frog that had been staring back at me all along. It glowered, and its tiny nostrils flared. With a sudden burp it puffed up its throat at me, bulging out a massive double chin. As the chin tightened, a visible stream of gas puffed out from the creature's eyes. I stared. I was not mistaken. A gas, not far different in color from the amphibian's damp skin, vented in quick streams from each eye. Soon the entire terrarium was a cube of drab smoke, and the continued venting could only be inferred by a faint whistle issuing from behind the clouded glass. The stench followed.

A door shut behind me and I whirled around. From an interior room, slipping an arm into his bulky coat as he walked, strode none other than Mr. R. F. Jackaby. He paused and eyed me in confusion as he buttoned up the coat. I, for my part, added nothing to the conversation save the eloquent, "Uh . . ."

His expression suddenly contorted and he broke the silence. "Oh good God! You stared at the frog, didn't you? Well, don't just stand there. Get the window up on your side. It'll be hours before it clears." He rapidly unclasped and drew up a window on the far side of the room. I glanced behind me, spotting another, and repeated the motion. The acrid stink crept from the terrarium and assaulted my nostrils, gradually easing into full force like a boxer warming up before a fight.

"Are you . . . ?" I began, and then tried again. "I'm here about the posting posted in the, er, post office. You . . ."

"Out! Out!" Jackaby snatched his knit hat from a hook beside the door and gestured emphatically. "You can tag along if you like. Just get out!"

We managed to reach the sidewalk before my eyes began to water, and I welcomed the fresh, cold air. I glanced back at the red door and hesitated, wondering if I should dart back in for my luggage. Jackaby pressed on down the lane, tossing his long scarf over one shoulder. After a rapid consideration, I left the case behind to hurry after the enigmatic man.

Chapter Three

I had to jog to catch up to Jackaby. He had nearly rounded the corner as I matched his stride. He moved his lips rapidly, mouthing thoughts he did not bother to share aloud. Wild locks of hair scrambled to free themselves from under his peculiar hat, and I couldn't blame them for plotting their escape.

"Do you work for the . . . er . . . the service?" I asked.

He glanced my way. "Service?"

"The investigative service. You're one of their detectives, aren't you? I knew it—didn't I say so? I said you must be a detective!"

Jackaby smiled. "And so I must." He turned sharply, and I followed at his heels.

"You wouldn't happen to know if they've filled the assistant's position, would you?"

"If they've what, now? Who are 'they'?"

I handed him the posting. Jackaby scowled at it for a moment.

"I think you must be a bit confused," he said. "But don't feel bad—it's a common state. Most people are." He folded up the advert and tucked it into his jacket, rounding another sudden turn. "My name is Jackaby. I am, as you said, a detective. I am not, however *with* the investigative service . . . I *am* the investigative service. Or, I should say, I provide it. That is to say, they are I and I am they. And you are . . . ?"

"Oh—Abigail," I answered. "Abigail Rook."

"Rook," he repeated. "Like the bird or like the chess piece?"

"Both?" I answered. "Neither? Like . . . my father, I suppose." This seemed to either appease or bore Jackaby, who nodded and turned his attention back to the cobbled road and his own thoughts.

We were taking a somewhat winding path for all the hurry Jackaby seemed to be putting into the trip, but we had already traveled several blocks before I spoke again.

"So . . . has it been filled?" I asked. "The position?"

"Yes," my companion replied, and I drooped. "Since the posting of the advertisement, it has been filled . . . five times. It has also been vacated five times. Three young men and one woman chose to leave the job after their introductory cases. The most recent gentleman has proven to be far more resilient and a great deal more helpful. He remains with me in a . . . different capacity."

"What capacity?"

Jackaby's step faltered, and he turned his head away slightly. His mumbled reply was nearly lost to the wind. "He is temporarily waterfowl."

"He's what?"

"It's not important. The position is currently vacant, Abigail Rook, but I'm not certain you're the girl for the job."

I looked at the mismatched detective and digested the turn the conversation had taken. His ridiculous hat fought a color battle with his long scarf. The coat that hung from his lanky frame looked expensive, but it was worn, its pockets overstuffed and straining. Their contents jingled faintly as he walked. It was one thing to be turned away by a stuffy suit in an ascot and top hat, but this was another matter entirely.

"Are you just pulling my leg?" I demanded.

Jackaby gave me a blank look. "I clearly have not touched your leg, Miss Rook."

"I meant, are you serious? You're really an investigator of—what did your sign say—'inexplicable phenomena'? That's really your building back there?"

"Unexplained," corrected Jackaby. "But yes."

"What exactly is an 'unexplained phenomenon,' then?"

"I notice things . . . things that other people don't."

"Like that business back at the inn? You never did tell me how you knew so much about me at a glance."

"Back where? Young lady, have we met?"

"Have we—is that a joke? Back at the inn? You somehow knew all about where I'd been traveling . . ."

"Ah—that was you. Right. Precisely. As I said . . . I notice things."

"Clearly," I said. "I am very keen to learn what you noticed about me, sir—as it obviously wasn't my face—and you'll find I can be very persistent when I've set myself to something. That is just one of the qualities that would make me an excellent assistant." It was a reach, I knew, but if I was to be given yet another brush-off, I would at least take my explanation along with it. I straightened up and kept stride, keeping shoulder to shoulder with the man—although, truthfully, my shoulder came up barely past his elbow.

Jackaby sighed and drew to a stop as we reached the corner of another cobbled street. He turned and looked at me with pursed lips.

"Let's see," he said at last. "I observed you were recently from the Ukraine. This was a simple deduction. A young domovyk, the Ukrainian breed of the slavic house spirit, has had time to nestle in the folds along the brim of your hat."

"A what?"

"Domovyk. Were the fur a bit longer, it could easily be

confused for a Russian domovoi. It seems quite well established, probably burrowed in more deeply as you boarded the ship. Ah, right, which brings us to Germany.

"More recently, you seem to have picked up a young Klabautermann, a kind of German kobold. By nature, kobolds are attracted to minerals, and take on the color of their preferred substance—yours has a nice iron gray coat. Fondness for iron is rare among fairies and their ilk. Most fairy creatures can't touch the stuff. That's probably why your poor domovyk nestled in so deep. Klabautermann are among the most helpful of their breed. See, he's made some repairs to the hem of your coat, there—probably his little way of thanking you for the ride. These charming fellows are known for helping sailors and fishermen. Henry Wadsworth Longfellow wrote about a cheeky little one who . . ."

I interrupted, "You mean to say I've got two imaginary beasties living in my clothes, even though I haven't ever seen them?"

"Oh, hardly imaginary—and I should think it's a good thing you *didn't* see that little chap!" The man allowed a throaty laugh to escape. "Goodness, it's a terrible omen for anyone blessed by a kobold's presence on a ship to actually lay eyes on the creature. You'd likely have sunk the whole vessel."

"But you see them?" I asked. "You saw them right away at the pub, didn't you?"

"Not right away, no. As you hung your coat, I did spot

the droppings on your lapel, which naturally I thought might . . ."

"Droppings?"

"Yes, just there. On your lapel."

I glanced down, brushing a few stray bits of lint from my otherwise spotless lapel, and then straightened, feeling foolish. "People pay you to tell them this sort of thing?"

"Where it is pertinent to the resolution of their problems, yes," replied Jackaby, resuming his brusque walk. "Some of my clients are most grateful, indeed. My property on Augur Lane was a gift from Mayor Spade. He was particularly happy to be rid of a nest of brownies who had settled in a corner of his estate—caused no end of trouble, those little ruffians. At least the mayor's eyebrows seem to have grown back faster than his wife's rosebushes."

"Your clients pay you in real estate?" I gawped.

"Of course not," scoffed Jackaby. "That was a . . . special circumstance. Most pay in banknotes, some in coin. It's not uncommon for some to pay with bits of gold or silver they happen to have on hand. I've more tea services and candlesticks than I can count. I much prefer the banknotes."

"But, then . . . why do you wear such dreadfully poor garments?" The tactless question slipped out before I could catch myself. My mother would have been appalled.

"Poor garments?" Jackaby scowled. "My dear woman, my wardrobe comprises priceless fineries."

I tried to determine if the man was speaking in earnest

or simply having me on. "Please don't take this the wrong way, sir—but that hat is a priceless finery?" I asked hesitantly.

"Silk is more precious than cotton because of the nature of its acquisition, is it not? Fine threads are collected from tiny silkworms over countless hours, whereas cotton can be pulled off nearly any farm in the States, and it ships by the boatload. My hat, Miss Rook, is made from the wool from one of the only surviving yeti of the Swiss Alps, dyed in ink mixed by Baba Yaga herself, and knit by my very good friend Agatha as a birthday present. Agatha is a novice knitter, but she put quite a lot of care into this hat. Also, she is a wood nymph. Not a lot of nymphs take to knitting. So, tell me if my hat is not more precious than the finest silk."

He was speaking in earnest. "Oh yes. I see." I nodded in what I hoped was a convincing manner. "Sorry. It's just—at first glance it doesn't look quite as impressive as all that."

Jackaby made a noise, which might have been a huff and might have been a laugh. "I have ceased concerning myself with how things look to others, Abigail Rook. I suggest you do the same. In my experience, others are generally wrong."

My eyes were on my companion as we rounded the corner, and I had to catch myself midstep to avoid barreling into a policeman. Half a dozen uniformed officers kept a crude perimeter around the entrance to a broad, brick apartment building, holding back a growing crowd of curious pedestrians.

"Ah," said Jackaby with a smile. "We've arrived."

Chapter Four

A tall, barrel-chested policeman looked down his hawk nose at us, and it became apparent that my companion held no more sway here than I did. Jackaby reacted to the obstruction with mesmerizing confidence. The detective strode purposefully up to the officers. "Eyes up, gentlemen, backs straight. Crowd's getting a bit close, I think. Let's take it out another five feet. That's it."

The officers on the far end with no real view of Jackaby responded to the authoritative voice by shuffling forward, pressing a small crowd of onlookers back a few paces. The nearer officers followed suit with uncertainty, eyes bouncing between their colleagues and the newcomer in his absurd winter hat.

Jackaby stepped between the nearest uniforms. "When

Chief Inspector Marlowe arrives, tell him he's late. Damned unprofessional."

A young officer with a uniform that looked as though it had once belonged to a much larger man stepped forward timidly. "But Marlowe's been inside nearly half an hour, sir."

"Well, then . . . tell him he's early," countered Jackaby, "even worse."

The hawk-nosed policeman with whom I had nearly collided turned as Jackaby made for the doorway. His uncertain gaze became one of annoyance, and, taking a step toward Jackaby, he slid one hand to rest on the pommel of his shiny black nightstick. "Hold it right there," he called. I found myself stepping forward as well.

"I beg your pardon, sir . . ." I should like to say that I mustered every bit as much confidence as the detective, using my sharp wit and clever banter to talk my way past the barricade. The truth is less impressive. The officer glanced back and I opened my mouth to speak, but the words I so desperately needed failed me. For a few rapid heartbeats I stood in silence, and then, against every sensible impulse in my body, I swooned.

I had seen a lady faint once before, at a fancy dinner party, and I tried to replicate her motions. I rolled my eyes upward and put the back of my hand delicately to my forehead, swaying. The lady at the party had sensibly executed her swoon at the foot of a plush divan. Out on the cobbled streets, my chances of a soft landing were slim. As I let my knees go limp, I threw myself directly into the arms of the brutish policeman, instead, sacrificing my last lingering scraps of dignity.

I gave myself a few seconds, and then blinked up at the officer. Judging by his expression, I don't know which of us felt more awkward. Anger and suspicion were clearly more natural expressions for him than care and concern, but to his credit, he looked like he was trying.

"Um. You all right, miss?"

I stood, holding his arm and making a show of catching my breath. "Oh goodness me! It must be all this fresh air and walking about. It's just been so much exertion. You know how we ladies can be." I hated myself a little bit, but I committed. A few other officers crowding around us nodded in confirmation, and I hated them, too. "Thank you so much, sir."

"Shouldn't you . . . um . . . sit down, or something?" the policeman asked.

"Oh, absolutely. I'll step inside at once, Officer. Yes, sir. I wouldn't want to stray too far from my escort, anyway. He does worry when I wander off. You're absolutely right, of course. Thank you, again."

The big brute nodded, looking a little less out of sorts now that he was being agreed with. I smiled graciously at the circle of uniforms and swept into the building before they had time to reassess the whole affair.

Jackaby regarded me with a raised eyebrow as I closed the door behind me. We found ourselves in a small but well-lit lobby. A wall of miniature, bronze-edged mailboxes stood to our left and a large stairwell, flanked by two fat columns, to our right. Ahead was a door marked EMERALD ARCH APTS: MANAGER with a window looking in on the front desk. Within the little office, another policeman was taking statements from a chap in a doorman's uniform. Neither paid us any attention.

"That ridiculous little performance of yours should not have worked," Jackaby said.

"You don't have to tell me that." I glanced back at the door. "I'm actually a little offended that it did."

He chuckled. "So, why did you do it? Surely there are employment opportunities that do not necessitate the brazen deception of armed officials."

I faltered a moment before I defended myself. "Not so terribly brazen," I said weakly. "I find most men are already more than happy to believe a young woman is a frail little thing. So, technically the deception was already there, I just employed it in a convenient way."

He surveyed me through narrowed eyes and then grinned. "You may just be cut out for the job after all, Miss Rook. We'll see. Stick close."

"Where are we going?" I asked.

"About to find out." He ducked his head into the manager's office. His voice and another responding one came to me in mumbles, and then he popped back out and gestured at the stairs. "Room 301. Shall we?"

Our steps echoed up the stairwell as we started up the first flight.

"So, that policeman just told you where to go?" I asked.

"Yes, very helpful gentleman," said Jackaby.

"Then, you really are working with the police."

"No, no, not on this case . . . not as of yet. I simply asked and he told me." Jackaby swung around the banister as he rounded the curve up to the next flight of stairs.

I thought for a moment. "Is it some kind of magic?" I felt stupid asking.

"Of course not." Jackaby scoffed at the idea. He paused to examine the banister, and then resumed his trek upward.

"No? Then you didn't, I don't know, cast some kind of spell on him or something?"

The man stopped and turned to me. "What on earth makes you think that?" he asked.

"Well, we seem to be sneaking into a crime scene, but you're not worried about rousing police suspicion, and all your talk about . . . you know."

"What has that policeman got to be suspicious about? There are half a dozen armed watchmen outside ensuring that only authorized personnel are allowed in. Not unlike your little feigned faint, I merely allowed his assumption to work for me. A far cry from magic spells, Miss Rook, honestly."

"Well, it's hard to know what to expect from you. I don't exactly believe in all this . . . this . . . this occult business. I don't believe in house spirits, or goblins, or Santa Claus!"

"Well of course not, that's silliness. Not the spirits or goblins, of course, they're quite real, but the Santa nonsense."

"That's just it! How can you call anything nonsense when you believe in fairy tales?"

"Miss Rook, I am not an occultist." Jackaby turned on the landing and faced me. "I am a man of reason and science. I believe what I can see or prove, and what I can see is often difficult for others to grasp. I have a gift that is, as far as I have found, unique to me. It allows me to see truth where others see the illusion—and there are many illusions, so many masks and facades. All the world's a stage, as they say, and I seem to have the only seat in the house with a view behind the curtain.

"I do not believe, for example, that pixies enjoy honey and milk because some old superstition says they do . . . I believe it because when I leave a dish out for them a few times a week, they stop by and drink. They're fascinating creatures, by the way. Lovely wings: cobweb thin and iridescent in moonlight."

He spoke with such earnest conviction, it was difficult to dismiss even his oddest claims. "If you have a . . . ," I spoke carefully, "a special sight, then what is it that you see here? What are we after?"

Dark shadows clouded Jackaby's brow. "I'm never sure

what others see for themselves. Tell me what you observe, first, and I'll amend. Use all your senses."

I looked around the stairwell. "We're on the second-floor landing. The stairs are wooden and aging, but they look sturdy. There are oil lamps hanging along the walls, but they're not lit—the light is coming from those greasy windows running up the outer wall. Let's see . . . There are particles of dust dancing in the sunbeams, and the air is crisp and nipping at my ears. It tastes of old wood and something else." I sniffed and tried to describe a scent I hadn't noticed before. "It's sort of . . . metallic."

Jackaby nodded. "Interesting," he said. "I like the way you said all that. The dust-dancing business, very poetic."

"Well?" I prompted. "What do you see?"

He frowned and slowly continued to the third floor. As we entered the hallway, he reached his hand down and felt the air, as if reaching over a rowboat to trace ripples in the wake. His expression was somber and his brow furrowed. "It gets thicker as we near. It's dark and bleeding outward, like a drop of ink in water, spreading out and fading in curls and wisps."

"What is it?" My question came as a whisper, my eyes straining to see the invisible.

Jackaby's voice was softer still: "Death."

Chapter Five

The hallway was long and narrow, concluding with a wide window at the far end. It was lit by oil lamps, which cast a sepia glow over the scene. A single uniformed policeman waited outside the apartment immediately ahead. He stood leaning against the frame of the open door, peering back into the room he guarded. A plaque above him declared it apartment 301. The smell, like copper and rot, grew more powerful as we advanced. Jackaby walked ahead of me, and I noticed his step falter slightly. He paused, cocking his head to one side as he looked at the policeman.

At the sound of the stairway door closing, the officer snapped to attention, then relaxed his stance a bit as he made eye contact. He watched our approach, but made no move to engage us. He was clean-cut, his uniform crisp and neatly ironed. His collar was starched, and his badge and buttons shone. His shoes, which looked more like the sharp-toed wingtips of a dress uniform than the sturdy boots of an average beat cop, were buffed so brightly they might have looked more at home on a brass statue than a living body.

"Good day, Officer," said Jackaby. "Marlowe is waiting for us inside. Don't want to keep him."

"No, he isn't," said the man, simply. His face was expressionless, studying Jackaby. By the light of the lamps I made him out to be just a year or two older than I. Curls of jet-black hair peeked out from beneath the brim of his uniform cap. He turned to acknowledge me with a polite nod, and his rich brown eyes paused on mine. He smiled shyly, turning his attention quickly back to the detective. My face felt suddenly warm, and I was grateful that he had looked away again.

"Ah, yes," responded Jackaby, not losing pace, "but he'll be wanting to see us in there, nonetheless. Bit of a surprise. He'll be thrilled."

"I doubt that very much," said the policeman. His accent was difficult to place—Americanized but faintly eastern European. "I know you," he said.

Jackaby's eyebrows rose. "Oh?"

"Yes, you're the detective. You solve the"—he sought for a word—"*special* crimes. Inspector Marlowe doesn't like you."

"We have a complicated relationship, the inspector and I. What's your name, then, lad?"

"Charlie Cane, sir. You can call me Charlie. The chief inspector is down the hall right now, talking to witnesses." He stepped aside, opening the doorway for Jackaby. "I know all about you. You help people. Helped a friend of mine, a baker down on Market Street. No one else would help him. No one else would believe him. He had no money, but you helped anyway."

"Anton? Good baker. Still saves me a baguette every Saturday."

"Be quick, Mr. Jackaby." Charlie glanced up and down the hallway as the detective slid into the room behind him. "And you, Miss–?"

"Rook," I answered in my most professional tone, hoping I did not sound as flustered as I felt. "Abigail Rook."

"Well, Miss Rook, will you be examining the room, also?"

"I–of course. Yes, I am Mr. Jackaby's assistant. I will be, you know, assisting."

Jackaby shot me a momentary glance from within the room, but he did not correct me. I slipped inside and was immediately overwhelmed by the coppery stench. The apartment had only two rooms. The first was a living area, populated by a small sofa, a writing desk, a bare oak table, and a simple wooden cupboard. Not many decorations adorned the area, but there was a dull oil painting of a sailboat on one wall, and a small framed portrait of a blond woman propped up on the desk.

The door to the next room hung open, revealing the grisly source of the smell. A small halo of dark crimson stained the ground beneath the body. The dead man wore a simple vest and starched shirt, both of which were dyed vivid red at the chest and tattered so thoroughly, it became impossible to discern where clothing ended and flesh began. I felt light-headed in earnest this time, but drew on all my practiced stubbornness not to succumb to a genuine faint. I forced my eyes away from the bloody scene, following the detective instead as he hastened around the first chamber.

Jackaby gave the spartan living room a cursory examination. Wrapping a finger in the end of his scarf, he opened and shut the cupboard, then peeked beneath the table. He lingered briefly by the writing desk, pulling out the chair and returning it. Beside the desk sat another chair, which Jackaby examined more closely, leaning in and delicately brushing a finger along the grain of the wood. Rummaging in his crowded pockets, he removed a blue-tinted vial and held it up, staring at the chair through the glass.

"Hmm." He straightened and quickstepped to the macabre scene in the bedroom. The vial disappeared back into the coat. I followed, breathing through the fabric of my sleeve—which helped only a little. Jackaby took a rapid tour of this room as well, checking in the closet and under the pillow before bringing his attention to the corpse. I tried to survey the room—to take a careful and deliberate mental inventory of the dead man's belongings—but my memory of that space remains a faded blur. Almost against my will, my eyes fixed themselves on the horrific sight of that poor body, instead, the picture burning itself into my mind.

"Tell me, Miss Rook," Jackaby said as he knelt to examine the victim, "what did you notice in that last room?"

I dragged my gaze from the slain body and back to the doorway as I tried to remember anything unusual. "He lives simply . . . *lived* simply," I corrected myself awkwardly. My mind peeled very slowly away from the corpse and began to find focus as I considered my surroundings. "I would guess he lived alone. It looks like he had a girl, though—there's a picture of one in a nice frame over there. Not much food in the cupboards, but a lot of papers on the desk, along with a very modern typewriter, several pens, and at least one spare inkwell. By the letterhead on his stationery, I take it his name was Arthur Bragg. The wastebasket is full of crumpled papers. I wouldn't be surprised if he was a writer."

"Huh." Jackaby glanced back at the door. "Wastebasket?"

I tried to read his expression without looking back at the body. What sort of detective didn't look in the bin? The men in my adventure magazines were always finding important clues in the bin. "Yes. Back there, just beside the desk."

Jackaby went back to looking at the body. He lifted a corner of the rug and peered beneath it. "What about the chairs?"

I thought a moment. "The chairs? Oh, of course—there are two at the writing desk. One where you would expect, but the other—he must have had company!" I looked out again. "Yes, I can see where it's been taken from its place at the table. Someone was sitting opposite him at his writing desk. That's why you were so interested in it. Is it strange they didn't sit around the table, instead? What do you think it means?"

"Haven't a clue," answered Jackaby.

"Well, have I got all the important bits? Did you notice something I missed?"

"Of course I did," said Jackaby, with such a matter-of-fact tone as to almost obscure the arrogance of the statement. "You entirely ignored the clear fact that his guest was not human. I suppose that could, in other circumstances, be inconsequential—but given the state of the man now, it seems rather pertinent."

I blinked. "Not human?"

"Not at all. Remnants of a distinctly magical aura are all over the chair, and even stronger on the body. Hard to tell what sort of being was here, but old, I can tell. Downright ancient. Don't feel bad, no way you could have seen that. Now then, what do you notice about the body?"

I paused. "Well, he's dead," I said, not wanting to look again.

"Good, and . . . ?"

"He's clearly lost a lot of blood, having been"—I swallowed hard, keeping my eyes on Jackaby—"torn open, like that."

"Precisely!" Jackaby grinned at me over the body. "An astute observation."

"Astute?" I asked. "With all due respect, sir, it's impossible to ignore. The poor man's a mess!"

"Ah, but it's not the wound that's strange, now is it?"

"It isn't strange? I suppose you see people with their chests ripped open every day?"

"What the . . . *detective* is saying," came a new voice from the doorway, hesitating on the word "detective," as if bestowing the title with great reluctance, "is that the blood that isn't here is more of a mystery than the blood that is."

I turned. A uniformed policeman with two silver bars on his sleeve stepped into the room, looking down sternly at Jackaby. Heavy iron handcuffs hung from his belt and clinked against his leg in a measured rhythm until he drew to a halt just a few paces from the body. He was clean-shaven, with a hard jawline.

Jackaby did not look up. He fished about in his pockets and continued examining the body through various vials and tinted lenses as he spoke. "Right you are, Chief Inspector," Jackaby said. "This carpet alone should be entirely saturated, and yet it's hardly stained except immediately about the torso. It looks as though the wound's been daubed. Just here, and all the way across, like someone's taken a towel to mop it up." He packed an oblong jade disk back into a pocket and got to his feet. Speaking more to himself, he added, "Only, why bother cleaning up the body at all if you plan on leaving the scene like this?"

"Thank you ever so much," said Chief Inspector Marlowe, "for providing me with deductions I had reached an hour before you trespassed onto my crime scene. And now, Mr. Jackaby, any reason I shouldn't have you in a cell for the remainder of this investigation?"

"What, just for paying you a friendly visit at work?"

"For that, and also for obstruction, trespassing . . . hell—I'm sure that god-awful hat of yours is worth a couple of charges all by itself. You still haven't thrown that rag away?"

"Obstruction? Is that what you call freely offering my invaluable insights?"

"There's not a lot of value in insights I can provide for myself."

"Wait, there's more than that," I piped up, instantly wishing I had stayed silently in the corner. "Er, he noticed something else . . ."

The chief inspector interrupted. "No, no, let me guess: the culprit is . . ." He paused for mock dramatic effect. "Not human?"

"As a matter of fact," answered Jackaby.

"Just like the thieves in the Winston Street Bank case?"

"They most certainly weren't human," Jackaby answered. "Welsh pixies, a small clan."

"And the bar fight at Mickey's Tavern?"

"Well, not the scrawny fellow, obviously, but I maintain that big bloke was a troll. Half blood at least."

"And the 'Grocery Ghost' who kept rearranging produce after hours?"

"Okay, I have already admitted I was wrong on that one. As we saw, that was Miss Maudie from Hampton Street, but you have to admit, the old girl is very strange."

Marlowe breathed in deeply and sighed, shaking his head, then turned his attention to me. "And you are?"

I gave the inspector my name and started to explain about my arrival and the job posting. He cut me off again.

"Another one?" He directed the question at Jackaby, then turned back to me. "A little advice, young lady. Get out before he drags you too far into his craziness. This business is not for the female temperament. Now both of you, I want you off this crime scene and out of my way. This isn't some two-bit bar fight–this is murder. Out!" He turned and called into the hallway, "Detective Cane, between this idiot and Mr. Henderson, I've had quite enough lunacy for one afternoon. Please show the man and his young lady off the premises."

Marlowe stepped aside, and Charlie Cane appeared, looking uncomfortable and fiddling nervously with the polished buttons on his uniform.

"Nice chat as always, Marlowe," said Jackaby pleasantly as he passed. Marlowe grunted. I followed my new employer into the hallway and the chief inspector slammed the door behind us.

"Well, he's cheerful today," Jackaby quipped.

"Oh, Marlowe is an exceptional chief inspector," Charlie replied.

"I'm sure he is," I said, "Detective Cane, isn't it?"

His gaze dropped, and he looked sheepishly aside. "It's Junior Detective, to be totally accurate, miss," he said. He met my glance again with a smile before he went on. "It really is an honor to work with Chief Inspector Marlowe. He's just a bit edgier than usual today. The new commissioner is supervising this case very closely. He makes Marlowe tense."

"Who's Henderson?" asked Jackaby.

"Who?" said Charlie.

"Henderson. Marlowe mentioned him. Something about lunatics."

"Oh, that would be William Henderson—room 313. He is . . . odd. We thought he might have some useful information, because he says he heard wailing early this morning, like someone crying very hard. Only, when the inspector asks him how long the cries persisted, Mr. Henderson looks at him funny and says they haven't stopped. He tells us all to listen, and says they're clear as anything, can't we hear them? Now, we all listen—and I have very good ears.

There is no sound. Henderson insists it's as loud as though someone were weeping in that very room, and shouldn't we do something about it? He begins to get agitated, so the inspector excuses himself, assuring the man we would look into it. Very odd."

"Interesting." Jackaby started on down the hallway, glancing at room numbers as he passed. I hurried after him.

"Wait," said Charlie, following. "I told the inspector I would take you out of the building."

"And so you shall," Jackaby called over his shoulder. "Expertly, I imagine, and to the letter of the instruction. However, I don't recall Marlowe giving any specific directions about time, nor about the route we take, so let's have a quick chat with someone odd, first, shall we? I do love odd. Ah, here we are!"

Jackaby rapped firmly on the door to room 313. After a pause, it flung itself open, and we faced a poorly shaven man with bushy, muttonchop sideburns, tired, sunken eyes, and a pair of bright red pajamas. Around his head a leather belt had been strapped, holding two decorative throw pillows tightly to his ears. Little fabric tassels on one of them swayed to a stop as he stared at us from beneath a furrowed brow.

"Well?" the man said.

Jackaby smiled and extended a hand in greeting. "Mr. Henderson, I presume?"

Chapter Six

Mr. Henderson stepped back to let us into his flat, which was a nearly perfect match for the victim's, except that this one had a worn sofa in place of the writing desk, and a mix of colorful fruit had been arranged in a bowl on the table. Mr. Henderson made no motion to remove the cushions from his ears, and instead shouted his disapproval at the police department for not having put a stop to the noise. He slumped onto the couch and scowled.

"We are not with the police department," said Jackaby. He pulled out a thin leather satchel and laid it on the table.

"Well," said Charlie, "I am."

"We are not with the police department, except for those of us who are," Jackaby revised. "Mr. Henderson, could you describe the cries you're hearing, please?" He untied the leather lace around his satchel and rolled it out on the table with a light clinking. From over his shoulder I could see that it contained three slim pockets, which housed metallic instruments of some sort.

"How can you not hear it?" the man demanded, still yelling. "Is it . . . Is there something wrong with me?"

"Just describe the sound, please," repeated Jackaby.

"It's so . . . so . . . so . . ." The man's voice wavered and softened with each "so," and his eyes fell downward. "So sad."

"Remove the cushions, if you would, Mr. Henderson," said Jackaby. He had selected a small metal rod that forked into two long prongs.

Henderson glanced back up. His eyes had welled slightly with tears, and his brow, no longer knit in aggravation, melted into a pitiful, pleading look.

"Mr. Henderson," repeated Jackaby, "the cushions, please."

Henderson slowly raised his hands and pulled the belt off his head. The cushions fell away. His eyes immediately slammed shut and his whole body flinched, tensing into itself as a silent wail apparently assaulted his ears.

"Where are the cries coming from?" asked Jackaby firmly. "Can you tell what direction?"

Tears dripped from Henderson's clenched eyes, and he shook his head, whether to answer "no" or to shake away the sound, I couldn't say.

Jackaby held the rod loosely and tapped the metal prongs against the table. A clear, pure, sustained note rang out. It was a simple tuning fork. Henderson's body instantly relaxed, and he nearly collapsed onto the sofa. He sniffled, and gazed up, wide-eyed. The note hummed pleasantly for several seconds, growing quieter and quieter. Before it could fully fade away, Jackaby tapped it again.

"And now?" Jackaby inquired.

"I–I can still hear it," stammered Henderson, his voice a mix of relief and confusion. "But more distant. Still so sad, the wailing. It sounds like . . ." He sniffed and cut himself off.

"Like what?" prompted Jackaby, gentle but relentless.

"Reminds me," the man continued with difficulty, "of the way my mother cried at Papa's funeral. Just . . . just like that."

Jackaby tapped the tuning fork again. "It's a woman's voice, then?" Henderson nodded. "And now, can you judge where it's coming from?"

Henderson concentrated, and his eyes drifted to the ceiling. "From above us," he decided.

"Directly?" Jackaby asked. "The apartment above yours, perhaps?"

Henderson focused again, and Jackaby tapped the tuning fork to help. "No," he answered, "just a bit . . . that way, I think."

"Excellent. We shall attend to the matter directly. While I

have you lucid, however, I would appreciate it if you could think back to yesterday evening. Did you happen to notice anything odd? Strangers in the stairwell, perhaps?"

Henderson breathed heavily and scratched his hair where it was still pressed flat from the cushions. "I don't think so. Nothing very odd. Her voice . . ."

"Anything before the voice? Anything at all?"

The man thought again, his head rocking back and forth. "I don't think so. Someone upstairs was playing the fiddle earlier. I hear them a lot, late in the afternoon. Not bad. Someone was at the hall window during the night, too. Probably that Greek from across the hall. He goes out to smoke cigars on the balcony–thinks his wife doesn't know. He isn't very subtle about it, tromps about like an elephant. Nothing strange. Although . . ."

"Yes?" Jackaby prompted.

"There was another sound . . . like . . . like–ugh–I don't know." His brow crumpled in frustration at the effort to recall. Jackaby tapped the fork again, and the man breathed, focusing.

"Like . . . something metal. *Clink-clink*. Like that. Probably just his watch banging on its chain, I guess. Not long after that, the crying started. She was so sad . . ."

"Thank you very much for your cooperation, Mr. Henderson." Jackaby flipped the satchel closed with his free hand and tucked it deep into his coat. He gave the tuning fork one final tap before striding toward Henderson. "I'll be back to retrieve this later," he said, holding out the fork, "but I think it's best if you keep it for now."

Henderson took the offering delicately, holding it carefully by the stem to avoid dampening the crystal clear tone. The rims of his eyes were nearly as red as his pajamas, but they were full of gratitude. He nodded, and Jackaby patted his shoulder, a bit awkwardly, and headed out the door.

Jackaby was already examining the window at the end of the hallway as I stepped out. He flicked the latch open, closed, and open again, and felt along the frame. A very slim balcony was visible just outside, housing a pot of dirt, which might presumably have contained a plant before the frost set in. Before I could ask if he noticed anything unusual, he was striding back down the hallway in the opposite direction. Charlie and I flanked him, quickstepping quietly past the closed door of room 301 and into the stairwell.

"I wonder how many floors we have above us," mused Jackaby as he mounted the steps.

"Should be just one more," I offered. "There were four rows of mailboxes in the lobby, and the numbers only went from the one-hundreds to the four-hundreds. So, unless there's an attic . . ." I trailed off. We had reached the landing. The stairs did indeed conclude with one more hallway door, and Jackaby turned to look at me with his head cocked to one side as I caught up.

"The mailboxes?" he said.

"Er, yes. In the lobby."

The corner of his mouth turned up in a bemused grin. "That's quite sharp, Miss Rook. Quite sharp, indeed."

"You think so?" I found myself eager to impress my strange new employer. "Is that helpful to the investigation?"

Jackaby chuckled, turning away to open the door. "Not in the slightest—but very keen, nonetheless. Very keen."

Chapter Seven

The fourth floor of the Emerald Arch Apartments was nearly identical to the third. Light stumbled meekly out of the dirty oil lamps, testing the floor without really diving down to brighten it. Jackaby hastened to 412 and knocked loudly.

"What are we looking for, exactly?" I whispered to my employer as we waited. I could hear the shuffling of motion from within the room.

"I don't know," answered Jackaby, "but I'm excited to find out, aren't you?"

The door opened to a middle-aged man in an undershirt, pressed trousers, and suspenders. He held a damp towel, and daubs of shaving cream clung around the corners of his jawline. "Yes?" he said.

Jackaby looked the man up and down. "No, sorry. Wrong room," he declared. "You're clearly just a man." With no further explanation, he left the confused fellow to his morning.

Jackaby rapped firmly on 411, and a woman answered. She wore a clean, simple, white dress buttoned neatly up to her neck, and her red hair was tied back in a prim bun. "Hello? What is it? I already told the last one that I didn't see a thing." Her accent was distinctly Irish, and edged with quiet annoyance.

"Simply a woman," said Jackaby after another cursory examination. "No use. My apologies." He turned on his heel and advanced toward number 410.

The woman, having been far less satisfied with the encounter than Jackaby, came out of her room. "And just what do you mean by that?" she demanded.

I did my very best to blend into the wallpaper as she stalked after the detective. Charlie, I noticed, had taken a keen interest in the points of his well-polished shoes.

"Simply a woman?" she repeated. "Nothing simple about it! I've had enough of the likes of you, going on about the weaker sex, and such. Twig like you, care to see who's weaker?"

Jackaby called backward without looking behind him, "I mean only that you're of no use at this time."

Charlie shook his head.

The woman bristled. "I am an educated woman, a nurse, and a caregiver! How dare you . . ."

Jackaby turned at last. "Madam, I assure you, I meant only that you are not special."

I cupped a palm over my face.

The woman reddened several shades. Jackaby smiled at her in what I'm certain he felt was a reassuring and pleasant manner following a reasonable explanation. He seemed prepared to let the whole thing wash away as a friendly misunderstanding. What he was not prepared for, apparently, was to be socked in the face.

It was not a ladylike swat or symbolic gesture. The force of it actually spun the detective halfway around, and his trip to the ground was interrupted only briefly by the wall catching him on the ear on the way down.

The woman loomed over him, all silky white linen and fury. "Not special? Simply a woman? I am Mona O'Connor. I come from a proud line of O'Connors, stretching back to the kings and queens of Ireland, and I've got more fight in me than a wet sock of a man like you could ever hope to muster. What do you have to say about that?"

Jackaby sat up, swaying slightly. He waggled his jaw experimentally, then snapped his attention to his attacker. Thoughts rolled across his gray eyes like clouds in a thunderstorm. "You said O'Connor?"

"That's right. Have a problem with the Irish, too, do you?" Miss O'Connor squared her jaw and looked down the bridge of her nose at Jackaby, daring him to confirm the prejudice.

Jackaby climbed to his feet, dusted off his coat, which clinked and jingled as the contents of various pockets resettled, and tossed his scarf back over one shoulder. "It's a pleasure to meet you, Miss O'Connor. I don't suppose you have a roommate?"

Mona's stance faltered. She looked briefly to Charlie and me, finding only equal bewilderment, and then back at the detective. He smiled at her again with charming, innocent curiosity. The left side of his face was red, and the outlines of four dainty fingers were slowly gaining definition. He was behaving in precisely the manner in which a man who had just been walloped across the face should not behave.

"An old relative, perhaps?" he prompted, continuing as though nothing had happened, "Or a family friend? Been around since you were just a girl, I imagine."

The red left Mona's face.

"Getting on in years, I expect, but hard to place just how many?" Jackaby persisted. "Been around as far back as you can remember, and yet she seems just as old in your memory as she is today?"

The rest of the color left Mona's face as well.

"How did you . . . ?" she began.

"My name is R. F. Jackaby, and I would very much like to meet her, if you don't mind," he said.

Mona's brow tensed, but her resolve had clearly been shaken. "My mum . . . My mum made me promise I'd look after her."

"I mean her no harm, you have my word."

"She's having one of her . . . one of her spells. I . . . Look, I'm sorry about—er—that business earlier, but I think you'd better come back some other time."

"Miss O'Connor, it is my belief that lives hang in the balance, and so I'm afraid the time is now. I promise to help in any way I can with her spell. May we please come in?"

Miss O'Connor, her guard now thoroughly shattered, walked back to her open door. She paused in indecision for just a moment, then stood aside and gestured for us to enter.

The layout of the apartment was familiar, but it felt cleaner and somehow more open than the other two. Soft daylight drifted through the white curtains to brighten a table with a simple brown tablecloth. This was topped with lace doilies, a vase of fresh flowers, a white porcelain wash basin, and a pitcher. The sofa was small, but well stuffed, with a thick quilt draped over it. In the corner sat a wooden rocking chair. The room was cozy and inviting, a striking contrast to the gruesome scene downstairs.

"Have a seat if you like," said Mona, and I gratefully accepted the invitation. As I sank into the cushions, I became aware of the toll that the morning's cold sidewalks had taken on my poor feet.

Officer Cane thanked the woman politely but remained standing by the door. In the light of the room, I got a good look at him for the first time. He really was quite young to be a police detective, even a junior one. While he held himself poised and alert, the angle of his dark eyebrows betrayed a hint of insecurity, and he had to periodically straighten his posture, as though actively resisting a natural urge to slink into himself. His eyes caught mine, and he looked away at once. I hurried my own gaze back to Jackaby and the woman.

Miss O'Connor trod gently to the bedroom door. Jackaby followed, pulling the knit cap from his head as he did. I craned my neck to watch as they slipped in. There were two beds in the room on opposite walls, and just enough room for a shared nightstand between them. The nightstand held a dog-eared book and a silver hairbrush. One bed lay empty, its sheets tucked tightly with hospital corners. The other contained a woman with long, white hair. She wore a pale nightgown and was propped up slightly on her pillows. She seemed to be rocking gently, but more I couldn't see as Mona and Jackaby stepped into the room in front of her.

"We have a guest," said Mona. "Mr. . . . Jackaby, was it? This is Mrs. Morrigan."

"Mrs. Morrigan. Of course you are," said Jackaby, gently. He knelt down beside the figure. "Hello, Mrs. Morrigan. It's an honor. Can you hear me?"

I shifted across the sofa until I could just see the old woman beyond Jackaby. She was slender and fair-skinned, her hair a medley of silver and white, but it was her face that captured my attention. Her thin, gray eyebrows contorted in a mournful expression. Her lips were thin and taut, and quavered slightly as she drew a deep breath. Then her head fell back, and her mouth opened wide in a tragic pantomime of a scream. My chest tightened in sympathy for the poor, tortured woman.

Her jaw trembled as she expelled the last of her breath, and I became aware of the overwhelming silence. She inhaled again slowly, and her whole body poured itself into another scream, but still not an audible whisper escaped her delicate lips.

A chill tingled up my spine. Beyond the obvious strangeness of the spectacle, there was something more profoundly unsettling about the woman's muted cries. An indefinable spasm of grief and dread shuddered through me. Was this the life that Jackaby led? Death and madness and despair behind every door?

"She gets this way, from time to time," Mona explained to the detective in a voice just above a whisper. "Always has. She can't control them. They're like seizures . . . only not like any I've seen in any of my medical books. Back home, she would go weeks, sometimes months without any problems. It was supposed to be better here, but we've barely had the apartment for a week and now this . . . It's the worst she's had. Hasn't stopped since yesterday."

"Since yesterday?" Jackaby asked.

"Yes, early yesterday morning, and on all through the night."

Mrs. Morrigan's body sagged as the air left her lungs again. Her eyelids flickered open for an instant, and she looked to Jackaby. Her hand reached weakly toward him, and he held it gently, the most human gesture I'd yet seen from the man; then her eyes closed, and the miserable cycle of silent screaming resumed.

Jackaby leaned in very close and whispered something in the woman's ear. Mona watched him with concern. Mrs. Morrigan opened her eyes again and gave the detective a somber nod. She resumed her muted cries, but her body relaxed slightly into the pillows. Jackaby laid her hand tenderly back on the bed and rose to his feet.

"Thank you," he said aloud, and stepped out into the apartment's main room. Mona followed, shutting the door quietly behind them.

The detective pushed his dark, unruly hair roughly backward and screwed the cap back onto his head.

"What did you say to her?" asked Mona.

Jackaby considered his response. "Nothing of consequence. Miss O'Connor, thank you for your time. I'm afraid I cannot help Mrs. Morrigan's condition for the moment, but if it comes as any consolation, this episode will resolve itself by sometime tonight."

"Tonight?" she said. "You seem so sure."

Jackaby stepped into the hallway and turned back. I stood up and slipped out after him. "I feel quite confident, yes. Take good care of your patient, Miss O'Connor. Good day."

We were at the stairwell before I heard her shut the door behind us. Charlie and I burst at once into questions. What had he said? What kind of seizures were those? How could he be so sure they would end tonight?

"She isn't seizing, she's *keening*, and she will stop tonight because by tomorrow morning Mr. Henderson will be dead." Jackaby's voice was without emotion, save perhaps a hint of interest such as a botanist might exhibit when discussing a rare orchid. "Mrs. Morrigan is a banshee."

The word hung in the air for several steps.

"Keening?" asked Charlie.

"She's a banshee?" I blurted. "That old woman? So she's our killer?"

"Our killer?" Jackaby stopped on the landing and turned toward me. I stumbled to a stop. "How in heaven's name did you make that leap?"

"Well, that's what you said, wasn't it? There had been something inhuman in the victim's room? Something ancient? And banshees . . . Those are the ones whose scream can kill you, right? Aren't they the ones who . . . scream you to death?"

My words petered out and slipped into the shadows, embarrassed to be seen with me. The look Jackaby was giving me was not unkind, but rather one of pity. It was a look that one might give to a particularly simple puppy who had thrown herself off the bed in pursuit of her own tail.

"So, not our killer?"

"No," said Jackaby.

"Well, that's good, then." I swallowed.

"Keening," said Jackaby, turning back to Charlie, "is an expression of grief for the dead." He turned and continued his explanation as we resumed our descent. "Traditionally, women called 'keeners' would sing a somber lament at Irish funerals.

"A few families, it was said, had fairy folk as their keeners. These fairy women, who came from the other side of the mounds, were called the 'women of the side,' which, in Irish, comes out something like 'ban-shee.' They were devoted to their chosen families, and would sing the most mournful laments if ever a member of the house fell dead–even if they were far away and news of the tragedy had not yet reached the homestead. As you might have guessed, Miss O'Connor's family was among these elite houses attended by a banshee."

Jackaby paused abruptly to inspect a scuff in the wood of the stairs. Charlie, who was hot on the detective's heels, had to catch himself on the banister to avoid toppling over the suddenly kneeling figure. Just as quickly, Jackaby stood and continued to climb downward. His gaze hunted the steps for something, but with the foot traffic of every tenant both coming and going, I doubted very much if any significant clues would present themselves here.

"Where was I?" he asked.

"Banshees," prompted Charlie. "Crying for the folks at home, even if a member of the family died far away."

"Right. So, the sound of the banshee's wail became an omen of death. Consigned to their role, over the years, banshees grew still more sensitive. These fairy women gained a precognition, sensing the very approach of death. Rather than keening for the deceased's surviving relatives, the banshees began to sing their terrible dirge directly to the doomed.

"They are still closely tied to their families, but as their power developed, it extended to all those in their presence. Any poor soul whose time drew near might hear the ominous cry, particularly those doomed to a violent and untimely end. Now, if you were an ill-fated traveler and you heard the wail, you knew death was on your heels. This makes them dreaded creatures, feared and hated by any who hear them, a treatment far disparate from the honor and appreciation they used to receive for their mourning services. Banshees themselves are not dangerous, though, just burdened with the task of expressing pain and loss."

I thought of Mrs. Morrigan's face, and was suddenly ashamed of my rash accusation. I was glad that Jackaby had shown her some tenderness, and I realized he had given her what little he could: his thanks.

"It is a kindness that you and I cannot hear the banshee's wail," he continued. "It is not meant for us. Henderson hears it because it is his lament, and his alone. Our victim in room 301 heard it also, I'd wager, before his untimely demise. Mrs. Morrigan has scarcely been given a moment's rest from her dutiful dirges."

We were rounding the last flight of stairs, and the brightness of the lobby spilled into the stairwell.

"Should we do something for him?" asked Charlie, suddenly. "If a murderer is coming for Mr. Henderson, we can't in good conscience just wait and let him be taken! Could we move him—hide him? Post guards around his room?"

Jackaby stepped into the lobby. By now the sun was high in the late-morning sky. Clouds blanketed a snow-dusted world, and the soft whiteness of it was blinding. "If it eases your conscience to try, then go right ahead. It will make little difference, though. If he hears the banshee's cry, then Mr. Henderson's fate is sealed."

Chapter Eight

Jackaby wrapped his scarf up to his chin and pushed open the front door of the Emerald Arch Apartments. Charlie stepped up quickly to hold open the door as I followed him. The crowd of curious onlookers had grown, and the police had acquired a few sawhorses and roped off an official barrier line. At the end of the sidewalk, Chief Inspector Marlowe had come outside and was speaking to a pretty young woman with blond ringlets and tears streaming down her cheeks. She blew her nose into a handkerchief and sobbed. I had been doing so well, keeping the fear and pity and horror stuffed down in my gut, but the woman's unmasked emotions churned them up and left me uncomfortable and queasy. I willed the feeling to pass. Marlowe was making no effort to comfort her, but listened as he flipped through the pages of a small leather notebook, occasionally nodding and scribbling additions. The chief inspector did not seem like the sort of man who could ever be overwhelmed by empathy. He would fit right in to the crime adventures in my magazines. He held the little pad like a shield, stoically barricading himself from the human tragedy. I wondered why Jackaby didn't carry a little notebook. It struck me that a detective should have a little notebook.

Charlie Cane was more interested in a shiny black carriage coming down the cobbled street. It had stalled as the driver shooed pedestrians out of the way. New Fiddleham was a growing city, and streets originally designed for the quaint, rural township it must once have been now found themselves easily congested with the traffic of everyday urban life. Gossip and chatter drew a bulky crowd as well, and despite the heavy police presence, onlookers spilled into the streets to watch the drama unfold.

"I appreciate all of your help, sir, but now I really must insist that you go," said Charlie, gesturing at the carriage. "That's Commissioner Swift's personal carriage. If he's actually coming out to a crime scene, you can bet Inspector Marlowe will be even less . . . cheerful."

Jackaby scowled. "Curious. The commissioner has taken quite an interest. Surely Marlowe has handled homicides unsupervised before."

"Not so curious," answered Charlie, looking more

uncomfortable about our continued presence as the carriage pulled nearer. "The mayor appointed Commissioner Swift a few months ago. First thing he did was push up quotas and double street patrols. He's trying to get into politics, very concerned about numbers and public image. The rumor is that Arthur Bragg was helping get him some publicity in the *Chronicle*. You can see why he'd be a little upset."

"You say the victim worked for the newspaper?"

"That's right. He was a reporter, mostly political stuff and local news. Really, sir, you need to get going now!"

Jackaby glanced down the sidewalk as the carriage pulled up to Marlowe. The inspector broke off his conversation with the weepy blonde and stepped toward it, standing at attention by the door. The girl looked lost and unsteady until another officer came to escort her away. I realized I had seen her face before. She was the girl from the photograph upstairs. The swell of emotions returned, and I fought back a lump in my throat.

"Right. Thank you, Detective. You've been a great help," Jackaby was saying. He nodded to the junior detective and hastened to the corner of the building. I waved a quick good-bye to Charlie, and his parting smile sent another surprising rush of warmth up to my cheeks.

I turned and hurried after Jackaby, rounding the corner almost on top of him. He had planted his back to the brickwork and was surveying the scene intently. "What are you doing?" I asked, glancing about and pulling myself into the shadows with him. The alleyway was wide, running between the Emerald Arch and a short brick building that smelled of fish. There were cans of refuse and old crates heaped along the wall opposite us, but nothing large enough to offer concealment, should we find ourselves in need of it. A slim balcony protruded from each floor directly above us.

"Well, Miss Rook, it's time for you to go," Jackaby said simply, glancing about the alley without bothering to look me in the eye.

I faltered. "So, it's a *'no'* on the job, then?"

"What? No, where did you get that idea?" He crossed to the pile of old boxes and picked one out with a sturdy wooden frame and a big, red fish emblem painted across the side. He set the box down beneath the balcony and picked up two more. He stacked these in a simple pyramid, then looked up. "If you're still in for it after this morning's business, then the job is yours . . . at least provisionally. We can call it a trial period."

After the small disappointment, the excitement of what he was saying began to percolate. "Oh, I'm in for it, Mr. Jackaby," I said. And then, after a pause, "What, exactly, am I in for?"

"Excellent, asking the right questions." He stacked three or four more crates in unsteady tiers as he spoke. "You'll come with me on some cases, like today, and spot little details that might be helpful. I will dictate findings for you to type up and compile into proper case files, and when I'm connecting the pieces, you will be my sounding board. I think better aloud, and I prefer not to talk to myself too much. Gives me headaches. Otherwise, you'll just run small errands for me, write up bills and receipts, manage the accounts, that sort of thing. Any further questions?"

"Why did you change your mind?" It just slipped out.

"Change my mind about what?"

"You said I wasn't the girl for the job, at first. What made you change your mind?"

Jackaby stopped arranging old boxes and looked me in the eye before answering. "Marlowe is a good man and a competent detective, but he notices what anyone would notice: the extraordinary. He spots bloodstains and mad men in red pajamas. I see the things more extraordinary still, the things no one else sees. But you—you notice mailboxes and wastebaskets and . . . and people. One who can see the ordinary is extraordinary indeed, Abigail Rook. Any other questions?"

I had just one more. "Why don't you have a little notebook?" I asked.

"What? A notebook?"

"Yes, for jotting down clues and leads and things. Terribly handy for a detective, I should think. Marlowe's got one. It has a leather cover and flips up top-wise. I wouldn't mind a notebook like that, myself. We should each have one. We'd look more like proper detectives, then."

"Firstly," Jackaby said with a sigh, "a 'proper detective' is about the last thing a *good* detective wants to look like, most of the time. Secondly, it isn't a bad idea on the whole, but I've used notebooks and I found them entirely useless. I'd give them to my assistants to type up, and none of them could ever decipher my handwriting. One of them rather rudely suggested it looked like the scribblings of a chimp."

"Well then, you could always read it out for me to copy—or not copy it at all, just use it for your own reference."

"Well, that's no good."

"Why not?"

"Because 'chimp' was generous. I can scarcely read a word I've written. I find it's far simpler to skip the exercise entirely. I can dictate my findings to you at the end of the day in the comfort of the office."

"Well, I should still like one myself, someday. I think I would look quite sharp with a leather notebook. Oh, and a magnifying glass. I would feel much more like a detective with a magnifying glass."

"I do have several of those, but why should you need to feel like a detective? I'm hiring you as an investigative assistant, not a detective. Would a magnifying glass help you to feel like an investigative assistant? If so, I would be happy to lend you one as you get adjusted to the role."

"Don't take this the wrong way, sir, but you have a way

of taking the joy out of an occasion, do you know that?" I buttoned my coat against the cold wind. "Shall we be off, then?"

"Not we, I have something I need to attend to here." The detective glanced up and down the alley once more. "Meet me back at my offices. I expect the smell should have become tolerable by now. Make yourself familiar with the place—just mind you don't slip in the pond. The mud is surprisingly slick."

"I didn't notice a pond . . . Is it around back?"

"No. Third floor. You can't miss it." Jackaby planted a foot on the wobbling pyramid, and quickly mounted the makeshift staircase.

"Wait, what are you doing?" I grabbed the top box with both arms, bracing it as the whole lot threatened to tumble.

Jackaby grabbed hold of a metal railing and swung himself up onto the narrow balcony. "I need to revisit room 301. If Arthur Bragg was a reporter in the middle of a story, and he wound up with a hole in his chest and short several pints of blood . . ." He let the sentence hang in the air.

"Of course," I called up, "He was probably killed for something he was writing about. But . . . why don't you want me with you?"

"Because"—Jackaby had planted one foot atop the thin, metal railing and was pulling himself up to the next balcony, his shoes scraping gawkily at the brickwork as he ascended—"you have—*oof*—been with me all morning and have not fainted, struck me with anything, or metamorphosed into an aquatic bird. I should very much like this to remain the state of things, at least for your first day."

"Ah," I replied. I was beginning to find it was easier to merely accept what the detective told me than to ask for explanations. "See you back at your office, then?"

Jackaby had planted his feet firmly on the third-floor balcony and begun to lift open the window. He stopped, eying the windowsill intently and mumbling something. "What is it?" I called up.

"Nothing. This is the window at the end of the hallway, I can see Mr. Henderson's door just there." He pulled the window open the rest of the way and slid a leg inside.

"Don't get nicked!" I cautioned in my loudest urgent whisper.

"That reminds me," he said, pausing. "There's a jar in my office marked 'Bail.' If you don't hear from me by tonight, just bring it down to the Mason Street station, would you? I'm usually in the first or second cell. There's a good girl. See you in a bit!"

The rest of Jackaby disappeared through the window, and an old, familiar sensation tickled its way up my spine. Until that moment, the events of the day had all been new and remarkable, but being left behind was one area in which I had countless hours of experience.

My father was highly respected in certain scientific circles, and his notoriety kept him perpetually away on business. I had my mother, of course, but her wildest ambitions involved parasols and cucumber sandwiches. Most little girls would probably have preferred playing dress-up with mommy to learning about their father's work—but most little girls did not have the intrepid Daniel Rook for a father. For him, "work" meant dashing off to exotic locales with groups of daring, khaki-clad adventurers. I could not count the times I begged him to let me see a real dig site, but to no avail. While he explored lost civilizations and unearthed the bones of monstrous beasts, I explored the garden and pulled weeds for a two-penny allowance.

I was not in my mother's garden, now. I was standing beneath a balcony in an alley that smelled faintly of old wash-water and dead fish, feeling my mind spinning from the day's events and teetering like an unbalanced top. This was different. I had in the span of the past hour experienced more genuine adventure than in all my time at home or my travels abroad. Inspector Marlowe had sounded just like my father. "This business is not for the female temperament," he had said—but Jackaby had not hesitated to point me toward the worst of it and ask for my opinions. It made me inexplicably excited that I would be working with this mad detective again. Looking back, I suppose I ought to have been less afraid of being left safely behind, and more afraid of the looming precipice ahead.

I walked back to the street and tried to get my bearings. The straightest path back to the odd little building on Augur Lane, I realized, would take me past the police barricade again. I decided that Marlowe would hardly notice or mind my muddling my way through the onlookers, so I chanced it, keeping close enough to the front of the crowd to watch the windows for any sign of my strange, new employer.

I caught no sight of him, but I did hope he would move quickly. Chief Inspector Marlowe was already walking back toward the front door, his cuffs beating their metronomic clink against his leg. He kept pace with a new figure, who must have been the commissioner. The man wore an expensive-looking suit, which demanded attention. It was just a bit old-fashioned, with notes of formal uniform to the fitted cut. The long coat was charcoal black and decorated with military epaulettes and red trim. On his head sat a velvety red derby with a slightly wide brim and a gaudy feather tucked in the dark sash. He carried a polished metal cane and walked with his chest puffed out and his chin propped up. The overall affect of the man was just a shade subtler than a sandwich board with the words BETTER THAN YOU written out in big block letters.

He was classically pompous . . . except, I realized, for his gait. The long coat and dense crowd blocked his legs from view at first, but as I moved in for a closer look, I could see there was something strange about the manner in which he walked. He leaned a bit too heavily on the cane for it to be merely a showpiece, for starters, but there was also a rigidity to the swing of his legs. I was nearly at the police rope before he passed, and I saw them at last. They had been painted black to blend nearly perfectly with his trousers, but the commissioner wore a pair of leg braces, which caught a faint hint of sunlight as he marched by.

I had seen a similar pair before, on a German boy during my time abroad. Although the disease was still fairly rare here in the States, the polio epidemic was already wreaking havoc across Europe. Whether out of strength or pride, the man refused to show any weakness, maintaining a rapid pace in spite of his impediment. Marlowe had to double-step occasionally to keep up.

"Don't think you do realize, Inspector," Commissioner Swift was barking. His voice was deep and angry. "In my town, right under my nose! Do you have any idea what Spade's campaign boys will do if I try to put my hat in the ring in the middle of this? I want suspects in cells, and I want them there yesterday . . ."

The tirade paused as Swift awkwardly negotiated the small step up to the doorway, batting Marlowe's hand away as the inspector instinctively reached to help. I realized, with a little guilty relief, that Jackaby would have more time than I had feared. The commissioner had three unpleasant flights ahead of him.

With that thought, I left the warmth of the gathering throng behind to wind my way back up the frosty cobbled streets toward Augur Lane.

Chapter Nine

By the time I found my way back to 926 Augur Lane, the sun was directly overhead and the snow had slunk back to hide in the shadiest corners of the streets. I stepped with greater confidence toward the building I would be calling my workplace.

The front door was even brighter red in the full midday light, and I was happy to find it unlocked, as before. Inside, the faint sulfurous stink had all but faded away, and the open windows had replaced it with crisp, fresh air. I hung my hat and coat on the rack, noting that my suitcase was still just where I had left it, and looked around the room for the second time. Sharing a wall with the doorway was a battered wooden bench, which could easily have been salvaged from a doctor's waiting room, but had about it a certain quality that suggested it might have been stolen from a church, instead. At the opposite wall sat the unoccupied desk, stacked with papers and overstuffed folders. To my right was the row of books and artifacts, including the terrarium, which my eyes now carefully avoided.

Toward the back of the room on the left wall stood a doorway flanked by two framed paintings. One painting featured a mounted knight driving a lance through a lizard the size of a small dog, an image I recognized as Saint George slaying the dragon. The other depicted a tumultuous sea in which a wooden ship was being towed through the waves by an enormous golden orange fish. Although painted in entirely different styles with nearly opposite color schemes, the two pictures seemed to belong together, held in unity, like the house itself, by some stronger force than aesthetic logic.

I crossed toward the door, but paused as I passed the desk. In a little valley of usable desktop, between the stacks of jumbled paperwork, lay an uncapped fountain pen. I took the two-step detour to scoop it up, not wanting it to dry out, and my eyes passed over the document on which it rested. The page was dated several months prior, written in tidy cursive, and read as follows:

Mr. Jackaby is quite certain that the whole affair will culminate in some unholy ritual this evening. He has been, as usual, unforthcoming about the details of the case.

The only link I have discerned between the incidents is the coincidental involvement of Father Grafton and a few members of his parish. My suggestion that we direct our inquiries toward the church was not met with enthusiasm.

When I pressed the matter, Mr. Jackaby informed me that my services will not be necessary in his current line of investigation, and insisted that, since I am so curious about it, I should go and ask my own "silly little questions" without him. I must admit to some nervousness, given the heinous nature of the case, but I suppose Mr. Jackaby would not send me on alone if he sensed any danger.

I shall be sure to record the results of my first independent investigation as soon as I return.

The author had not, in fact, recorded anything further at all. I found a few more pages in the same handwriting, but all of them from earlier dates. I brushed the nib of the pen with my finger, and a few flakes of long-dry ink crumbled off. I capped the pen and returned it to the desk, trying very hard not to read the whole thing as ominous. There were enough voices in my life telling me I couldn't *this*, or shouldn't *that*, or that I wasn't up to the task—the last thing I intended to do was start agreeing with them.

I shook the nervous thoughts from my mind and returned my attention to the door. With a push, it opened onto a hallway that zigged and zagged until it came to four doorways, two on either side, and a spiral staircase at the far end. I peeked into the first door.

Rows of books reached to the ceiling and lined the walls of a beautiful library. Central bookshelves had been arranged to allow light to pour down the aisles from alcove window seats, and the space felt warm and comfortable. I could have spent hours curled up on a soft chair in that room, but slipped back into the hallway to investigate the others.

The adjacent room was an office. It was well lit, but a mess of files and books. As I leaned in, the eerie sensation of being watched came tingling up my spine. Spinning around, I found the hallway as barren as ever. I pulled the office door closed, beginning to feel a bit like a trespasser. I considered leaving the other rooms alone altogether, but when I saw the last door was already open a crack, my curiosity got the better of me.

The door yielded to my gentle nudge, then struck something hard and would open no farther. I poked my head in the gap. It was a laboratory. Along the walls and windowsills, beakers and test tubes filled with myriad colors were nestled in complicated brass fixtures. Sunlight shone through them to paint the walls in calico spots. The carpet comprised more stains than original patterns, and was singed in quite a few places. The room smelled oddly sweet and acrid—like bananas and burnt hair.

I couldn't shake the creepy feeling that I was not alone,

though the sole inhabitant of the laboratory appeared to be a battered, armless mannequin, propped up on one side of the room. I craned my head to see around the door and found myself suddenly attacked, two massive rows of gleaming white teeth gaping over my face. I pulled back sharply, my shriek cut short as I bounced the back of my head off the door frame and then rapped my forehead on the door before retreating successfully into the hallway.

I breathed heavily, staring at the gap, waiting for the creature to appear. Nothing happened. Still rubbing the back of my head, I peeked in again to find the seven-foot skeleton of an alligator, suspended on cables from the ceiling. I had let Mr. Jackaby's talk of the supernatural infiltrate my imagination. The bony beast above me was no more dangerous than the ones in the natural history museum back home.

I pulled the laboratory's door shut with a squeak and turned to the spiral staircase. Willing myself to calm down and breathe evenly, I climbed the steps up to a poorly lit hallway on the second floor.

Feeling even more like a prowler in the semidarkness, I tried the first door on my right, hoping for a little light from the windows. I found, instead, precarious towers of treasures, trash, and bric-a-brac. A mounted stag's head had been propped up against an expensive, newfangled phonograph, an assortment of silk neckties draped over the bell. Chess sets toppled into tea sets, and tea sets into toolboxes.

A bed was nearly hidden beneath the bulk of the collection. Some light, at least, petered past the towering clutter, so I left the door open as I crossed to the room opposite.

This door opened to a bedroom that must have been the same size, but it felt easily twice as large because it was immaculately tidy. The bed had fresh linens and was topped with a plush comforter. Curtains with lace edging hung closed at the window, and as I crossed the floor to open them, I was startled by a sharp gasp. I turned to look for its source, my eyes straining to make out anything in the darkness. I threw back the curtains and whipped around. I was alone in the room, but the tingling in my spine was back, and rapidly creeping up my neck. My heart pounded.

"Hello?" I squeaked. "Is someone there?"

Across the hallway, one of the piles shifted. A silver saucer slid away from its service and to the floorboards with a clang. It rolled past the doorway and just out of view down the hall, where it revolved to a ringing stop.

There had been no gasp, just the sound of shifting clutter. I stepped into the hallway to retrieve the dish. The bedroom door slammed shut at my heels, and I spun. The light beneath the door vanished, exactly as though the curtains beyond had been pulled quickly shut, and I was caught by an icy chill.

In my rush to return to the well-lit office on ground level, I discovered that it is exceedingly difficult to bound both rapidly and gracefully down a spiral staircase while wearing a dress. As a result, my return to the first floor was executed in a thoroughly undignified somersault. My shoulder aching and my hair a tangled mess, I found my feet at last, and retreated to the safety of the office.

I took the seat behind the desk and waited for the tingles to leave my spine and my pulse to return to normal. A dusty chalkboard stood against the wall. I tried to make out any words, but they had been smeared to obscurity, if they had ever been legible at all. Several notes had been circled and connected in a sort of web, but all that remained now were the ghosts of the lines.

Ghosts.

I glanced up at the ceiling. Directly above me sat the impeccably tidy room with its polished floors and neatly tucked bed. And something else.

I shook my head. It wasn't that I did not believe in ghosts; it was that I believed in them in the same noncommittal way that I believed in giant squids or lucky coins or Belgium. They were things that probably existed, but I had never had any occasion to really care one way or another. I had never given ghosts much thought—except, perhaps, as a frightened child gazing into shadows at bedtime.

Jackaby, I was rapidly discovering, had a way of opening that corner of my brain. It was a quiet little corner in which I had lived when I was younger. It was a corner in which anything was possible, where magic was not an improbable daydream, but an obvious fact—if still only just out of reach. In those days I had known there must be monsters in the world, but I would happily accept them, knowing that, by the same logic, there must also be wizards and wands and flying carpets. I had never really closed that part of my mind, just slowly stopped visiting it as I grew older. I had left it unlocked like the jumbled treasure room upstairs, waiting for someone to come poking about.

Where was Jackaby? Surely he should have returned by now. I thought about Swift and all those steps, but even the hobbling commissioner must have reached the room after such a wait. I found the mason jar, which Jackaby–or one of his previous assistants–had indiscreetly labeled BAIL MONEY in bold letters, and pulled it off the shelf. Stuffed in wads and rolls, there must have been over two hundred dollars in the thing! I gawped at the sum. How much should I bring? I had never bailed anyone out of jail before. I wouldn't feel safe walking down the street with half a year's wages in my pockets.

Fortunately, before I had to make a decision, I heard the lobby door bang shut. I tucked the jar back on the shelf and zigzagged quickly down the crooked hallway. Jackaby had just hung his hat beside mine on the rack when I poked my head into the lobby.

"Oh, hello, Miss Rook. Had a chance to look around a bit?"

"Just a bit," I hedged.

"Good, good." He hung up the scarf, which dangled

Chapter Ten

Jackaby filled me in on the details of his return to room 301 as we walked back down the crooked hallway. He had been able to successfully slip in and out without detection, and had uncovered a few papers of interest.

Arthur Bragg had produced reams of scribbled notes, most kept in his own shorthand. Amid the papers on his desk were details of recent political debates and annotated minutes from city hall meetings. He had notes from interviews with Mayor Spade and with Commissioner Swift. Both men, as best Jackaby could tell from his quick glance at Bragg's shorthand, were discussing the upcoming mayoral election.

"Sounds like Detective Cane was right," I said. "Bragg

must have been Commissioner Swift's connection at the newspaper."

"So it would seem."

"I see why Swift was so angry about it being right under his nose! It wasn't just a murder in his city—he let his personal newsman get killed before his free publicity even hit the stands."

"Yes, well, it seems Mr. Bragg had been looking into something else as well."

Jackaby reached the end of the hallway and gave the door to his laboratory a shove. It squeaked open, and he pushed past whatever had been blocking it, sending several ripe red apples rolling across the carpet.

"Oh, blast, it's overflowing again," he muttered, ducking absently under the skeletal alligator as he plowed in. "Mind your step. Help yourself to an apple if you like."

I remained in the doorway. A heavy black cauldron sat on the other side of the door, teeming with fresh fruit. I hadn't had a proper meal since yesterday, but something about the room's lingering smell of burnt hair and unknown chemicals quashed my appetite.

Jackaby crossed the room and pulled off his coat, draping it casually over the mannequin. From its pockets, he pulled out a few of the vials I had seen earlier and nestled them into waiting slots on the big metal rack. He continued, selectively removing items, like the slim vials I had seen him peering through, and replacing them with new ones. New artifacts found their way into the myriad pockets as he darted about, among them a Chinese coin, a set of rosary beads, and a little vial with something that rattled inside it. I gave up following his movements as he restocked.

Without the coat, the man looked even lankier. He seemed to be built entirely of angles, from his long legs to his hard cheekbones. He wore a simple, clean white shirt with no necktie, and a pair of plain brown suspenders. His wild hair looked coal black in the dim light of the room, and atop his gaunt frame it gave him the figure of a spent match.

"What else was Bragg onto?" I asked.

"I don't know yet. But I believe the answer may lie in this." He produced a folded piece of paper and handed it to me. "I found it concealed beneath the leather blotter on his desk. Tell me what you make of it." I opened it and turned it around.

"It's a map," I said.

"Brilliant. Already making yourself an invaluable asset to the organization."

I went on. "It's not a proper, printed map. It looks like Bragg traced it, but it's got a good bit of detail. The coastline looks all squiggly in the right places. There's us in the center." I pointed to the spot where Bragg had marked New Fiddleham. "And it looks like it goes out fifty miles or so above and below us. It's too distant for street details, but he seems to have blocked out the nearby cities and county lines."

All across the simple chart, the late Arthur Bragg had inscribed a dozen *X*s in red ink. They were scattered on all sides of the city, some clustered in twos or threes, others far off on their own. In fine script he had written *C.Wd.* beside most of them, and *N.Wd.* beside a few. Each was marked with a date. The dates went back as far as three months prior, and as recently as just one week past. "What do you suppose these notes mean?" I asked.

"That is what I intend to find out." Jackaby, apparently satisfied with the restocking of his pockets, left the coat on the mannequin and crossed into the hallway. I stepped aside as he passed, and followed him into his office.

He pulled a dusty rag off the chalkboard's frame and gave an ineffectual couple of swipes across the surface. Having rearranged the chalky film to his satisfaction, he plucked a white stump from the tray and poised to write. "We'll start with the dates," he said. "Read them off to me. Start with the earliest."

I read the earliest date aloud, October twenty-third, and scanned the numbers for the next oldest, and the next. I glanced up after four or five. "What's that you're drawing?" I asked.

Jackaby scowled. "Recording the dates. Keep going."

"Is that an elven language or something?"

He stood back from the chalkboard and stared at it blankly. "No."

"Are those pictograms? What's that bit you just finished? The one that looks like a goose tugging at a bit of string?"

"That's a seven."

"Oh." We both looked at the board. I tilted my head. "Oh right–I see. I think."

Jackaby handed me the chalk and plucked the paper from my hands. We traded positions without further comment and recommenced. Shortly, with Jackaby reading off numbers and locations while I wrote, we had produced a list of twelve dates. On average they were five or six days apart. Beyond that, no discernible pattern existed. Jackaby moved on to the abbreviations.

"*C* and *N*," he thought aloud. "The *Wd.* is consistent, whatever it means. What could *C* and *N* signify?"

"*Central* and *Northern*?" I suggested. "It is a map."

"Possible, but they're certainly not accurate, if that's the case. Look, there are two marks around Glanville, south of us, and the southernmost of those is an *N*. What else could they be?"

"Let's see, Bragg was covering the election, and he interviewed the current mayor. *C* for *Current*, perhaps, and *N* for what? *New?* Maybe he was taking a poll?"

"That's good–only most of these marks are out of our district. In fact, all of them are. Look. We've got three up in Brahannasburg, four in Crowley, two each in Glanville and

Gadston, with one more out in Gad's Valley. That's at least four separate jurisdictions with their own . . ." Jackaby froze. He stared at the map in his hands.

"What?" I asked. "Have you worked something out?"

Jackaby's eyes were dancing back and forth, chasing thoughts. "What? No, nothing. Maybe nothing. Possibly nothing. Just a hunch. I'll need to pop out to send a telegram or two. You're welcome to stay and settle in if you like."

My eyes flashed to the ceiling as Jackaby folded the map and headed into the hall. "Before you go," I ventured, "tell me, have you got anyone else staying in the building? Lodgers or tenants of some sort?"

"Oh, ah, hmm." Jackaby stumbled toward a response. "Yes, yes, I suppose I do, indeed," he called out from across the hall.

"That's fine, then. Anything I should know about them?"

"Which one?"

"'Which one'? How many people have you got living here?"

Jackaby popped his head back through the doorway. His mouth opened as if to speak, and shut again, his lips pursed in concentration. "Well," he managed at last, "that depends on your definition of *people* . . . and also of *living*." He pulled on his baggy, brown coat. "It's complicated. Fetch you a meat pie while I'm out?"

I gave earnest consideration to my definitions of *people,*

and *living,* and found the prospect of remaining on the property less and less appealing. "Wouldn't it really be best if I accompany you on your errands?" I said. "For . . . learning purposes?"

"Suit yourself, Miss Rook."

My employer was on his way with no further discussion, and I hurried after.

Chapter Eleven

My stomach was growling audibly as Jackaby paid the vendor for two steamy meat pies. I was all the more grateful I had come along, and that the little pie shop had been en route to the telegraph office.

They were sturdy things, with a thick crust that held together and made them fairly easy to eat as we walked. Jackaby held his gingerly with the end of his scarf, blowing on it to cool it down. Far too hungry for patience, I devoured mine with less grace, and with manners that would have made my poor mother blanch, losing more than a little crust and hot filling to the cobblestones.

"So, what we know thus far," Jackaby said suddenly, as if the ongoing conversation in his head had bubbled over and simply poured out his mouth, "is that our culprit left poor Mr. Bragg with a wicked chest wound and a grieving girlfriend, and he made off with a good deal of the fellow's blood. From the look of it, just the blood. The heart and other organs appeared to be intact, and his wallet and watch were still safely in his vest pockets."

"Who steals blood?" I asked, wiping my mouth.

"More creatures than you might think, and many you would never suspect. Blood is a hot commodity in many circles, used for any number of things. Legends suggest a certain Hungarian countess actually bathed in the stuff back in the sixteenth century. Earned her titles like 'the Blood Countess,' and 'the Bloody Lady' among the terrified townsfolk."

"You think Arthur Bragg was killed by a sixteenth-century Hungarian countess?"

"Of course not. The Bloody Lady was human. We're looking for something decidedly supernatural. True, though, it's likely our culprit appears human enough. He or she clearly stopped to sit in Bragg's chair for a spell before dispatching the poor fellow."

"So, we're looking for someone who looks human. Hardly narrows it down, does it?"

"On the contrary, it does so quite considerably, Miss Rook. We've eliminated a good many species in one deft stroke. Also, it seems likely we are in pursuit of an exceptionally heavy creature, or one who wears particularly stout footwear."

"Heavy footwear? I'm sorry, you've lost me."

"The footprints, of course," Jackaby answered. "Did you not see them? I am quite certain that the figure who made those marks also visited Arthur Bragg's room. The aura was unmistakable. This doesn't prove anything absolutely, of course. A great many people might have visited the man's room before his untimely demise, but it is a decided point of interest. The marks were solid enough–surely even your eyes must have been able to pick them out."

"And yet they did not. Perhaps you'll be kind enough to just describe them?"

"Deep gouges were cut in the wooden stairway, alternating in a clear step pattern. They left indentations in the carpet as well. I'm rather surprised any of those were still visible, actually. By the time we had our turn, the police had been traipsing up and down the scene, shuffling most of them to oblivion. The stairs, though, bore distinct marks. An ordinary pair of leather brogues could scarcely mar the wood. It stands to reason, then, that we have a person of interest who is either inordinately massive, or wearing shoes cut from some especially dense material, like steel. Given the size of the tread, I would guess the latter."

"That's brilliant! Our killer wears metal shoes! That's real enough–even Marlowe would have to admit that's a solid clue."

"Of course it's real. We should avoid assuming prematurely, however, that the marks are our killer's. The recency of the footprints puts their bearer here near the victim's time of death, but they could have been made just prior to Bragg's demise, or by an unwitting witness. Traditionally, fairy folk avoid drawing attention to themselves, so any of their kind who stumbled upon Bragg's body would be understandably reticent to submit testimony to an armed official and might simply have fled as quickly as possible."

"And you're absolutely, positively certain we're looking for someone . . ." I still felt silly talking about wild folktales and real crimes in the same breath. "Someone supernatural?"

Jackaby gave my skepticism a severe admonishing glance.

"Okay, fine," I said. "So, how many supernatural creatures are known for metal shoes?"

He gave the matter a moment of thought. "I can think of . . . eleven or twelve offhand. Double that, if you consider that the Knights of Ålleberg were a dozen in number, and clad in full armor when they became ghosts. Unfortunately, we also cannot be so hasty as to eliminate other possibilities. Rabbinical golems, for example, are creatures forged of clay. If hardened properly, some ceramics have a density to rival steel."

I stared at the detective. "How do you know these things?" I asked.

"It is my business to know. Were I a fisherman, I could tell you about . . ." He paused, looking blank for a moment.

"Fish?" I suggested.

"Quite so."

We arrived at the telegraph office. It was a thin structure with a high ceiling, seated tightly beside the post office. I found my mental map of New Fiddleham slowly filling in with details. It was difficult to believe that it had been only a handful of hours since I had plucked Jackaby's posting from the board next door. That little slip of paper had turned out to be my ticket into a more remarkable world than I could have imagined.

Jackaby strode up to an operator, and I hung back a respectful distance while he conducted his business. The operator was an older man, in possession of very few of his teeth and none of his hair. Jackaby dictated a telegraph and the old man read it back, and while I couldn't make out its full content, I couldn't help but hear the rhythmic whistle and clop as the old man punctuated each sentence with a "Stop." From a bench by the window, I watched the foot traffic flow past, and the occasional cart or carriage rattle along the cobblestones.

I thought about the strange details of the case so far, from Bragg's missing blood and mysterious map to the suspicious footprints made by curiously heavy shoes. If my employer was correct, the poor man's murderer also looked human, but was actually a very old—what? None of it made any sense. Perhaps, if I really did have a nice leather notebook that flipped open top-wise, I could jot down all the information in neat, orderly lines, and it would fall into place. Unbound, the clues shifted and slipped through my mind, ducking away as I tried to focus on them.

"Young lady . . ." A woman with a high, nasal voice shattered my concentration. I emerged from my thoughts to find a sour-faced character wearing a tiny, fashionable bonnet pinned up with more flowers and ribbons than there was hat to hold them all. She cast a slow glance under drooping eyelids at my employer, and then continued in a conspiratorial whisper. "I do so detest idle gossip," she said, "but I feel obliged, one woman to another, to inform you that the man you are accompanying is not the most suitable companion. I don't know what he's told you, my dear, but he has a reputation for being"–she leaned in close–"uncouth."

I nodded. "Yes, ma'am, thank you for that. I think that being 'couth' may actually be somewhat overrated. As it happens, I am now in the employ of Mr. Jackaby, and accompanying him is a part of my job."

"Ah," said the woman, and then tutted in disapproval. "A girl your age really shouldn't resign herself to working for a living. You should be thinking about your wedding. It's not too late for a pretty thing like you to find a good, respectable husband to look after you."

"I prefer to look after myself, ma'am, but thank you. I appreciate your concern for my well-being, but some of us have more pressing matters to attend to than practicing our curtsies and turning foolishly sized bonnets into topiaries."

The woman harrumphed. "Perhaps you are fit company for that man, after all." She sneered and bustled out the door. I had been impolite, but I tried not to smile as I watched the pile of colorful blossoms atop her head bouncing away in rhythm down the sidewalk. It would be easy to imagine a domovyk living unnoticed in a hat like that.

"Coming, Miss Rook?" Jackaby was behind me, his task complete. He made for the exit without waiting for an answer, and I bounded after him and onto the sidewalk. A sound caught my ear as I exited, a sort of rattling clank. It might have been anything, a horse's harness or a loose door latch, but my mind dashed to what Mr. Henderson had said about the noise outside his room the night Bragg was murdered. *Clink-clink.* Another detail to add to the jumble in my mind. I wished that the woman in the floral bonnet hadn't distracted me from my thoughts.

"I think I really do need a proper notebook if I'm to be any help as a detective," I said, matching step with Jackaby.

"You're not a detective," said Jackaby. "You are an investigative assistant."

"All the same, it wouldn't hurt," I said. "I met a woman, while you were at the desk, who didn't seem to think I should be working for you at all."

"That's fair. I'm not certain if you should be working for me at all, either. How did you respond?"

"Rather rudely, I must admit."

"Hmm," he grunted. "You may find it not worth your

trouble to engage in that sort of argument in the future. She is not the first to be put off by who I am and what I do, and she will not be the last."

"So what are you?" I asked. "A magician? A wizard?"

"I told you, Miss Rook, I don't go in for that sort of thing. I'm a man of science."

"Well, what do you call what you do?"

"I call it ratiocination. Deductive reasoning. The logical connection of . . ."

"Not that bit of it. I'm talking about the other side of it. What do you call people like you who can—you know—detect invisible things?"

"Ah." He nodded. "The term I use is *seer*. It's not a perfect title. It's been used to define all manner of fortune-tellers and prophets over the centuries, but it's simple and apt. I see. I am a seer. *The* Seer, in fact, in this usage. The one and only, for the moment. I've looked into it a great deal, and there doesn't appear to be anyone else who can see like I see. There have been others in the past, but never two at the same time. It is as though the ability leaves when one vessel dies and is reborn in another."

"How could you possibly know that? How do you know there isn't some fellow in China right now who thinks he's the only one—and another in Australia, and one in France?"

Jackaby sighed and his pace slowed. "I held out hope for many years that there were. I had questions of my own and wanted answers. There are certain groups, very old groups, that take an interest in these sorts of things. They found me. I was given answers, though not as many as I would have liked, and not without a price. I am the steward of a very old and venerated role, one that will remain long after I am gone."

"Why you?"

He grunted. "That was one of the answers I would have liked, but did not receive."

"Did you ever meet the seer before you?"

Jackaby stopped. His face looked gaunt and his storm gray eyes were miles away. He breathed in deeply, and then, slowly, he resumed walking. "The ability can manifest anywhere in anyone. The next seer could as easily be a boy down the road as an old woman on the far side of the globe."

"You did, though, didn't you? Who was he?"

Jackaby did not speak for several paces.

"She," he said at last, quietly. "I prefer not to discuss the matter." There was a dark finality to his tone, so I swallowed my curiosity for the time being, letting another block of cobblestones pass beneath our feet before I spoke again. "Do you think you could teach me? To see past the illusions?"

"No," said Jackaby, almost before I had finished speaking. "Probably no. Almost certainly no. It is, as I just explained, an ability unique to me. The sight resides within a single host at any given time."

"Have you ever tried?" I asked. "Maybe I can't learn to do it exactly like you do . . . but we could see how much I am able to pick up."

Jackaby scowled, but I could see the scientist in him was intrigued by the idea. "I suppose we could establish experimental parameters, measure sensitivity under consistent conditions and changing variables, introduce external stimuli . . ." He was beginning to regard me with the same focused attention he directed at his peculiar artifacts and vials of curious chemicals. It was both promising and deeply unsettling. "I shall give the prospect my consideration," he concluded. "If I decide to keep you on at all, of course." He turned his eyes back to the sidewalk.

"It can't be easy," I said, "tracking this stuff down, all on your own. Not much help to be found if no one else can even see what you're looking for."

"Quite so," said Jackaby. And then he stopped short. "No. Not entirely alone."

"Well, I'm glad to be along," I replied modestly.

"Not you, Miss Rook. But since you mention it, there is someone who sees things—not precisely the same way I see them, but in a similar fashion . . . sometimes. She's called Hatun. It might very well prove enlightening to know what sort of things she's seen lately." We had been winding back toward the office, but Jackaby now turned, taking a side street in the opposite direction.

"Another seer? You just said . . ."

"Not exactly a seer, no. She . . . oscillates. There are basically three ways she sees the world, and she sort of bounces among them. At times she perceives the world just as any simpleton does—just as you do."

"Thanks for that."

"Other times, though, she sees things almost as I do, the world behind the glamour. It isn't always as clear for her, I think. It's just a feeling she gets, a hunch or premonition, and she lets her imagination fill in the blanks. Good imagination, though. She's often right on track, even if she doesn't know what track she's on."

"What's the third?"

"Third?"

"The third way she sees the world?"

"Oh, right. How shall I put it? The first way is the predictable way, and the second way is how the world *really* is. The third is . . . the *unpredictable* way, and how the world really *isn't*. All sorts of nonsense and madness in that one. Decidedly less helpful. It can be a bit tricky, determining which version she's in—and, of course, they do overlap a bit."

"Sounds complicated."

"She is that. But Hatun is a good woman. Once, in the middle of the night, someone slipped in and pried up every last cobblestone from one of the alleyways off Mason Street. An entire alley, secreted away in one night. Scarcely two blocks from the police station, no less!"

"And she helped catch the criminals?"

"Hah! Better! She was discovered, a few days later, carting a bulging burlap sack full of the stones off to some special place in the woods. A police officer was sent out to ask her about it, and she smiled and patted his arm and told him it was all right, that there wouldn't be any more bad luck. She had been warning people for weeks beforehand that the hexagonal-cut stones were emanating hexes. Genuine concern and consideration for her fellow citizens, mind you. She pulled them up herself, stone by stone, and stashed six bags of them in plain sight behind the masons' building until she could lug them off to a safe place. No one thought twice about spare stonework on a masons' lot. Clever planning and selfless efforts. Must've worked herself ragged."

"And the stones were causing bad luck?" I asked.

Jackaby shook his head with a wry smile. "Only for the unfortunate city grunts who had to lay them twice. Octagons, the second go-round, by special request of Mayor Spade. I certainly took an interest and investigated the matter, but I can assure you, there wasn't a hint of anything malevolent about the original batch. They were stones. She's always doing that sort of thing. Protecting the city from the demons in her head. She once cautioned me that the weathercocks were in league with one another. Just felt I ought to know."

"So she's just a mad woman?"

Jackaby hesitated, and when he spoke, his answer had a soft earnestness to it. "Hatun sees a different world than you or I, a far more frightening one, full of far more terrible dangers, and still she chooses to be the hero whom that world needs. She has saved this town and its people from countless monsters countless times. That the battles are usually in her head does not lessen the bravery of it. The hardest battles always are."

We had come to the edge of town, where architecture ended and a swath of grasses and shrubs separated the city from the forest. Not far from the road, a little bridge hopped over a winding creek, and a thin footpath snaked into the trees. As we left the road and drew closer, the first thing I noticed was that the creek had frozen over. Snow dusted its solid surface, along with a few leaves and windblown branches. The second thing I noticed was a slumped figure by the base of the bridge. She was fishing in the frozen creek . . . or at least, holding a pole and letting the hook scrape lazy lines in the frosted surface. The metal sinker bounced along the impurities in the ice, tinkling like a wind chime. "Good evening, Hatun," Jackaby called out amiably as we approached. "Are they biting?"

Chapter Twelve

H atun looked up and smiled at the detective. "You know good and well the fish aren't biting. I made a promise to try, though, at least once a week. Token gesture, but better a cold backside than an angry you-know-who. Even if he is just a little fellow." She tapped her nose with her finger in a conspiratorial gesture.

"And you're good to remember," Jackaby told her. Then, to me: "She made a promise to a troll . . . Calls the thing Hammett, if I recall. When she does catch the occasional little something, she leaves it under the bridge for him. She's been at it since early fall."

"Another one of her imaginary dangers?" I whispered.

"Oh no. Quite real. This is his bridge. He's a diminutive thing, but all the more nasty and ill-tempered for his size.

He has brought an untimely end to more than a few lost house pets and unfortunate local fauna. He seems to have a fondness for cats, though—rides a stray orange tabby when he needs to get about."

"A troll?" I said. "Seriously?"

"Scoff if you like, but if you're keen on keeping all of your digits and extremities, you would be well advised to steer clear or pay him an offering."

"All right." I suppressed my skepticism again—an exercise I was finding necessary more often than not while working for Jackaby. "Well, trolls . . . eat people, don't they? Could Hammett be our killer?"

"Interesting thought. I can't see a full-grown troll leaving a body without at least gnawing the bones a bit first. It'd be as if you or I ate an orange peel and left the fruit in the center. As for Hammett, he's not exactly a menacing figure, for all his pugnacity. He would be happy to crunch the lot of us between his teeth, but I've seen him lose in a fair fight with a particularly robust badger. So . . . doubtful." He turned his attention back to Hatun, who had tucked the fishing pole under the little bridge and come across to meet us.

She stood a foot shorter than I, with curly gray hair tied back in a sloppy bun, and the wrinkled face of someone who had weathered many years outdoors. She was dressed in bulky layers of shirts, petticoats, and wraps, all tattered and faded into complementary shades of soft pastels and subtle grays. She stood with a proud, erect gait, and an expression of benevolent confidence, looking almost stately in spite of her rags.

"Hatun, I would like you to meet my new associate, Miss Abigail Rook. Miss Rook will be working closely with me on cases for the foreseeable future. Feel free to speak openly before her."

Hatun looked squarely and a little suspiciously at me, and then shuffled a half step to one side and then the other. She watched my eyes intently during the exercise. "Hmm," she said. "Well, then. Nice to meet you, missy. I expect you two are looking into that business at the Emerald?"

I glanced to Jackaby, who seemed unperturbed by her behavior or her accurate guess. "Yes, in fact," he answered.

"How did you know?" I meant it as a proper detective's question, but I'm afraid it came out as an awed whisper, instead.

"Of course she knew." Jackaby gestured impatiently back toward city. "There are at least a dozen uniformed men and scores of pedestrians making a noisy scene not three blocks from where we stand. If that mill weren't in the way, you could probably see them from here."

"Oh, think you know so much?" Hatun shook a finger at the detective. "Well, I'll have you know I saw a lot more than boys with badges and a lot of silly rope. I was by there last night, and I looked the devil in the eyes, I surely did.

I'm guessing you saw it, too, eh? Can't ignore what you see with your own eyes, can you? Not you."

"You saw him?" Jackaby's eyes widened. "Hatun, you mean to say you actually saw the murderer last night?"

"Murderer?" Now it was Hatun's turn to look surprised. "Oh dear. I guess must have, at that. I hadn't realized. Who did he get?"

"Bragg," I answered. "Arthur Bragg. A newspaperman. Did you know him?"

She shook her head. "No. Poor soul. But I'll say a few words tonight."

"I don't suppose you've spoken to Marlowe or any of his officers yet?" asked Jackaby.

"Oh no. Been keeping to myself. Kept my shawl on all tight all night, didn't want anyone finding me after what I saw."

"You were hiding in your shawl?" I asked.

Hatun gave the pale blue knit shawl around her shoulders an affectionate tug. "Only street folk can see me in this, beggars and homeless, like. Never had much cause to watch out for them—they're good souls, the most of 'em. For everyone else—well, it doesn't make me invisible or nothing, just impossible to notice." She smiled proudly.

Jackaby and I exchanged glances.

"Erm, *I* found you," said my colleague.

Hatun gave him a knowing wink. "You don't exactly follow the rules when it comes to finding things, though, now do you, Detective?"

Jackaby looked to me again. "Miss Rook? Are you able to . . . ?"

"Yes, of course I can see her."

Jackaby turned back to Hatun. "I'm afraid it may not be working properly," he said with a pitying look. "Now, what is it you saw at the Emerald Arch last night, precisely?"

"Oh, stuff it with the snooty faces." Hatun closed the gap between us and looked me up and down. "Young lady, that's a lovely dress."

"Thank you, I–"

"Where do you live?"

"Well . . ." I hadn't yet found proper lodgings, and having only had gainful employment for a matter of hours, hadn't yet felt up to asking Jackaby for a week's advance. "I'm working on that."

The woman stuck out her tongue at Jackaby. "See? Homeless. It's working fine."

Jackaby raised an eyebrow in my direction, but persisted with the matter at hand. "The Emerald Arch, Hatun? What did you see? Be specific."

"Well." She glanced quickly around and lowered her voice. "It was getting late in the evening. The sun had gone, and the lamps near that corner were dark. They need new wicks, that whole block, they're always going out–but the moon was near full, and it brightened up the street pretty well. I was only out to see if I could scrounge something for Hammett. He does threaten to turn me to stew, but it gets cold out here and I worry about him. Poor thing's had a cough for weeks. So, I was just across the street behind Chandler's Market—Ray just throws out the bones and fish heads—and I hear a sound coming from that Emerald Arch building. I look way up and see a dark shape at the window—not the top one, but at almost-the-top window. The window creaks up and someone sticks his head out and looks up and down the street."

"Did you get a good look at his face?" Jackaby pressed.

"Oh yes. I'll never have that face out of my mind. So, his head comes out and he's got evil, evil eyes, and terrible, sharp teeth. He looks up and down the street, but I have my shawl on, see, and he doesn't see me. That awful head ducks back inside for a second, and then out comes his leg and he starts to step out onto the balcony. Well, about then, I backed up to stay as far from that creature as possible, and I backed right into a crate of old scrap shingles some fool left in the alleyway. The things clatter to the street, and the beast just leaps back into the window and pulls it shut."

"You're quite certain that what you saw was a creature of some sort, and not a man?" asked Jackaby.

"He was a beast, all right. Nothing human about that face. Strange, though, he dressed like a man. It was dark, and he was good and high up there, but I could see his trousers and a suit jacket. Normal kind of clothes, I think, except his shoes. His shoes were shiny metal. Coming out of the window, their soles looked like the hot side of an iron, and they clanked as he stepped onto the balcony. I stuck around in the alley for a long time, to see if he'd come back, but he never did. Must've gone out the front, instead."

Jackaby's face was clouded with thought. "He did indeed, Hatun. His trail resumed on the interior stairwell. Was there anything else?"

Hatun informed us that she had returned home after that, and hadn't seen the creature since, nor anything else out of the ordinary. "Do be careful though," she added. "The chimneys and stovepipes have not been singing as often lately. That's never a good sign for the city. They know something's wrong."

Jackaby thanked her for her time and counsel, and offered her an apple, plucked from somewhere up his sleeve. With a few mumbled cordialities, we left the woman to her frosty bridge and returned to the streets of New Fiddleham.

We had walked several blocks before I interrupted Jackaby's intense concentration. "You were right," I said. "About the shoes, I mean. Even if she doesn't get it all right, she saw just what you predicted. So, they are metal. And this is good, right? We've narrowed things down—eliminated more possibilities?"

"Yes, indeed. Except that it isn't good at all."

"No?"

Chapter Thirteen

By request of my employer, the contents of chapter thirteen have been omitted.

~ Abigail Rook

Chapter Fourteen

Back in his home on Augur Lane, we passed through the quiet lobby—my eyes still willfully avoiding the frog—and down the crooked, green hallway. Instead of continuing to his office, Jackaby pushed open the door to the library. Soft light played in through the alcove windows at the far end, and the detective didn't bother with the lamps. He began plucking books from the shelves. Some were massive, impressive-looking, leather-bound volumes, and others seemed little more than pamphlets.

"May I help?" I asked.

He set down an armload on the table next to me and glanced up. "What? Oh. Yes, of course, of course, that's why I hired you. Let's see, there should be a few useful titles down that aisle. Look for the *Almanac Arcanum,* and anything by Mendel."

He bustled off around the corner, and I perused the spines nearest me. Neither the authors' names nor the titles of the books seemed to have been taken into consideration in Jackaby's shelving method. "Is there a system to these? How do you find anything?" I called.

The detective's voice came from the next row over. "I have a simple and utilitarian method of arrangement. They're sorted by supernatural potency and color of aura. You're in beige, just now."

"You know, I could get these all catalogued and sorted properly for you if you like. I used to spend a lot of time in libraries, back in school. I bet it wouldn't take more than a week or two."

His head appeared suddenly at the end of my row. "Good heavens, no! No no no, I have them precisely where I want them. Just—just see to it you don't move things around much. And don't lose any of my bookmarks. Oh, and don't go into the Dangerous Documents section." He gestured toward an area blocked from sight by a corridor of bookshelves, from which the shadows seemed to fall a little darker than was absolutely natural. "And don't—"

"Perhaps I should just carry these to your office," I offered, patting the stack of books Jackaby had already selected, "where you can conduct your research more comfortably?"

"That sounds like a marvelous idea. Thank you, Miss Rook."

In all, we brought a stack of eleven or twelve volumes and three large charts into the office before Jackaby seemed satisfied that he could suitably bury himself in his work. He ducked into the jumbled laboratory across the hall and brewed a pot of exceptionally strong black tea before diving in. The tea service he returned with did not suit the detective. It was a delicate set, painted in soft pastels with understated floral patterns and curling, feminine accents.

"I hope you don't take milk. I appear to be out," he said, pushing a few papers aside to make space for the tray on the corner of his desk.

"I'm sure I'll manage. Thank you, sir."

"Also, there was an incident with the sugar last month. You'll find a few lumps in the dish, but they have been thoroughly caramelized. I'm afraid the thermochemical decomposition is irreversible, but they're still technically sugar." Several squiggly, molasses brown tendrils stuck out of the sugar bowl, frozen stiff at odd angles as though a minute octopus had been beaten into stillness by the dainty silver spoon.

"Quite all right," I said. "Is there anything I ought to be doing to help?"

Jackaby had already planted himself in his thick leather chair and begun scanning through the first book on the stack. Making no indication he had heard me, he nibbled absently on a curl of browned sugar, and was otherwise entirely immersed in his research. I sat a bit awkwardly on the chair opposite and sipped at my cup, finding comfort in the familiar habit, as he riffled through pages, tucking scraps of paper here and there as makeshift bookmarks.

My idle eyes scanned the books and decorations around the room. For all the interesting artifacts and volumes they held, I realized there was one thing missing. Not a single photograph, nor portrait painting—not even a simple silhouette—adorned the walls. Even Arthur Bragg's lonely bachelor apartment had held a photograph of a woman. The woman he loved. The woman who loved him. The woman who sobbed in the street when he was gone. The memory caught in my throat. I wondered which was sadder, leaving someone to cry after you when you were gone, or not having anyone who would miss you in the first place.

My gaze landed again on the bail jar, stuffed with bank notes, which pulled me away from feeling sorry for others and reminded me to feel sorry for myself, as well. Meeting with Hatun had bluntly reminded me of my current state of homelessness, and I tried to consider the best way to broach the topic of cash before we completely lost daylight and parted ways for the night. Whether from the potent tea or the helpless idleness, I began to feel a bit jittery, waiting for Jackaby to come up for air from his reading.

I poured a second bitter cup from the beautiful teapot and slid back into my seat. A glimmer of light on the wall caught my eye, and I looked around to see what might be reflecting it. When I glanced back, the glimmer had grown, expanding beyond the surface. I stared. My brain ground into action and made sense of what I was looking at: a face. It was a woman's face, silvery and pale, and then a smooth, slender neck, and then a body, clad in a simple gown, every inch of her incandescent and immaterial. She slipped from the wall like a swimmer rising from a pool, only it was her form and not the surface behind her that rippled delicately in the wake of the motion. Gently, fluidly, a ghost entered the study.

I froze, and the cup dropped from my fingers. My mouth gaped, but I found I had forgotten how to make a sound. Fortunately, the scalding sting of hot tea across my thigh pushed its way through my stunned stupor, reminding me. The sound that I made was "Aaayeeaarrgh!"

This caught Jackaby's attention.

The detective quickly pressed a chalky rag into my hands and righted the armchair. I did not recall standing but had apparently done so with great haste, the toppled furniture lying in evidence. I dabbed at my sore, damp leg, staring at the spectral figure as she drifted halfway through the desk to scoop up the teacup that had bounced beneath.

"If you're going to have guests," the ghost said with a sigh, "would it be so hard to give me a little advance warning?" Her eyes were dark with heavy lids. She had soft cheekbones and gentle features, framed neatly by twin locks of hair, which swept her cheeks on either side. The rest was tucked behind her ears and spilled down her back and shoulders in silvery waves, like a mercurial waterfall. She had a slim, spritely figure, and her movements were as smooth as smoke in a soft breeze. She placed the cup on the tray with a gentle *clink*, and drifted to a seat on the windowsill. Through her opaque figure, I could see the swaying branches of a weeping willow in the yard.

"How rude of me. Jenny, this is my new assistant, Abigail Rook. Miss Rook, this is Jenny Cavanaugh. I do apologize for not formally introducing you sooner, but Miss Rook and I are currently engaged in matters of life or death, you understand."

"I do," she said wistfully. "More so than you, I imagine. We actually met, while you were out. Well—sort of met. I take it you didn't tell her about me, either? Not ashamed of me, are you, Jackaby?"

"Oh bother. Of course not—other things on my mind. Did you get on well?" Jackaby's attention had returned to the volumes on his desk, and he began absently rolling out one of the charts. Jenny's shadowy eyes remained fixed on the window.

"We did not get on well, for your information," Jenny said. "Nor poorly. We didn't get on at all, because a lady doesn't fraternize with strangers who come unannounced into her bedroom. She's lucky I didn't take her for a thief." Then, with that special tone usually reserved for old, accustomed arguments, she added, "Although I wouldn't have minded if she were a common thief. Maybe then she would have stayed across the hall and made off with some of the rubbish you've allowed to take over the guest room before she came traipsing into mine."

"It's not rubbish. I have things exactly where I like them, thank you."

My eyes, apparently the only ones actually looking at anybody, bounced back and forth between them as they bantered as casually as neighbors over a hedge.

"Right. Because there's no better place for my grandmother's settee than under a dirty tarpaulin covered with crumbling rocks."

"Runestones," corrected Jackaby, still without bothering to look up. "I've told you, they're a rare and significant record of the ancient Scandinavian gods."

"Really? Because the last one you bothered to translate was a dirty joke about a group of rowdy drunkards."

"Yes, those are the ones. The Norse really knew how to pick their deities. Those crumbling rocks, I should point out, are making more use of that sofa than either you or your late grandmother, just at the moment."

There followed an awkward pause, punctuated only by the occasional flip of a page or shifting of books on Jackaby's desk. After a short while, it seemed the detective had forgotten he had been conversing at all. His lips formed words occasionally, silently mouthing private thoughts meant to remain between him and his dusty papers.

The ghost, Jenny, stayed perched on the windowsill, watching the world beyond growing dim. Behind her silvery complexion lay a very human woman. By her features, she could not have been much older than I was. For all her bluster, she looked tired and quietly sad.

"I'm sorry about the room," I said. "I didn't know."

She turned her head just a fraction in my direction. "It's fine."

"And about the tea. You just—I wasn't expecting . . . you."

"I know. That's why I did it." She dropped to the ground, or just above it, and began to drift toward Jackaby's door. "You wouldn't have seen me at all, if I didn't want you to, dear. I didn't let the last one see me for a week."

"Well, I'm glad you did. That is—I'm very pleased to meet you, Miss Cavanaugh."

She paused at the threshold and looked back over her shoulder. Her gaze flickered to Jackaby, who remained engrossed in his work, and then turned to me. "Are you, really?"

Now that the initial shock had subsided, I found her growing less frightening and more intriguing. Once one got past her shimmering translucence and weightlessness, it was difficult to find anything really disturbing about the striking, opalescent lady. I wondered, perhaps a little jealously, if she had looked as beautiful in life. Her flowing gown made me acutely aware of my own plain dress, with its muddy green hem and fresh tea stain. For the first time since England, I wished I had chosen to wear something less practical—something with a corset and ribbons. If I had a figure like Jenny's, I might actually enjoy dressing up and would certainly never need to worry about being treated like a child.

I realized I was staring and held out a hand. "I am charmed."

She did not return the gesture, but turned away instead and slid through the door. Because it stood ajar, she only truly slid *through* a small part of it. From the hallway, she gestured for me to follow.

I glanced at Jackaby, whose dark hair peeked over the top of a particularly massive leather tome with Celtic knotwork on the cover.

"Oh, he'll be at it for hours," she said wistfully. "Come on."

I stepped into the hallway, and she continued toward the spiral staircase. "Have you met Douglas?" she asked as she swept up the steps.

"Who?"

She paused halfway around the turn, and a smile danced across her eyes. "You should meet Douglas."

Chapter Fifteen

Jenny led me straight to the third floor. I stopped abruptly as I reached the landing, marveling at the space before me. Where the stairs on the previous two floors had opened into thin, dimly lit hallways, this level was wide-open. Interior walls had been knocked out on either side, leaving only the occasional column to support a high ceiling. Broad windows on every wall allowed light to pour in, and the scene they illuminated was astonishing.

I stood on a hardwood landing that extended ten or fifteen feet, but which seemed then to warp slightly, melting abruptly into grass and mud. The rest of the floor was a rolling, living landscape. Where the hallway should have been, there remained a solid path of wood, laid with a few narrow oriental runners. A slender margin on either side of the carpeting showed floorboards, but then quickly gave way to damp earth on the left and right. Some of the columns, I realized, were sprouting thin branches, and I wondered momentarily if they bore leaves in the spring.

The dominant feature of the space was the massive pond occupying the majority of the floor. It lay just left of the pathway, an oblong pool of greens and blues, bent slightly like a kidney bean, with a little island in the middle. The island was covered in shrubbery and held what appeared to be a tall armchair with dark plum upholstery. The pond must have been twenty feet across at its widest, and from the look of it, several feet deeper than was physically possible, given the dimensions of the building and the height of the ceiling on the floor below. A few golden orange fish darted about beneath the surface.

Here and there around the earthen floor sat desks and cabinets, half enveloped by vines and weeds. Chairs, chests of drawers, and even paintings on the walls were fringed with moss, as though nature had crept in through an open window and caught them by surprise during the night. They simply became a part of one lush, well-furnished landscape.

"I was against it, at first." Jenny's voice came from just over my shoulder. "Jackaby didn't exactly consult me. He has a way of acquiring a lot of favors, especially from his more unconventional clientele. Now, though, I can't imagine the place without it. On a clear night you can throw back the drapes and let the stars catch in the ripples, and the water bounces their light right back up to the ceiling. It's really quite beautiful. For a man who professes to be entirely rational and scientific, he can't seem to steer clear of the impossible and magical."

The last rays of the setting sun were bleeding red and orange across the sky, and faint waves of the warm light played across the ceiling above the pond. It made the room feel serene and ethereal. My gaze gradually found its way back to Jenny, who was watching me with pursed lips.

"Do you have feelings for him?" she asked.

"Feelings for who?" The image of a certain young policeman popped involuntarily into my mind, and my cheeks flushed as I pushed the thought away.

"For Jackaby, of course."

"Oh—goodness, no!" I had not intended my response to sound quite so aghast, but the question had caught me by surprise. My reaction seemed to please the ghost, however, and her expression softened.

"You needn't be quite so shocked at the idea. He is a good man . . . and a not unattractive one."

"I suppose," I said, with some difficulty. "Perhaps if he could be convinced to burn that atrocious hat."

Jenny laughed, a bubbling, honest laugh. "Oh, I know! I know! I've given up on that battle. Don't worry—he'll wear it less often come spring." Her pretty giggle was infectious, and I found myself chuckling, too. "There is someone, though, isn't there?" Jenny asked.

"I—well, I haven't—no. Not really." Strong cheekbones, deep brown eyes, and curls of jet-black hair beneath a police cap snuck back into my mind, and my cheeks grew hot again. "No."

Jenny sighed. "Don't waste time. Life is too short for un-requited love. Take it from an expert." She swept across the woodwork and greenery toward the center of the room. Her weightless steps stirred the blades of grass like a faint breeze. "Fetch a bit of bread from the chest, would you?" she called back.

I glanced behind me and found, against the wall, a simple wooden crate containing a few loaves of dry bread. I selected one and trotted along the path to catch up. The floorboards tapered off into a grassy mound, where the ghostly lady sat perched on a wrought-iron park bench facing the pond. She patted the seat for me to join her.

"Why did you come here, then?" she asked as I sat down.

"It was your idea," I said. "It is nice, though, you're right. Very peaceful."

"Not to the pond, silly. Why did you come to work for Jackaby?"

"Oh, that—well. It happened rather quickly, I guess," I said. "I've been in eastern Europe for much of this past year, and only recently docked in the States. Just looking for work, I suppose. Any job would do, so long as it paid for a roof over my head. And there was a posting . . ."

A mallard fluttered over the surface of the pond toward

us, etching a shallow wake with one webbed toe before landing at the water's edge. I broke a chunk off the loaf and tore it up as I spoke, tossing the crumbs into the nearby grass.

"Now that I've gotten involved—I don't know. It's all rather exciting, of course, and more than a bit unbelievable. I should very much like to help solve mysteries and save lives. I fancy there are worse ways to earn a day's wages."

"He's quite mad, you know. But adventure can be very appealing."

I nodded, watching the duck waddle up the bank and begin nibbling at the crumbs. "My father was a bit of an adventurer," I found myself telling her. "Although I'm not sure he would fully approve of my current situation."

I chose not to mention that I had carefully avoided knowing what my parents thought for the past several months. Since making the decision to abscond with the tuition money to fund my travels, I had deliberately kept out of touch. I had sent an occasional postcard, assuring them of my safety and well-being, but never with a return address, nor any way to trace my current whereabouts with any real precision.

My mother worried, I knew, but my father . . . For my entire life, I had revered the man, and for my entire life, I had heeded his command to stay behind as the dutiful daughter while he marched into discovery. It was not that his word no longer held its power over me, but just the opposite. Secretly, I feared that if he gained the chance to summon me back home to safe monotony, I could only oblige.

Jenny's voice gently broke the silence I had left. "Spending too much time around Jackaby can be . . . dangerous. That doesn't frighten you?"

"Well, yes, it does a bit, I suppose," I admitted. I had been getting similar warnings all day, from that unpleasant woman at the telegraph office to Inspector Marlowe–even Jackaby didn't seem to think I could handle the job. "But today–I don't know how to explain it. It was so easy to get caught up in it. It felt so natural. Like how you think things ought to be when you're a child and you've been reading storybooks and listening to fairy tales. I guess I forgot about being frightened because it felt good to finally be in the adventure."

Jenny sighed and tossed her head back. She said something very softly, which might have been, "And that's what makes him so dangerous."

The duck polished off the bread crumbs and sauntered up for more. He was a stately fellow, with a deeply black head and back, accented in greens and purples. His wings were brown and hung like a prim vest over his white underbelly. His chest was a dappled, reddish color, and it puffed out slightly, like a cravat, tapering away into the white beneath. He came within a few feet and waited, expectantly. I tossed him another handful of crumbs.

"There was a woman," I recalled. "After Jackaby and I left, there was a woman crying. The victim had a picture of her in his room. The whole thing wasn't sad—I mean, it was grisly and tragic—but it wasn't really sad until there was that woman crying. That part didn't feel like the adventures you read about in books. Jackaby says it isn't over, either. We met a man today who Jackaby believes will be dead by morning."

Jenny nodded solemnly, and we watched the duck peck at the bread crumbs for a bit. "You aren't the first assistant he's worked with, you know."

I nodded. "He told me. A handful of them quit on him . . . and wasn't there someone who stayed on?" I remembered the cryptic journal page I had stumbled upon downstairs, and a grim thought occurred to me. "Is that you, then? You didn't—you know—during one of his cases, did you?"

She raised an eyebrow. "Die? No, that happened long before I met Mr. Jackaby. And I never worked for the man, if that's what you thought. This place was my family's. A number of occupants attempted to move in before he did, but apparently having a resident ghost isn't good for property values, and word spreads. The lot fell to the city, and that Mayor Spade fellow called on Jackaby in the hopes he could do some sort of exorcism. That was how we met." She smiled at the memory.

"I take it he didn't exorcise you?"

She laughed softly. "No, he didn't exorcise me. He spoke

to me. Like a person. He made a pot of tea—even asked my permission to use the kitchen first, and just made a pot of tea. We sat at the table and chatted. It was the first proper chat I'd had in a decade. He poured me a cup and just let it get cold in front of me while we talked about this and that. He was very straightforward. He had no qualms about Spade trying to sell the place, told me the man had every right to. 'If every dead person decided to keep their property, we'd have nowhere for the living to live,' he said, which was fair. But he told Spade that I had every right to stay as well. 'No malevolent spirits, no call for eviction,' I think he said. And that was that. A week later, Spade gave the place to him."

"That's quite an arrangement," I said. My bread crumb offerings had slowed, and the duck waddled closer, giving me significant looks.

She shook the fondness from her face with a roll of her eyes. "That was before he tore up the kitchen for his silly laboratory. It was such a pretty kitchen, with tiles and lace curtains—and you've seen it now. Nearly beat yourself senseless at the sight of those garish bones he's got strung from the ceiling, not that I blame you."

I massaged the back of my head at the memory. "You saw that, did you?"

Her eye twinkled in amusement, but she moved on, thankfully. "At least this floor turned out for the better. Wide-open and beautiful, it's the opposite of that mess of a laboratory. But that's Jackaby in a nutshell. Science and magic, beauty and bedlam, things that ought to be at odds—they just don't follow the same rules when Jackaby's involved. For all his faults, he really is a remarkable man." She looked out over the rippling pond while she spoke, and her silvery expression betrayed a hint of longing. "I don't exactly get to go out and about much," she continued, "so this place has really been a lovely escape. Of course, most of the junk he had stored up here migrated to the rest of the house. I've stopped trying to tidy up after the man . . . and the guest room—!" She stopped suddenly with a gasp.

"What, what is it?"

"You need somewhere to stay! You can finally get him to drag his rubbish heaps up to the attic! Do you keep a clean room, Miss Rook?"

"I—er—I'm not sure I'd feel comfortable asking for room and board. I've only just been hired on as it is."

"Douglas takes room and board! Jackaby can't turn you down. It's perfect!"

"I don't know," I hedged. "And who is Douglas?"

"You're the new Douglas. He used to be Jackaby's assistant, just as you are now. These days Douglas just tends the archives." She gestured at the cabinets against the wall, the tops of which were carpeted with moss and wildflowers.

"Where does Douglas sleep?"

Jenny giggled at a joke I didn't get. The duck ceased waiting for me to toss another handful and flapped his wings in a brief flurry to land gracelessly on my knee. The bird was not small, at least a foot and a half from beak to tail, and his perch put us more or less face-to-face. He stared at me, and not the bread in my hand, and his tiny eyes bore into mine.

"Douglas?" I wagered.

A reddish orange bill bobbed once. One wing craned out, and the bird wobbled unsteadily to keep balance. Talons on the ends of his webbed feet poked into my leg uncomfortably.

"Well?" Jenny giggled again. "Go on, then. Don't be rude. Abigail, meet Douglas."

I took the duck's extended feathers with my right hand and shook them carefully. Douglas returned to a more dignified stance, briefly preened, and then snatched the remaining half of a baguette and took off. He swooped in a lazy arc to land on the plum-colored armchair in the center of the bushy island and peck at the bulky morsel.

"Jackaby felt really guilty about Douglas," Jenny told me when he had flapped away. "He used to be a person, of course. Jackaby sent him in alone to check out a lead that might have been nothing, but Douglas stumbled right into the thick of it. By the time Jackaby realized his mistake and hurried to help, it was too late. All he could do was shout out a warning before Douglas was hit with a powerful wave of untempered magic."

"Don't tell me," I said. "He warned him to . . ."

"Duck." It was Jackaby's voice that finished the sentence, and Jenny and I both turned to see him step off the path and onto the grassy hill. "That's right, and the irony that my attempt to help Douglas became the final mark of his curse was not lost on me. I vowed never to let anything distract me until I had found a way to reverse his metamorphosis." The detective came to stand just behind the bench, scowling at the memory.

"My goodness," I said. "But, then . . . are these recent murders somehow connected to the case that transformed Douglas?"

"What? No. The incidents have nothing at all in common."

"Then, what made you abandon your vow?"

"I didn't abandon it! I fulfilled it," he answered. "The solution presented itself after an exhaustive evening's research and one short trip into the country for supplies."

"Then, why is Douglas still a duck?"

"You can bloody well ask him!"

"But . . . he's a duck."

"He's stubborn is what he is."

"It didn't work," Jenny chimed in.

"Well, of course it didn't work," snapped Jackaby. "He has to want to change back! It has to be his own will."

"But . . . why should he want to stay a duck?" I asked.

"Because," Jenny answered, "no one wants to let go of

himself. Douglas may have all of the memories of a man, but he is a duck."

"It's not as though he came by it naturally," Jackaby grumbled.

"It wasn't his choice to lose the life he had—it was taken," said Jenny. "But it is his choice whether or not to lose the life he has now—to lose himself."

"He would still be himself! He would be Douglas. He just has to decide to be human, again."

"No." Jenny's voice was patient. "He would be a different Douglas. The Douglas who has to make that decision would be gone."

"Utter foolishness. It's birdbrained stubbornness."

"Don't be so hasty to impugn a stubborn spirit, Detective," she said meaningfully. "You're speaking to one."

Jackaby rolled his eyes and sighed. "Fair enough, fair enough," he conceded, "but don't think being dead makes you the authority in every argument."

"No, but being right tends to. No one wants to let go of themselves, whatever form they may take—and I do know a little something about that." Jenny rose from the bench and began to descend, slowly, through the grassy ground. "And now, I think I'll leave you two to your business. Don't forget to ask about the room, Abigail!" In another moment her silvery hair melted out of sight beneath the floor.

"What was that about a room?" Jackaby asked.

I stood. "Nothing. Find something in your research?"

"Too much." He brandished a small crumpled envelope and handed it to me. "And we've gotten our telegrams."

"Ah, excellent. Did your hunch lead to something after all?"

"Oh yes." answered Jackaby. "Yes, indeed, Miss Rook. It seems the plot is much larger and more wicked than we'd feared."

Chapter Sixteen

The envelope contained telegrams from three cities. Contacts in law enforcement, the identities of whom Jackaby did not feel compelled to reveal, had responded quickly from Brahannasburg, Gadston, and Glanville. The telegraph office had collected and sent the posts all together, per the detective's request. Two or three more would likely arrive soon, he told me, but from just one he could extrapolate the content of the rest. They all bore the same message in various shorthand phrases, and the message was simple: *murder.*

I looked over the pages while we climbed down the spiral staircase back to Jackaby's office. *CONFIRM INCIDENTS IN BRAHANNASBURG -STOP-* read the top sheet. *DETAILS FIT DESCRIPTION -STOP- NOVEMBER ELEVENTH BUTCHER COD NECK*

WOUND -STOP- DECEMBER FIFTH POSTMAN COD CHEST WOUND

-STOP- DECEMBER TWENTY-SEVENTH TRANSIENT COD CHEST

WOUND -STOP-

"Cod?" I asked as we descended.

"Cause of death," he said simply.

ALL INCIDENTS UNSOLVED -STOP- NO RELATED CASES ON

RECORD -STOP- ASSISTANCE WELCOME -STOP- There the message ended. A quick glance at other pages revealed similar notes with varying dates and occupations of victims from Brahannasburg and Gadston.

"My God," I said, reading over the pages a second time. "But there are so many!"

"Yes. Mr. Bragg seems to have been following a trail of serial murders extending back for several months, probably longer. The marks on his map, *N. Wd.* and *C. Wd.,* denote neck wounds and chest wounds. It seems our killer favored the chest. All of them appear just beyond the jurisdiction of New Fiddleham, which shows that the killer made an effort to keep the authorities in the dark. Bragg's attempts to connect and shed light on these deaths only brought him to his own, it would seem."

Back in Jackaby's office, the detective unfolded the dead reporter's hand-drawn chart and placed it on top of a massive, finely detailed map already shrouding most of his desk. He rummaged in a drawer and produced a small box of pins with fat, shiny heads. He emptied the box onto the surface and compared the two maps.

In the flat section of his desk, we could see that the two maps corresponded well. Bragg had been diligent in his copying. Jackaby began marking each of the original *X*s with a pin on the larger map, jamming the points deep into the wood and effectively tacking the chart in place for the time being. From across the desk I scooped up a few pins and helped him finish the job.

"That's the lot," I said.

"Not quite," said Jackaby.

I scanned the original map again and counted out the marks. Jackaby swept the extra pins back into the box while I checked. We had stabbed all twelve points. The detective handed a single pin to me, with a somber, purposeful look. I took his meaning and, leaning in to find the right section of the city, plugged Arthur Bragg's own pin into the map. Thirteen shiny markers stood like polished gravestones.

"Bragg was not marked on his own map for obvious reasons. What else do you notice that sets his death apart from the other murders?" he asked.

I looked at the map. Bragg's pin looked very alone in the center of the chart. The others stood in little groups of twos and threes, circling his like school-yard bullies.

"He's the only one in New Fiddleham," I ventured.

"Very good. What do you make of that?"

A frightening thought occurred to me. "It means . . . that the murderer kills a few victims in each city, then moves on to the next. Now he's here in New Fiddleham . . . and he's only just begun!" I had been to the theater, and knew very well that a revelation like that one merited a dramatic chord from the pipe organ and a collective gasp from the audience, but in the real world, the words were left to stand on their own.

"Clever," responded Jackaby, "but also wrong." He pulled a ball of twine from the top drawer and glanced up at the board, where our list of dates still sat in neat, chalky rows.

"October twenty-third," he read, and tied the end of the string to the corresponding pin in Gadston. "And next was here, on the thirtieth." He drew the twine to the opposite side of the map, looping it around a pin in Crowley. "Then November fifth, down here." The line cut across the map again, down to Glanville, then up to Brahannasburg. He brought the string back and forth. The murders were never in the same town twice in a row, rarely even in an adjacent town, but always bouncing around to alternating corners of the map. The end result resembled a sloppy starburst, with lines zigzagging across New Fiddleham. Finally, Jackaby snipped the end and tied it to the lonely pin in the middle of the mess.

"He planned his marks to delay detection for as long as possible," Jackaby said. "Weeks, even months would pass before he returned to the same location, allowing time for attention to die down. Because he jumped jurisdictions, we might have seen even further months of this before police forces finally began to work out that they were even tracking the same culprit. Thanks to Bragg's stumbling onto the plot, the killer was forced to break his own rule in a rather significant way."

"How's that?" I asked.

"He killed where he lived. By the pattern of deaths before now, he had avoided New Fiddleham, but he clearly gravitated around it. Police tend to look with suspicion at a man in the center of a pile of dead bodies, and so our killer carefully perpetrated his crimes just beyond their vision. His home is here, though. I'm quite certain of that."

"What—here in town?" I asked, my eyes darting inadvertently to the window and the dimming light of the early evening. The moon was low in the sky but already clearly visible in the waning daylight, an almost perfect orb of white framed by the sinister, dark fingers of barren branches. "Wouldn't it be easier for a monster to hide out in the forest? Lurk about in the shadows and come out at night, or something?"

"It's possible, certainly—but we have reason to suspect we are looking for a man, and a man of property," Jackaby said. "Hatun claims to have gotten a good look at the murderer. The creature she described may or may not actually exist, but I believe she was there as our villain attempted to flee out the window. He left his traces on the windowsill, but not on the balconies below, which corresponds with her account. Now, if you were a cold-blooded killer, capable of tearing a hole through a grown man's chest, would you be worried about facing a hobbling, gray-haired old lady?"

"I suppose not."

"Ah, but if you could not see who or what awaited you? Then, like our cautious fiend, would you not find an alternative escape, just to be safe? If the culprit looked down upon the alleyway and saw nothing, as Hatun says, then that shawl of hers may have the power to alter perception, after all. If the villain could not see Hatun, then he has a home, and if he has a home, we can be confident it is within New Fiddleham, and if he dwells within New Fiddleham, then not a soul in the city is safe." Jackaby finished at a rush, and stopped, at last, to breathe.

I wanted less and less to be out and about finding lodging tonight. "But why should he begin to hunt in New Fiddleham?" I asked. "Maybe this was a special circumstance. Bragg was onto him. As you said, the reporter was probably only killed because he had begun to piece together the other murders."

"You mean, as we've just been doing?" Jackaby asked with a raised eyebrow. "I see your point, but the killer must have known his plot would only delay things for so long. Now he must know that he is at the end of his free rein. Like a caged goose, he will be more erratic, more unpredictable, and more deadly to anyone caught up in the trap with him."

"A goose?" I asked.

"Yes. Geese are terrifying. Whatever the metaphoric animal, we who have taken up Bragg's research find ourselves most squarely in the creature's sights. I think it may be prudent to heighten the building's defenses, and our own, until this affair is over. It's only a matter of time before the villain gets wind of our inquiries around town and pays us the same visit he paid Arthur Bragg."

A chill ran up my spine, and I darted a nervous glance over my shoulder. I began to speak, but was cut off by a sudden, deafening clamor of crashes and thuds from the floor above. The detective and I exchanged wide-eyed looks, and then he snatched a gnarled, wooden club from the shelf behind the desk and hurried into the hall to investigate. I scanned the office frantically, finding nothing intimidating to wield, and settled for a particularly heavy book. I carried it like a shot-putter, hefting the clumsy thing by my ear. My wrist was shaking, but I remained tensed to launch it fiercely at any ne'er-do-wells.

My nerves vibrated like a plucked harp, and I silently cursed the spiral stairwell as I crept upward in a cold sweat. The last turn revealed a massive heap of artifacts splayed across the passageway. They had clearly tumbled from the cluttered room on the right, and out into the hall. A china plate with gold inlay was still wobbling to a stop, and the feathers drifting slowly downward suggested that a ruptured pillow was probably somewhere in the mound.

Jenny stood in the doorway, her knees vanishing into the

side of the upturned phonograph, which lay toppled and propped on its bell. The ghost's expression was difficult to read. Her face, a study in silver, seemed flushed, her cheeks and nose darkening to an iron gray. Behind her, Douglas flapped to a landing on the curved headboard of the bed, which had been half unearthed since my last visit. He had two silk neckties draped across his neck like ceremonial vestments.

"What–?" Jackaby began.

"Oh, hello," said Jenny, smiling sheepishly. She wore a pair of lacy silk gloves, whose substantiality stood out in odd contrast to her translucent figure. "Just helping you get started. Got a lot to move. You'd be surprised how tricky it can be to stay solid while you're trying to maneuver the big, awkward stuff."

Douglas quacked and wobbled on his perch.

"Oh, like you were any help!" Jenny jabbed a silky white finger in his direction, then turned back to us. "I knew you would say yes, of course, Jackaby. So Douglas agreed to help me find space in the attic." She looked from the detective to me, reading expressions. "You are staying here, aren't you?"

"I haven't–," I started, but Jackaby burst in at the same moment.

"Of course she's staying here! Where else would she stay? That's no reason to go throwing my things across the house!"

And with that it was settled. Jenny clapped her hands together and smiled brightly, and Jackaby turned to look at me. "What in heaven's name are you doing with my copy of *Historia Lycanthropis?*"

"I–what?" I answered eloquently.

"That book. What on earth are you doing with it?"

"Well, you had the stick."

His eyebrows furrowed. "This is a shillelagh. It was cut from Irish blackthorn by a leprechaun craftsman, cured in the furnace of Gofannon, and imbued with supernatural powers of protection. That"–he gestured to the book–"is a book."

"It's heavy, though. A leprechaun? Like, the tiny fellows who keep pots of gold at the ends of rainbows?"

"Don't be asinine. I mean a real leprechaun. That volume is a sixteenth-century original printing. I hope very much that you didn't intend to use it as a projectile."

I held out the *Historia Lycanthropis,* which he collected on his way back to the staircase. "Jackaby," I said before he disappeared down the passage, "thank you."

"Whatever should you be thanking me for?"

"Well, for the lodging–and also for taking me on. Thanks."

"Don't thank me. Just do your best not to die, would you? Oh, and one more thing, Miss Rook. Promise me, if you do become a pigeon or a hedgehog or something, you won't get all stubborn about it. Now then, I've a few things to take care of around the place. Why don't you help Miss Cavanaugh sort out your room?" His voice faded as he trundled away down the stairs.

Jenny and I spent the remainder of the evening carrying an eclectic assortment of objects up to the third floor. Some of them found homes among the greenery, and others we hauled into an even more crowded attic. Douglas spent the time eating bread crumbs and squawking in disapproval about where we positioned the furniture. Jackaby spent it securing storm shutters and "maintaining safeguards," which seemed to consist of circling the house with salt, rye, holy water, and garlic.

Across town, Mr. Henderson–the man who had heard the banshee's silent scream–spent the evening dying. To be more accurate, he spent a very brief portion of the evening dying, and the rest of it being dead.

Chapter Seventeen

I awoke in the morning to the sound of dishes clattering somewhere below me. For just a moment I was back in my parents' house, my mother making breakfast in the kitchen. I was safe and everything was normal. The faint smell of something burning brought my eyes open, and my disoriented mind tumbled back into a strange, messy room, thousands of miles from home. For all the work Jenny and I had done, every corner was still cluttered with surplus chairs and old desks, their surfaces busy with ornate candlesticks or wooden masks. We had concentrated on the collection crowding the bed, first–and it had been all I could do not to simply collapse into it once its surface was clear. When I finally did, I had barely touched the soft linens before slumber took me.

I had slept in my underthings again, having laid out the sad, green walking dress to air. With the dawn light peeking in through the curtains, I rubbed the sleep from my eyes and reached for it. My dress was gone. My suitcase was still at the foot of my bed, where I had left it. I hefted it onto the mattress and clicked it open with a sigh.

Several underskirts and one very rigid corset later, I stepped out into the hallway in a red evening gown, a gift from my mother for my sixteenth birthday. The bodice was constricting, the buttons were snug, and the neck was high and tight around my throat. The hem swept the floor, and I felt like a porcelain doll with the layers of lace around my collar–not to mention the ridiculous, full sleeves that puffed out so much at the shoulder that they actually restricted my peripheral vision. Even through all the layers, I could feel the oversized bow bobbing up and down on my back-side with every step. I considered returning to the room and emerging instead in the filthy work pants–but no, I had spent enough time in those ruddy trousers to know I would be no more comfortable in them.

I navigated the stairwell carefully and found the door to the laboratory ajar. Jackaby was inside, humming tune-lessly and shuffling an iron skillet over a small burner. He snatched a pepper mill from amid the jars and bottles around him, and gave it a few twists into the skillet. The counter was littered with eggshells and bits of vegetables, and dusted here and there with powders of various hues. I pressed into the room, and Jackaby turned as the squeaky door announced my entrance.

"Ah, good morning, Miss Rook. Omelet?"

"Er–perhaps in a bit. Thank you, Mr. Jackaby." I pulled out a chair to sit, awkwardly navigating the inconvenient bustle and bow into the seat, and tucking the skirts beneath me. "I don't suppose you've seen my other dress, have you?"

"No, although Jenny mentioned something about laundry this morning. She's quite good with the wash . . . all the more impressive given that she can only physically interact with relics of her own belonging. I believe she wears an old pair of gloves for the exercise. It would be nice if she would remember her little impairment and wait for assistance when rearranging my things, but she is impossible to reason with. You can have a look out back and see if it isn't on the line."

I shuffled to the window and peeked out. My simple dress, indeed, hung on a clothesline outside, along with my stockings and handkerchief. The petticoat looked crisp and white, and the green skirt had lost its cloudy hem of dust along with the dark oval tea stain from last night, but they were still visibly damp, and dripping lightly into the grass. In this cold, I would be lucky if they were dry by sundown.

"Drat," I said. "That is to say, very kind of her. I should be thankful." I turned back, and my sweeping hem caught the leg of the mannequin's base, suddenly spinning the fabric figure toward a rack of glassware beside my employer.

I reached to catch it, far too slowly—but Jackaby's reflexes were fortunately much sharper. He stalled the figure a few inches from the expensive beakers and pipettes with one hand, then righted the mannequin and glanced down at my bulky red gown for the first time.

"What in heaven's name are you wearing?" he said. "I do hope you do not intend to dress in such a manner while we're working."

I swallowed. My cheeks felt hot and the satin collar was growing tighter about my neck. "That's just it," I said. "This sort of thing is all I have. Well, and a few boys' things—some trousers and the like—but I obviously can't walk around town in those."

"It seems you can barely manage to walk around in that," Jackaby said, turning back to his cooking. He picked up two identical red containers and sniffed at each of them. "If you need some ladies' things to wear, you might ask Douglas to help you."

I raised an eyebrow. "Douglas used to wear ladies' things?"

"Not that I'm aware of, no—although I would much prefer to see him in a frock than in feathers these days. He keeps a record of my previous cases, including ledgers. I received a chest of clothes some time ago as payment from a client with no money to speak of. They belonged to the fellow's late wife, I believe, or possibly his mother. Just ask Douglas—I'm sure he'll remember. Does this smell like paprika or gunpowder to you?" He stuck one of the red containers under my nose, and I sniffed experimentally at the holes in the top.

"Paprika?" I guessed, never having had occasion to handle either.

Jackaby nodded and tipped a generous helping into the skillet. Then, for good measure, he tapped in a few from the other container, too. He flinched and covered his face as the powder cracked and popped violently in the greasy pan. When it did not explode, he straightened up, wafting the pleasant aroma under his nose with a smile.

I excused myself to go see a duck about a dress.

Douglas was agreeable, as birds go, and upon my uncertain inquiry he guided me to a mossy chest toward the back of the pond. I thanked him kindly, and he flapped off, back to his perch on the little island. I pulled open the chest and exhumed a dusty, black dress. It looked like something a puritan grandmother might have considered a bit old-fashioned. I held it up to my shoulders anyway. The client's late wife—or possibly mother—had apparently been as tiny as she was dowdy. A soft giggling bubbled up behind me.

The ghost was resting comfortably on a grassy log, her shimmering head propped up casually on one hand. "Oh! I didn't . . . Good morning, Miss Cavanaugh," I said.

"'Jenny' is fine." She smiled. "You really shouldn't wear those, you know."

"I did ask."

"I'm sure you did, dear. You shouldn't wear them because they're dreadful."

"Oh," I said. "I suppose you're right. Although, if I were about a foot shorter and twenty pounds lighter, I might have made a fetching Pilgrim. A tiny, fetching Pilgrim."

"I think you look positively darling in that pretty red outfit—but it is really more of an evening gown than a day dress, isn't it?"

"I haven't much choice. Everything I have with me is either pretty or practical, except maybe the one you washed. Thank you, by the way."

"If you don't like them, why did you pack them?"

I sighed. "They were the first things I saw in my closet. Before I ran off on my own, my mother used to love to dress me like a paper doll in showy gowns from her favorite dressmaker. I never had to think about what to wear, because it never much mattered what I thought, anyway. I might have had more to choose from if she had packed for me, but I also would have needed a separate carriage just for hatboxes. It was one of her deepest fears that some passing gentry might see her daughter dressed in *rags*. That was what she called any outfit that did not have a wire frame, lace fringe, and five layers of fabric. I had a few school uniforms, at least—and I rather liked those—but they were worn out even before I left, and built for sitting in desks, not for clambering over rocks. They tore easily, and the hems got all tattered to ribbons. By the end of the first month, they really were rags. I spent the rest of my days at the dig site in boys' trousers."

"You didn't!"

"I did. And I loved it . . . at first. It was part of my big act of defiance, all bold and brazen and exciting. I can assure you, though, it stops feeling liberating after months of hard, dusty work. Now I just wish I had some dresses that were a little less . . . dressy."

"Well then," said Jenny, "when you find you must choose between two conflicting options, just do what Jackaby does. Take both." She patted a neat pile of folded clothes beside her with her slender, gloved fingers. "As I was going to say, if you need more functional attire, try these. You're a little smaller than I was, I think, but if you like, I can show you how to bring them in. It isn't as though I've any use for the things any longer."

I picked up the first garment. It was a rich, chocolate brown skirt, made of sturdy cotton—not as hardy and rough as denim, but thicker and more practical than any of my own. I held it to my waist. It hung well off the ground. My mother would be mortified at the thought of my bare calves, open to the world. I was delighted at the idea of not tripping over myself when stepping up to a curb.

"It's just a day dress, nothing fancy," said Jenny. The next item was an understated shirtwaist. It had been sewn with a minimum of unessential embroidery, but without losing its feminine lines. A long, fitted coat had been cut to drape smoothly over the shirt, coming in at the waist and then flowing loosely into the skirt. Laid out in front of me, the outfit looked infinitely more comfortable than my current options, and it was simple but elegant.

"The waist cinches up in the back, and there are pockets sewn into the hem, here and here." Jenny gestured to the skirt.

Pockets! I was thrilled. I have never understood the aversion to pockets in ladies' fashion—as though it has become some great shame to appear as if one might actually need to possess anything.

"These were yours?" I asked, feeling immediately indelicate about my use of the past tense. Jenny did not seem to notice. She nodded.

"Drab, I know."

"Not at all—they're brilliant!"

She smiled again. "I have some other skirts and aprons if you prefer. Not as much fun to wear, but they served me well helping out around the laboratory."

"Laboratory? You were a scientist?" I asked.

Jenny's smile faltered. "My fiancé was the scientist, but I was studying. I dare say it helped to prepare me for sharing a home with Mr. Jackaby. Well—as much as anything could prepare one for Jackaby."

"And your fiancé? What happened to him?" I was beginning to let myself feel like I was gossiping with an older sister.

Jenny pursed her lips, and did not answer. I instantly regretted the question. After several moments, she smiled politely. "Do try them on, why don't you?" she insisted.

I turned around to unbutton the billowy red gown, and found a large, prim mallard perched on a mossy cabinet just behind me.

"Goodness–Douglas! Are you going to–erm–fly off or something?" I said to him.

Douglas bobbled his head from side to side, looking very much like a simple bird.

"I don't see why he should," Jenny called from behind me, playfully. "He is a duck, after all. Besides, I watched *him* dress on more than one occasion when he wasn't," she added with a nostalgic smile. "Not a bad figure. I suppose it's really only fair."

I felt my cheeks growing hot. "Rather bold," I said.

She laughed. "Free spirit, Abigail. Losing one's body has that effect."

"You didn't seem so blithe about privacy when I stepped into your room by accident."

Her mischievous grin vanished into a dour pout. "That's different," she said, but relented with a shrug. "But if you insist. Come on, Douglas, let's give the girl some space." She tossed her arms up and dove backward, like a swimmer into a pool, pouring smoothly into the mossy floor behind her. The greenery trembled slightly, as if kissed by a gentle breeze, and in the blink of an eye the only sign that the spectral lady had ever been present was the pair of white gloves, pressed softly into the moss. Douglas waddled to the edge of the cabinet and dropped into a shallow glide. From the other side of the ivy curtain I heard his webbed feet splash down in the pond. Out of courtesy, I retrieved Jenny's gloves and laid them folded on the log for her return.

The clothes fit brilliantly, and smelled faintly of pine and perfume. Jenny had even thought to provide a pair of thick, wool stockings, which cushioned my sore feet marvelously. I thanked Douglas for his discretion on the way out, keeping carefully to the hardwood path to avoid wetting my new, warm, woolen footwear. I padded down the staircase, and was nearly to the ground level when I heard the rapid knocking from the front room. Jackaby stuck his head out of the laboratory as I entered the hallway.

"Oh, Miss Rook, good. Go and see who it is, would you? Nearly finished with the eggs." He made no indication that he had even noticed my change in attire.

"I thought they were nearly finished before I went upstairs," I said as I passed.

"Different eggs," he said, sliding back into the room. "The last ones were somewhat . . . uncooperative."

I slid into the lobby and opened the bright red door to find an agitated Junior Detective Cane on the doorstep.

"Officer Cane!" I stepped aside and gestured for the young man to enter. "Please, come in! My goodness, you look dreadful! Have you slept at all?"

"I've not had a chance." He removed his hat as he slipped into the room. "Thank you, Miss Rook. You, on the contrary, are looking quite well." I felt my cheeks go warm again, and I found myself lifting a hand to my hair, wishing I had stopped to brush and arrange it before coming back downstairs. "Is Mr. Jackaby in, miss? I'm afraid it's rather urgent."

I led the man back down the hallway, and poked my head in the laboratory door. "It's Charlie Cane, Mr. Jackaby," I said, putting into my tone that touch of professionalism my tousled hair and stockinged feet might have lacked.

"Who?"

"The police detective from yesterday. He says he has some urgent news."

Jackaby plodded over to the doorway. "Oh, right–you." He looked Charlie up and down with a modicum of suspicion.

"So, I take it our friend in the red pajamas is dead?"

Charlie nodded. "Mr. Henderson, sir. Yes, sir."

"Shame." Jackaby nodded, thoughtfully, but without surprise. "Same manner of death as the last one?"

Charlie nodded again. "Just the same. Only more blood, this time, sir."

"That accounts for the stains on your knees, then," said Jackaby. "I take it you've been to examine the corpse?"

The last word seemed to thump into Charlie like a sandbag. I watched as he breathed in deeply, collecting himself.

His knees were, indeed, stained a deep merlot, but it was hardly discernible against the dark blues of the uniform fabric. Looking more intently, I noted that the mirror polish of his shoe had been marred by a smudge of red across the pointed toe as well. "I was there," Charlie said. "I was there all night, and I couldn't save him."

"Of course you couldn't," Jackaby answered dismissively. I shot my employer a stern glance. The junior detective looked stricken. Jackaby caught my expression and reached out stiffly to pat Charlie on the arm. "No one could have saved him," he amended. "No escaping it, once he heard the cry. Good of you to try, though. The silver lining to this tragedy, of course, is that we have a new, fresh crime scene. After Miss Rook and I have had a quick breakfast, we'll come see what clues our villain has left for us, this time."

Charlie shifted his feet impatiently. "Detective, surely time is of the essence! A man is dead!"

"Lamentably so, and no amount of hurry and bother will revive him. He will still be dead when we reach him, I assure you. Now, a good bit of hot breakfast will only help to improve our faculties and ensure that we don't miss—"

But the detective's sentence was cut short by a sudden, deafening boom, and the crunch of an iron skillet lodging itself halfway through the wall, its black handle poking out into the hallway at a jaunty angle, the metal visibly vibrating from the impact. The ringing silence that followed was broken by a few tinkles and thumps from within the room, and a half-dozen ripe, red apples rolling into the hallway.

"Too much paprika?" I offered.

"On second thought," Jackaby continued with nonchalance, "it wouldn't do to weigh ourselves down before we'd even gotten started, would it?"

Charlie's mouth opened and closed wordlessly as he blinked at the pan.

"Yes, just a quick bite should do the trick. Apple?" Jackaby bent and retrieved one, and I accepted the proffered fruit.

"I'll just fetch my shoes, then?" I asked.

"Do hurry," Jackaby instructed. "Time is of the essence, Miss Rook. A man is dead."

Chapter Eighteen

The Emerald Arch was even more heavily guarded than it had been the previous day. The police presence appeared to have doubled, and official-looking rope now stretched around the entire building. A glance down the alleyway as we passed proved that there would not be a repeat of Jackaby's sneaky business with the balconies, unless he felt like pulling his maneuver in the company of three uniformed officers. From what I had seen of the strange detective in the last twenty-four hours, he might have even pulled it off. In fact, it would probably have come to them giving him a leg up and wishing him all the best.

Charlie marched us past the guards at the front door. I recognized one of them as the thick, hawk-nosed policeman we'd slipped past yesterday. His pinched, suspicious expression hadn't changed. "Cane," he said without affection, but this time he didn't try to stop us as we followed our escort past the cordon.

"O'Doyle," Charlie answered in a matched tone. That being the apparent limit of their cordiality toward each other, we passed quickly and were soon through the front doors. Charlie had already shared a few details of the scene as we rushed through town, but it had all been a blurry, fragmented mess of information. As we entered the stairwell, Jackaby asked the detective to repeat his story from the beginning, leaving nothing out.

"Well, let's see. I suppose it began after I left you yesterday, sir," Charlie began. "I returned to my post outside Mr. Bragg's room—that is, the late Mr. Bragg's room. When Chief Inspector Marlowe arrived, I told him that I thought it would be wise to post guards tonight to protect Mr. Henderson. He asked me why. Now, you must understand that the chief inspector is very . . . selective about what he is willing to believe. Some of the other men are more open-minded—Officer Porter told me he attended a séance once, and I've even seen Lieutenant Dupin knock on wood—but not Marlowe. Marlowe does not even believe in luck. I couldn't very well tell him about the banshee, so I just told him that something Henderson said when I revisited his room made me believe he had information about the murderer, and that he was too afraid for his life to come forward.

"The chief inspector just looked angry about that, and asked when I had spoken to his witness without permission. I told him we just stopped by on our way out, and that you had actually had a calming effect on the poor man. That was a mistake. He got all red and asked why the hell I had let that lunatic crackpot—sorry, sir, his words—wander around the building against his orders. He reminded me who was in charge, and told me he would have my badge if I couldn't recognize the chain of command.

"It was my fault. I should have been more careful with my words. Commissioner Swift had arrived, as you know—he came into the hallway while we were speaking, breathing hard as he came out of the stairwell. Having the commissioner around always puts Inspector Marlowe on edge. I apologized and assured him it would not happen again. Then I asked if he would still be placing any officers to watch Henderson. That was another a mistake. He used quite a few unpleasant words to tell me no. Well, I could not argue with the chief inspector, especially with the commissioner present . . ."

"But you couldn't stand idly by while a man's life was in danger, either?" Jackaby offered. "You came back anyway, didn't you?"

"I had to try to help him. Yes, I returned after my shift had ended and all of the rest of the police had gone."

"Your time might have been better spent comfortably at home with your family."

"I have no family here, Mr. Jackaby, and I can think of no better way to spend an evening than in service to my city."

"That sounds terribly lonesome," I said. "I mean, isn't there anyone . . . ?"

"My life is . . . complicated," said Charlie. "I find it much more convenient to live alone."

I might have liked to know a bit more about the stoic policeman, but Jackaby pressed forward with the matter at hand. "So, Henderson was already dead when you arrived?"

"No, not at all. I knocked on his door to check, and he opened it, looking a bit tired and holding on to that tuning fork, but otherwise healthy. I did not wish to alarm him, so I told him I was just keeping an eye on the whole building. He bade me good night and went back inside, his lock and deadbolt clicking soundly after the door was shut. I took up a position in the hallway. I knew he was still there for several hours, because I could hear the chime of the tuning fork every minute or so on the other side of the door.

"My hearing is very good, sir, and I was watching and listening for anything strange at all in the building. It must have been close to midnight when there finally came some sort of clinking sound from the stairwell. It was terribly familiar, but I couldn't place when I had heard it before. The hallway was dark, and I kept to the shadows as I crept over to investigate. The floorboards must have given me away as I got nearer, because when they creaked under my footstep, the noise stopped. I raced in and had a look, but there was nothing in the stairwell.

"I did not dare leave the third floor with Henderson unguarded, so I slipped back down the hallway toward my post. I could see his door clearly as I came nearer—the hallway lights are kept lit at night, and the moonlight through the window was even brighter. As I drew close, I could swear I heard a noise in his room, just a bump in the night. So, quiet as a mouse, I listened at the door. I must have listened for five or six minutes, not moving, barely breathing, but not another sound came from Henderson's room. That was when I knew something was terribly wrong."

"You knew something was wrong because you . . . *didn't* hear anything?" Jackaby asked.

"Sorry to say, it took a few minutes to realize it, but yes, sir. Specifically, what I did not hear was the ping of your tuning fork. Henderson's room was, as they say, as silent as the grave. I knocked first, and announced myself, just as we're taught to do. I got no answer and the door was still locked tight, so I had to"—Charlie, ahead by a few paces, shot a glance over his shoulder at Jackaby—"to kick it in. It was a horrible sight, Detective, and the smell! He was there, still wearing those red pajamas, only the red was spreading across the floor. More than the last one, much more. The window was wide-open, and the room was so cold, you could see the heat rising off the body in thick, steamy clouds.

"I scanned the room and hurried to the window, but there was no one in sight. I heard him, though. The sound rang like horseshoes on pavement, but the rhythm was a man's steps. He was moving fast, so fast he was blocks away before I could even pick out a direction from the echoes. I was too slow. Too slow and too late.

"I looked around for any clues, but there was nothing at all out of the ordinary—except, of course, the body bleeding on the floor. I ran for the station on Mason Street and sent a runner to alert the chief inspector. I brought a few of the night shift back with me, and then waited for Inspector Marlowe to arrive."

We reached the third floor just as his story came to an end. A guard had been posted at either end of the hallway. As we approached the first, he narrowed his eyes, but he gave Charlie a nod of recognition and let us pass. That same strong, coppery smell spilled through the hallway, and I noticed Jackaby was feeling at the air with his hands, just as he had when we approached the first victim.

"Speaking of Marlowe," Jackaby said, his hand still gently coasting beside him, "where is the old boy? I should think he would be keeping a tight grip on the scene this time."

"He is." The voice came from the doorway ahead as the chief inspector stepped into the hallway to meet us. In spite of his midnight awakening, Marlowe looked as clean-shaven and pressed as he had the day before. The hand-cuffs still swung from his belt as he moved, and the silver bars on his uniform caught the morning light streaming through the hallway.

"Ah, Marlowe, good morning!" said Jackaby, a little too cheerfully. "You're looking well."

"And you look like you've been dragged through hell, as usual. Enough pleasantries. I've had a short night and a long morning, and I'm overdue an explanation."

"Ah, yes. Don't be too hard on the junior detective—it isn't his fault. We were just in the area and thought it would be rude if we didn't stop by to—"

"Detective Cane is not working behind my back . . . not *this time*." Marlowe shot a finely sharpened glance at Charlie, who shrank into the collar of his uniform. "He brought you here on my orders. He didn't tell you? I mean that I am overdue an explanation about this." The inspector stepped back and gestured toward the open door of room 313.

The door was splintered and raked with gashes, and the frame had come apart around the lock. The smell was strongest here, metallic and sickly sweet, like pennies and spoiled fruit. Inside, beside his worn sofa, lay the body of Mr. Henderson.

My breath caught in my throat. This body was worse than the last one, and the blood was everywhere. A splash of deep burgundy had painted a sloppy scar across the wallpaper, and it had dripped dark lines back down to the floor. The late William Henderson's bright red pajamas were dyed an even deeper crimson, and the wound on his chest was a match to Arthur Bragg's, down the hall. The blood had poured across the room, rivulets tracing the corners of the floorboards and mapping the topography of the room with dark pools. My vision swam and my stomach lurched, but try as I might, I could not pull my eyes from the horrible scene. Marlowe stepped forward, cutting off my line of sight, and I blinked and breathed again, the trance broken.

"May I?" my employer asked, and Marlowe nodded his permission to enter. Jackaby stepped carefully into the chamber, taking wide, uneven strides to avoid the spill. I remained by the doorway behind Marlowe while Jackaby examined the body. He followed a trail of drips to the window and glanced out.

The chief inspector watched closely, but he did not interrupt or question the detective as the man danced around the crime scene, peering through the vials and lenses he produced from his pockets, and even leaning in to sniff the windowsill. Jackaby moved with all the gangling grace of a newborn foal, but he kept clear of the puddles of liquid evidence. At length, he hopscotched his way back to the door, where he knelt and ran a finger gently across the splintered gashes in the wood. With one fluid, almost imperceptible motion, he plucked some small sample from the splinters and, like a street magician with a tricky coin, made it vanish in his hands before he rose.

"You said you saw no one in the hall, and the door was

still secured from the inside when you forced your entry?" he asked, turning around.

"That's right," Charlie confirmed. "I found the window open, inside."

"And the scene has not changed since your first impression?"

Charlie looked inside and swallowed hard, nodding. "It's spread. But otherwise, yes, it's just the same."

"Not forgetting something?" Inspector Marlowe prompted his detective, not taking his eyes off Jackaby.

"Oh. Yes, sir. Of course, sir. There has been one item removed as evidence." Charlie grimaced and pointed to Henderson's hand, which was clenched, but empty.

Marlowe nodded and reached into his own pocket, producing a small cloth packet. "Mr. Jackaby," he said, shifting the bundle from one hand to the other as he spoke, "you've had a look around. Anything to share?"

Jackaby glanced from Charlie to Marlowe before answering. "We are obviously faced with the same villain. Rushed, this time, but otherwise consistent in every detail."

"And what details would those be?" Marlowe pressed. His voice was flat, and his eyes locked on Jackaby like a raptor on a field mouse. "Be specific."

"The chest wound, most obviously, and the removal of blood. Avarice is clearly not a motive in either killing–there is a rather expensive pocket watch on the end table, just there, by the window, but the culprit passed it by, just as he left Mr. Bragg's wallet. He also left Mr. Henderson clutching my tuning fork, which I assume is the object you have tucked in your handkerchief now, an item of considerable value to me, and one I would like back when this business is all over."

Marlowe raised an eyebrow a fraction of an inch, and made no motion to relinquish the parcel. "Would you, now? Anything else to say?"

"I *would* also mention the residual supernatural aura, which is exceptionally strong and clear inside the room, but we both know you'll dismiss it as hokum, so I refrain from wasting any time describing it."

"Your restraint is appreciated," said Marlowe drily. "But what was that you said about the blood? You were right that the last victim was surprisingly clean–but you can hardly say the same about Henderson."

"You must have noticed the smearing on the body?" Jackaby asked. "And the trail?" Marlowe's face was impassive and unreadable, and after a pause Jackaby resumed. "Just there, along the torso, and continuing a short way up the side of the sofa. The rest of the blood appears to have dropped, splattered, or run in a natural fashion, but there you can see it's been smeared. Someone was soaking up a bit of it, perhaps with a simple rag. There are then droplets of blood on the arm of the sofa marking a trail, obscured briefly by that pool, but resuming on a straight course for the window. One can only deduce that the culprit daubed some item in the wound, then ran for his exit. I imagine the trail continues on the pavement below. If followed, it might just lead to–"

"It doesn't," Marlowe interrupted. "I followed it myself with two of my best detectives."

Jackaby glanced at Charlie again for a moment, and addressed his next question to him. "And all three of you lost the scent?"

"Detective Cane was not present during the pursuit," Marlowe cut in. "But yes, the blood droplets petered out by Winston Street. I was able to track his footprints a few blocks farther, to Market, but there the trail became impossibly lost." The inspector continued to stare at Jackaby, his gaze locked as tight as a pair of manacles.

Jackaby, whether by mere affectation or true obliviousness, paid no mind to the inspector's focused attention. "Interesting. And why wasn't he present during the pursuit?"

Marlowe blinked. "What?"

"Detective Cane. He discovered the body, after all. Is there any reason he was not involved in the search?"

Marlowe flashed a stern glance at Charlie, who slunk back slightly like a scolded puppy. "Junior Detective Cane was otherwise occupied."

"Ah, I believe I understand." Jackaby nodded. "Just how long did you keep your detective incarcerated?"

"That's not what I said."

"Yes, but it is what you meant. You did not trust your

detective, just as you do not trust me. I'm sure you questioned him first, which was wise. Probably did so before you bothered to follow the legitimate lead, though, which was not. Is it any wonder the trail went cold? Having been cooped up in a cell certainly accounts for his increased agitation as well. Was he released exclusively to fetch me, I wonder?" Jackaby seemed almost amused at the thought.

Inspector Marlowe's brow furrowed, and his eyes developed the menacing sort of shadows usually reserved for dark alleys in bad neighborhoods. Jackaby continued.

"You did have him followed as he called on me, of course. Yes, I thought I recognized Lieutenant Dupin keeping an inconspicuous distance as we passed Fourth Street. It becomes evident that you did not summon me for a professional consultation, Inspector. I thought, perhaps, you might have realized you were out of your depth and actually sought my input, but we both know that is not the case. So, you've had time to observe me at the crime scene, and your men have had plenty of time to ransack my establishment. Would you like to actually ask me any questions before tossing me in lockup?"

"I think that can wait until we've reached the station," Marlowe said with a grunt.

The watchmen from either end of the hallway suddenly appeared at the door. Jackaby stepped out as calmly as one might exit a coach, presenting his wrists to be handcuffed.

"What?" My mind reeled at the sudden, extreme turn the

day was taking. This was madness! "Mr. Jackaby—can they do this? You haven't done anything! Inspector, please. He hasn't done anything!"

Marlowe delicately folded back the corner of the handkerchief in his hands, revealing the metallic sheen of the fork, and a crimson stain, which could only be blood. He made a show of thinking about the object for a few moments while Jackaby was shackled. "Don't worry, Miss Rook." He turned to me, flipping the cloth back over the tuning fork. "He won't be leaving alone. I did warn you not to let him drag you into his craziness, didn't I?"

Marlowe's heavy, iron handcuffs were icy cold as he clicked them onto my wrists. As we drew into the lobby, we passed a small crowd of tenants being herded into the office by uniformed officers. A woman in a canary yellow dress made a point of alerting as many of her neighbors as she could nudge that we were passing through. They shuffled and watched our approach, in no hurry to be interviewed, but eager to eavesdrop. A reporter had set up a camera by the doorway, and he flashed a photograph as we arrived. Marlowe barked at him to put it away, and an officer crossed to block his view, but I tucked my head as deeply into my coat's collar as I could, flushing with embarrassment. Jackaby, for his part, seemed unflappably comfortable, striding with as much confidence as if he were leading the policemen and not the other way around. The reporter didn't try for any more photographs, but the nosy gossip in yellow had found her way over to him. She was stealing glances at us, and I saw her mouth form the words "that girl" with haughty disdain, before another figure burst from the milling crowd.

Mona O'Connor shoved past her neighbors and planted herself in front of Jackaby before any of the officers could intervene. She jabbed a finger into his chest accusingly. "You! You lied to me!"

"I assure you, Miss O'Connor, I did nothing of the sort. This is all a misunderstanding. If you don't mind, we do need to be getting along." His calm was mesmerizing, and if not for the cuffs jingling on his hands, I might have forgotten he was under arrest. Mona was not placated.

"You did! You lied to me!"

The guard on Jackaby's arm attempted to position himself between the two, mumbling an ineffective, "Step back, please, madam. Out of the way. Step back." An officer from the lobby came to assist, tugging at her arm. She jerked it away and persisted.

"You told me she would be better by morning!" she cried out as we began to move forward again.

Now Jackaby's unflappable expression faltered. His eyes went wide and his brow creased. He attempted to stop, and the officer behind him gave him a shove. "Mrs. Morrigan?" he called over his shoulder as we were pressed toward the door. "You mean to say she isn't?"

"Worse!" Mona's voice hollered past the uniform now

bodily restraining her. "A hundred times worse! The worst she's ever been!" The officers finally restrained the woman and succeeded in ushering Jackaby and me out the door.

Jackaby's face was ashen as we reached daylight. He did not speak again until the two of us had been loaded into the back of the police wagon. The policeman slammed the doors, and we were alone on hard wooden seats, which stunk of stale beer and vomit.

"It's bad?" I asked.

He breathed in slowly before responding. "Each night Mrs. Morrigan has wailed, a life has been brutally ended. If she wails, now—wails a hundred times worse, now—then yes, I imagine it is very bad, indeed."

Chapter Nineteen

"Well, look on the bright side," I said, after the officer had slid shut our cell doors and clicked tight the locks. "At least we're in jail."

In the adjacent cell, my employer pushed back a handful of dark hair and raised an eyebrow in my direction. The processing officer had taken our personal effects, and Jackaby looked exceptionally frail in the barren cell without his silly hat and coat to hide in.

"True, we've been locked in here," I continued. "But you could also say the murderer has been locked out there, which is something."

It wasn't as bad as I had feared. Jackaby and I had been stuck in separate holding cells, of course, but the enclosures ran along the wall, connected on either side, so I didn't feel entirely alone. Aside from my employer and me, the lockup contained only one other inhabitant—a peacefully snoring drunk with cheery red suspenders who lay on the far side of Jackaby. Our cells faced not the drab cement slab I had envisioned, but instead a simple, carpeted walkway, bordered by a couple of desks with official-looking documents sorted neatly in trays. An officer sat at the nearest one, stamping papers with a satisfying *thup-thup*. In the corner was a small table with a few coffee mugs and a half-eaten cake with bright white frosting. Tacked on the wall above it was a handwritten *Happy Birthday, Allan*. I had heard of offices feeling like prisons, but in this case our prison felt, rather anticlimactically, like an office.

"I would rather be at home on this occasion," said Jackaby.

"I'm just thankful the constables can't go calling my parents to bail me out," I said. "I don't want to know what they would think if they could see me now."

"Why should you mind what some old constable thinks of you?"

"Not the constables, my parents. I can't imagine how all this would look to them."

"Does it matter, considerably, what your parents think?"

"Well . . . of course it does. They're my parents. How did your parents react when you started being—you know—you?"

Jackaby ran a finger along the thick bars of the cell, a

scowl twisting his brow into a knot. "My home, unlike this jail cell, has been fortified against the sort of dangers presently at large in the city. I would feel far more secure within the premises of my own property on Augur Lane."

"I saw you setting up 'fortifications.' I think bricks and steel might actually be a slightly more effective deterrent than a pinch of salt and powdered garlic. Besides, we don't exactly make easy targets; we're surrounded by police."

"I suppose that's fair, Miss Rook, and true enough," answered Jackaby, "unless, as I am beginning to suspect, our villain wears a badge."

I glanced at the officer on duty behind the desk. His little stamp continued to *thup* rhythmically. He was a portly, rosy-cheeked man with a walrus mustache, the bristles of which were smattered with white frosting. "Do you think that's likely?" I asked.

"It is a decided possibility."

My mind flashed back to the crime scene. "The door," I said. "Charlie said he'd had to kick it in."

"Hmm? Yes, that's right. He also reasoned, logically, that the murderer must have entered and escaped through the window."

"Then whose claws raked into Henderson's door?" I asked.

"Ah." Jackaby leaned his back on the bars and watched the drunkard snoring for a few moments. "You noticed that, did you?"

"The thing was in poor shape, all splintered and cracked. It had clearly been forced open, as he said, but footprints are footprints and paw prints are paw prints. I know you spotted them, too."

"Indeed. I managed to collect a few small hairs, as well, but until I have my coat back, and can return to my laboratory to test them, they might as well be turnips, for all they'll tell us."

"But why would Charlie lie?" I asked, lowering my voice as a door opened on the far side of the office. Inspector Marlowe came in, trailing a pair of uniforms. "It doesn't make sense—he's been the most helpful of the lot! What's he hiding?"

"That is an excellent question," said Jackaby. "It seems the detective has a few secrets."

"Funny," said the chief inspector, from the doorway, "that's precisely what I was thinking about you. Maybe you really can read minds, or whatever it is you do." He drew to a stop in front of Jackaby's cell.

"Ah, Marlowe," answered Jackaby, "so good of you to join us. I'd offer you refreshments, but I'm afraid we're all out in here."

"There's cake in the corner," I offered, helpfully.

"Good, yes. There does appear to be cake, as my young associate observes, in the corner."

"Enough, both of you," Marlowe snapped. "I have tolerated your lunatic claims and your blatant disregard for authority. I will not tolerate withholding evidence in the middle of a homicide investigation."

"We've done nothing of the sort," said Jackaby, a bit haughtily. "You've done the withholding. You've got my tuning fork—which, I remind you, I would like back. We have withheld nothing."

"Oh, no?" The inspector held out a hand, and one of the uniformed men shuffled forward to hand him a folded paper. Marlowe opened it slowly. "Then I suppose this map, found in your office on Augur Lane, is not drawn on Arthur Bragg's personal stationery, and written in the victim's own hand?"

"Oh, that," said Jackaby. "Yes well, that wasn't *withholding* so much as *borrowing*, or possibly *safekeeping*."

Marlowe said nothing, but filled his expression with even more reproach. The officers who had taken position at either side of Marlowe wore matching, humorless scowls that suggested a lifetime of taking themselves too seriously. One of them also had several large, pale gray splatters across his shoulders, which suggested Douglas the duck had excellent aim. They had drawn to a halt, but the swampy, sulfurous smell that accompanied them was gradually creeping its way into the cells.

"Oh, don't look so put out," said Jackaby. "You could have asked for it."

"I've got plenty to ask," Marlowe replied. He shot a glance my way and added, "Both of you. But we'll be conducting this interrogation one at a time. Jackaby, I think it's time you and I had a little talk."

Marlowe nodded a silent command, and the cop with duck-poop epaulettes marched to the cell door and stood at military attention. "Detainees will move away from the door!" he barked. Jackaby, already halfway across the cell, rolled his eyes at the officer and took one more step backward. The man unlocked the door and slid it ajar. Jackaby stepped out, and the guard eyed him with suspicion as he slammed it shut. This fellow managed to make Marlowe seem fun.

Jackaby, Marlowe, and the overzealous guard disappeared down the hallway, leaving the second cheerless policeman to keep an eye on me, presumably because I could get into far too much trouble if left to my own devices in a locked, eight-by-ten cell. It sank in that I had, in fact, been left alone in an eight-by-ten cell, and I began to feel a swelling sensation of helplessness. I fidgeted, worrying the fringe on my new dress.

This was all so preposterous. I don't know why I felt more secure in the presence of a strange man I had known for less than a day—particularly one whom I had been warned to avoid by nearly everyone I had met—but I hoped that they would be back soon, all the same.

I extended a polite smile to the man guarding me. He returned a blank stare—not simply the expressionless look you might adopt while waiting in line at the bank, but a deeply, aggressively blank stare. He held the sort of posture attainable only by those who have had their sense of humor surgically removed. His uniform looked crisp and free of droppings, but a familiar sulfuric stench still rolled off him.

"Hello," I ventured.

The officer did not respond.

"So, you had a look around Jackaby's place? Pretty crazy, isn't it?"

Still no response.

"Be honest now. You stared at the frog, didn't you?"

The officer remained silent, but his nostrils twitched involuntarily. He continued to direct his maliciously blank stare toward me.

"I thought so." I smiled and leaned back on the slab of a bench behind me.

Chapter Twenty

I spent the next hour staring at a small patch of gray sky through the cell window and quietly drumming on the bench with my fingers. I had just perfected my timing so that the regular *thup* of the desk officer's stamp fit neatly into the rhythm, when the door finally burst open and Jackaby's voice preceded him through the hallway.

"Well, of course you would think that, if you're just going to measure a man's stability on whether or not he can taste banana when there are no bananas physically present. Narrow-minded and dismissive, as always, Inspector."

The guard with the dirty shoulders pulled open Jackaby's cell door, delivering the detective back inside with a shove. He slammed it closed, and then crossed over to unlock mine. "You're next." He jabbed a meaty finger in my direction, then stood rigidly at the door, waiting for me.

I whispered across the bars to Jackaby as I rose, "Shall I tell them the truth?"

"Have you killed anyone?" he asked, quietly.

"No, of course not!"

"Then I can't imagine why you shouldn't."

The corridor was quiet, punctuated by the occasional *clickity-click* of a typewriter in one of the offices we passed. I felt like a girl in grammar school, treading the long hallway to the principal's office with a hall monitor sneering over me all the way. The guard directed me into a room at the end of the hall. The little chamber was slightly larger than the cell had been, but managed to look even more drab and less inviting. The space lacked even the small, barred window that the cell had possessed, leaving nothing to puncture the dull grayness of the walls. The only light came from a single gas lamp, high on the wall behind Marlowe, who was sitting at a table reading over his notes. I took the chair opposite and waited for the chief inspector to speak. The policeman who had brought me in took his position in front of the door, as if I might leap up and race through the police station at any moment.

The table was plain wood, stained and battered, but sturdy. On it sat the handkerchief-bundled tuning fork, Bragg's map, and Marlowe's notebook. The latter lay open as Marlowe reviewed some previous entry. I definitely needed a notebook like that. The chief inspector took his time before slowly closing the book and setting it beside him on the table.

"So, Miss Abigail Rook." He spoke evenly and leaned his elbows on the table, his fingers steepled under his chin. "You only recently arrived in New Fiddleham, is that correct?"

"Two nights ago, yes," I answered. "I arrived by boat late in the afternoon."

"Inauspicious timing, Miss Rook. Late in the afternoon, two nights ago, Arthur Bragg was still alive. That is–right up until he wasn't. Had you met the man before then?"

"I never did meet him. Only saw his body, up at the apartment yesterday."

"Are you staying at the Emerald Arch Apartments, Miss Rook?"

"No, sir. I've taken a room in Mr. Jackaby's building on Augur Lane."

Marlowe raised an eyebrow. "Is that so?"

"Yes, sir. He's hired me on as his assistant."

"And invited you to live in his home. Is there any more to the nature of your . . . relationship?" He managed to keep his voice cold and emotionless, but something about the way he paused before the word "relationship" left it laden with unspeakable impropriety.

"What? No!"

Marlowe nodded and made a note. "Why were you at the Emerald Arch Apartments, if not to look for some place to stay?"

I did my best not to let the inspector's blunt questions and stony bearing get me flustered. "I–I had just started working for Mr. Jackaby–or rather, I think I began working for him while we were there. I was following him on his investigation."

"Indeed?" Marlow made another note. "Impressive that you should come so quickly to find employment with a man who just happened to be involved in a murder . . . one that took place the very night you arrived in town. Did you seek him out because you were interested in getting a second look at the crime scene?"

The blood was pumping in my ears, and I was quickly beginning to resent the inspector's implications. "With all due respect, sir, I would be employed by half a dozen other respectable townspeople if any of them had been hiring. Mr. Jackaby had work for me, that's all–and I'm glad he did, Inspector. He's a bit strange, it's true, but at least he's a competent investigator. His methods don't include locking up everyone who tries to help." I realized I had let Marlowe throw me completely off balance, and I sat back nervously, waiting for his rebuke.

To his credit, the chief inspector took my comment in stride. He simply made another quiet mark in his notepad, and continued in the same even tone, a faint touch of gravel in his voice.

"Speaking of Mr. Jackaby's methods, do you recognize this?" He pushed the map across the table toward me.

"Yes, sir," I answered, meekly.

"Care to explain it?"

"It's a map. Mr. Bragg seems to have been researching a string of deaths just outside of New Fiddleham. We believe it's probably why he was killed."

"A compelling piece of evidence. Care to explain how it came to rest in the offices at 926 Augur Lane?"

"Oh, yes. I guess Jackaby discovered it in Mr. Bragg's room, and thought it might be worth looking into."

"And so he stole a crucial piece of evidence?"

"Well, I don't think he exactly meant to steal it. I'm sure he was planning on . . ."

"Was this before or after I discovered the two of you contaminating the crime scene?"

I swallowed. "After."

"Before or after the two of you ignored my order to leave the premises and went, instead, to speak with a witness—a witness who was brutally murdered the following night?"

"Er—after that as well, sir," I admitted.

"Why don't we start at the beginning, Miss Rook."

And so we did. I told him everything, from the kobold on my coat to the silent screams torturing Mr. Henderson, and the effect of Jackaby's tuning fork. I had explained all about Mona and the banshee, and had just reached old Hatun with her shawl-of-partial-invisibility when there came a knock at the door. Marlowe, in spite of his furrowed brow and occasionally rolling eyes, had listened to it all, jotting notes in his book. "We'll get back to you in a moment," he told me, and nodded to the policeman at the door.

The guard opened it a crack and then quickly stepped away, letting it swing wide. He popped instantly to attention beside the doorway. Commissioner Swift stood in the hall, looking thoroughly out of place in the plain, practical quarters of the police station. He wore the same expensive black coat with red trim and matching rosy derby. His collar looked starched, peeking up to frame a dark paisley cravat. He leaned heavily on his polished cane, straightening slightly as Marlowe and I turned to look.

With stiff but purposeful steps, Swift strode into the interrogation room. He fought against his leg braces to affect a normal gait, gritting his teeth every time the mechanism gave out the slightest squeak as he moved. He marched to the table beside Marlowe.

The chief inspector looked as surprised to see him as I was. "Commissioner," he managed with a respectful nod. "What can I do for you?"

"You can carry on, Inspector. I'll just be overseeing things. Who do we have here? I thought you were interrogating the infamous Mr. Jackaby." The commissioner picked up Marlowe's notebook and flipped back a few pages, scanning the scribbled entries.

"This is his associate, sir, one Abigail Rook. I was just taking a few statements."

"So I see." Swift scowled at the notepad and flipped another page. "A banshee? A magic shawl? Really? Trolls, Miss Rook?" His voice dripped with sardonic incredulity as he raised his eyes to mine over the top of the book.

"Just the one troll," I replied timidly. "I'm told he's very small."

"We were nearly finished here," Marlowe stated, reaching for the book. "If I may?"

Swift tossed it back to the table, ignoring Marlowe's hand. "You *are* finished here. I won't have my chief inspector wasting his time listening to fairy tales while some madman hacks my city to pieces. Do you have any idea how bad that makes me look? Any idea how far I will drop in the polls every time a body turns up in my jurisdiction?"

"Yes, Commissioner. I understand, but . . ."

"But nothing! I want you and your men back out in the streets where you belong, finding answers! Finding me a killer!"

Marlowe, out of self-preservation, bit his tongue before speaking, and I took the opportunity. "Does this mean I'm free to go?"

Swift darted a glance at me as though he had already forgotten I was in the room. "You? Certainly not. Marlowe, keep the both of them locked up tight until this is over. Should keep them out from under foot so you can do your damned job, and teach them a lesson for wasting our time. At least we can tell the press we've already taken the prime suspects into custody. The public likes fast action. Justice is swift and all that. Oh, that's not bad. I should have my campaign boys do something with that. Dixon!"

The commissioner moved stiffly to the door, hollering down the hallway until a scrawny man in a suede suit and straw boater hat popped into view. The two of them disappeared from view around a corner, and the sound of the commissioner's booming voice faded away.

Marlowe slowly shut his notebook and slid his chair back from the table. "This isn't over," he said. Collecting the bloody tuning fork and Bragg's map, he walked out the door.

The dirty uniform escorted me back to my cell, and I plopped down on the bench. A barred window on the wall across from us had been opened to let in some fresh air. It had begun to rain while I was in interrogation, and the pitter-patter from the window was pleasant, if a bit chilly.

"Did you have a nice time?" Jackaby asked, leaning against the bars between our adjoining cells.

"Did I have a nice time? Being interrogated for a double homicide at a police station on my second day of work?"

"That's a *'no,'* then?"

"It was . . . illuminating," I conceded. "I shouldn't have thought a young lady would fit the role of murder suspect for a man like Marlowe. It's almost refreshing to be mistreated equally."

"Oh, not at all," Jackaby said. "Culture and lore shape our societal expectations—and Marlowe has no doubt internalized countless archetypes of wicked women. La Llorona and her slaughtered children, Sirens and their shipwrecks, Eve and the apple."

"Thanks, that makes me feel much better." I slumped against the wall.

"So, Marlowe has his vigilant eye on you, as well, does he? I suppose he'll even have poor Douglas pilloried before this is over."

I proceeded to tell him about the commissioner's dramatic entrance and exit, and the extension of our custody.

"I should have liked to see Marlowe sweating for once." Jackaby chuckled.

The wind was picking up and it whistled against the buildings, spattering the windows with rain. Apparently the weather had grown too warm for more snow, but only just. I shivered involuntarily, but not from the cold. The processing officer had taken my long, fitted coat, but the heavy shirtwaist Jenny had lent me was thick and warm, and suited for the cold weather. Something else was sending tremors down my spine. It could not be more than midday, but the sky was growing dark as more clouds rolled in.

"Well, I guess we'll be here for a while," I said, trying to remain light. "I suppose we should make ourselves comfortable. At least they feed you in jail, right? It'll probably be the first proper meal I'll have had since making port."

Jackaby looked focused on his thoughts. His eyebrows

were knit in concentration. "Hmm? Oh yes. It's not bad, if you're partial to creamed corn."

"Should've gotten myself arrested sooner—could've saved us the trouble of clearing out a room for me, eh?"

The wind was really wailing now, and a sudden, hard gust danced through the station house, sending a stack of paperwork flying around the room. The portly duty officer latched the window tightly and quickly busied himself sorting out the mess. Even with the windows sealed, the angry gale roared against the panes.

Jackaby was sitting on the bench in his cell, but his eyes were a million miles away.

"Quiet a moment," he said, putting a finger to his lips. He shut his eyes, and his head cocked to the side as he listened. I listened as well, though it was getting impossible to hear anything over the howling wind.

And then, like a match struck in the dark, my mind made sense of the sound. It had been growing steadily louder on the tails of the storm. I felt the blood drain from my face as icy tingles shot down my spine and danced through my extremities. A drop struck my cheek, and I brushed away my own hot tear.

"You hear it, too?" Jackaby's voice came somberly through the wind.

I nodded solemnly. "So sad," I managed.

"Yes," said Jackaby. "Mrs. Morrigan has a remarkable voice."

At the mention of the banshee's name, a burst of lightning lit the little window, and the thunderclap was not far behind. I slumped in my seat, my head reeling, and listened to the banshee's cry—listened to the sound of our own deaths riding after us on the storm.

"Cake?"

My misty eyes found focus. The policeman with the walrus mustache was holding a tray with a few cheerful slices of birthday cake. He pushed one through the slot at the bottom of my cell.

"It's just gonna go stale, anyway," he said, kindly. "And we get ants."

Jackaby managed a weak smile as the man slid one to him as well. "Thank you, Officer," he said. "Many happy returns."

Chapter Twenty-One

The following hours, during which the stormy winds continued to harass the station-house walls, felt like days. We were half a mile from the Emerald Arch, but, like currents against a sinking ship, the banshee's wail continued to wash over us in rhythmic waves. I recalled the image of Mr. Henderson, pillows belted to his ears to drown out the sound, and his actions seemed much less like madness now.

The song was a whirlpool, powerful and disorienting, and pulling me ever deeper. At times it was melodic, sung with beautiful, sweeping tones of exquisite sorrow–but then it would collapse into the wretched discord of a woman in the throes of anguish, and back again. There was no break between the two, and the further into the lament I fell, the more I saw them as one and the same. It was my mother's voice, and it was my voice, and it was no voice at all. No words in any language could have more precisely conveyed the sadness and foreboding flooding through my senses. It was the last song I would ever hear.

With great difficulty, I pulled my mind back into the dim police station. I looked into the next cell at Jackaby, who was standing by the thin, high window, looking out into the tempest. How long had he been there? Minutes? Hours? It was a blur. He looked inexplicably calm.

I pulled the scratchy, woolen blanket tighter about my shoulders, wondered briefly when I had received it, and walked over toward him. His breaths were deep and even. His storm gray eyes flashed for an instant with the brilliant reflection of lightning outside.

"What do you see?" I asked through the bars.

"Nothing," he answered softly. "Just the rain."

"Aren't you afraid?" I asked, wiping my eyes with the wooly corner of the blanket.

He looked at me for a moment and smiled gently. "Of course I am."

"You don't look it."

"I suppose I am curious, first. I'll let myself be afraid when my curiosity is satisfied—and as my curiosity will only be satisfied when I've looked our murderer in the face, it is unlikely I shall need to spend much time in fear."

"Ah," I said. "That's convenient."

"Quite."

I followed his gaze out the window. "So," I said, "we're going to die."

"Well, of course we are, Miss Rook. Don't be dense. Everyone dies."

"Tonight," I said.

Jackaby sighed. "Yes."

"Any thoughts about what sort of creature we should be expecting?" I asked.

"Many thoughts, yes."

"Any conclusions?"

Jackaby's eyes narrowed, and he glanced my way. There was a glimmer of something in his eyes. Madness? Excitement? Hope? The banshee's melancholy melody howled through the trees and I shivered, holding my attention on that glimmer like a hot ember in a pile of cold ash.

"There is someone who has aroused my curiosity," he mused, turning away again. "Just a theory. Suspicions with no proof."

"Someone—a suspect? Who?"

Jackaby's answer, if he had intended to give me one at all, was interrupted. The banshee's wail came to a crescendo as the wind picked up. Icy chills danced up my back, and even the detective winced. The door at the far side of the room swung open, and Junior Detective Charlie Cane stepped inside.

He nodded to the portly policeman on duty, who had abruptly tucked a slim dime novel into his top drawer and was now making a show of shuffling through important-looking paperwork. Charlie made his way directly toward the holding cells. His shoulders were damp from rainfall, and his eyes were even more tired than when last we'd seen him, red-rimmed and hung with heavy bags.

I glanced at Jackaby, who was following the young detective's approach intently, as a cat on a windowsill might follow the movements of a stray dog below. Charlie? Could the sweet man whose intentions had felt so earnest really be the villain we were hunting? The villain hunting us? He had lied about the claw marks on the door, I remembered. Jackaby was right; the detective was keeping secrets. I fixed him with my steeliest gaze and waited for him to speak. Charlie did not seem to notice. He stopped near the bars of Jackaby's cell, heavy shadows collecting beneath his brow, his head hung down. He breathed deeply for several seconds, and a few drops of rain plunged from his damp hair to spatter the pointed tips of his polished shoes.

"Well, Miss Rook, Mr. Jackaby," he said at last, "this is it." His voice was grave and ominous, a tone only amplified by the wailing winds and icy air, but it was not menacing. It echoed the weariness written across his face. With a heavy sigh, his head finally rose, and those bloodshot eyes looked into mine.

He read my expression silently for several seconds, and I read his. Confusion, at first, crept in, crinkling his eyebrows as he glanced between Jackaby and me. Then some dawning comprehension smoothed his brow.

"You can hear her, can't you?" he asked.

"That's right," I answered, my trembling fear turning to indignation. "Just like Bragg. Just like Henderson. So we're next, are we?"

Charlie nodded, still without the menacing countenance of a killer stalking his prey, but with a resigned and genuine sadness. "Yes, Miss Rook, it seems we are."

It was not the taunt of a hunter, but rather the lament of prey. My suspicions wavered, and then fled like shadows from the light of dawn. "*We*? You mean you can hear the cries as well?"

He nodded.

Of course. How selfish Jackaby and I had been to think we endangered only ourselves by sticking our noses into the case. If the killer was a cornered animal, lashing out as we attempted to close in on him with each new clue, then we had brought Charlie right with us into range of the beast. Publicly, he had been as much a part of the search as either of us.

Jackaby stepped up to the front of his cell, closing the distance until he was nearly nose to nose through the bars with Charlie. My employer's expression had not changed, and he continued to scrutinize the young detective, peering into his reddened eyes and tactlessly surveying the state of the man's hair and clothing.

"Jackaby," I said, "it's coming for him, too. He can hear the banshee's wail. Whoever—whatever that monster is, it's coming for all of us."

He ignored me, finally ceasing his examination to fix Charlie with an aggressive stare. "Are you in control?" he asked in a hushed but forceful whisper.

Charlie looked momentarily confused by the question. "I won't allow my emotions to get in the way of my duty, if that's what you mean, sir," he said. "I can face death."

"That is not what I mean. I mean, *are you in control?*" Jackaby repeated the phrase with intensity. Charlie's eyes widened in surprise. He glanced at the officer in the desk behind him.

"You know?" he whispered in alarm, then shook his head and laughed softly at himself. "Of course you know. Yes, Detective. I am always in control, I assure you."

"Don't go getting any big ideas, Cane. I'm still running this show," barked a rough voice from behind Charlie.

He spun to face Marlowe, who had entered from the hallway. The clanking handcuffs still hung from his belt, but it seemed that when he wanted to, the chief inspector could tread remarkably quietly for a man of his stature.

"You're coming with me. Back to the Emerald Arch. Now."

The inspector did not slow his pace to wait for Charlie

to keep up, but continued straight on through the entry-way, jamming his navy blue uniform cap onto his head as he moved.

Charlie gave us one last pitiful glance, and then drew himself up, jogging after Marlowe and out the door. I turned to Jackaby. "I don't suppose you're going to tell me what that was all about?"

"No. I don't think I will. Don't worry, I'll keep you apprised of anything urgent."

I slumped back on the bench, lacking even the energy to argue. "Not that it matters. All three of us will be dead by morning."

"I'm afraid it may be even worse than that," Jackaby said flatly.

"Worse than death?"

"Worse than the three of us. Or didn't you notice? No doubt he hurried out to avoid our taking notice, but the chief inspector's eyes were as puffy as yours. He's been crying."

"Then—Marlowe hears it, too?" I said. "But that's terrible! He and Charlie are both running straight back to the scene."

Jackaby cleared his throat and nodded for me to look around. In the cell beyond Jackaby's, our inebriated neighbor in red suspenders had awoken and was sullenly picking at the crumbs of a piece of cake. Between nibbles, the man sniffled and wiped his nose on his sleeve. Tears had cleaned twin trails down the grime of his cheeks. I whirled around. At his desk, the portly policeman wiped his eyes with a handkerchief and then leaned heavily on his elbows, his hands sliding up to cover his ears.

They could hear the banshee's wail. All of them.

Chapter Twenty-Two

We have to warn them!" I swiveled back to face Jackaby, who looked remarkably composed for one who had just realized that a wholesale massacre was descending upon the town.

"You hear the keening, as well. Has it been of great help to you, knowing the sound is a portent of your impending extermination?"

I scowled at my employer, then deflated. He was right. I did not know how much time I had already lost, succumbing to the lilting wails. They had been possible to overlook when they were just a feeling in the back of my skull, an intangible sadness on the breeze—but knowing their full meaning had given the notes a dismal weight. I was going to die, and worse, I was going to squander my last minute thinking about the fact that I was going to die. "Ignorance is bliss, is that it?"

"That's insipid. Happiness is bliss—but ignorance is anesthetic, and in the face of what's to come, that may be the best we can hope for our ill-fated acquaintances."

The howling wails of the banshee were becoming more distinct from the wind and rain with each passing minute. The storm seemed to be abating. Wisps of rain, rather than heavy sheets, struck the small, barred window. The mournful cries, however, had not diminished in the least. They were, in fact, becoming unbearably intense. I had just crossed to peer out the window when another wave of sadness slammed into me. My eyes clenched shut, and I felt my knees give out and crack into the floor. With my hands clamped over my ears, I forced my eyes open and peered around.

In a muffled semivacuum of sound, with the echoes of the last cry bouncing about my head, I tried to reorient myself. The man in the far cell had curled into a fetal position and was rocking slightly. Jackaby was shouting something about his tuning fork at the desk officer, but the portly man had slouched back in his chair, keeping his hands clapped to either side of his head. I took my hands tentatively away from my own ears, only to be caught by another terrible wail.

I forced my eyes open again, my vision swimming slightly. Jackaby had abandoned his efforts with the policeman, and looked as though the task of simply standing upright was commanding all of his willpower. There was no noise at all now, save the sorrowful voice of the banshee in my ears. As the song and scream entwined, the painful beauty of the melody came into focus.

On the crest of the building wave, a few last thoughts—tumbling wishes and regrets—breached the surface. I longed to see my parents one last time, and tell them that I loved them—that I was sorry. I imagined my mother, scooping me into a deep hug, as she had done when I was small. The image changed, and she became my father, and he held me still more tightly in his big broad arms. Again the vision gently shifted, and now he was the handsome Charlie Cane, and I could not be bothered to shy away from the thought of his embrace. Gradually my mind cleared until nothing but the mournful sound remained.

So, this is it, I thought. *I am about to die.* A strange peace washed over me. The harrowing song reached its peak and came toward a lilting end, the melody drawing at last to one elegant final note. I breathed in deeply and let my hands fall to my sides, opening my ears to the long, sustained finale. The tones of pain and fear subsided, and it was a sound of pure release and relief. As if on cue, a beam of sunlight cut past the last dwindling raindrops and through the little window. Then, just as the trembling note began to soften, the voice abruptly stopped.

It was a jarring shift, like falling out of bed in the middle of a dream. Mundane sounds returned suddenly, alien at first in their normalcy: the soft slosh of water in the gutters, the pitter-patter of droplets slipping from the wet branches, the heavy breathing and occasional sniffle of the man in the far cell. Wondering, briefly, if I was dead, I blinked and patted down my torso. Finding no gaping wounds, I looked dumbly to Jackaby.

He glanced about the station and then met my eyes. "Interesting," he said.

"We're alive," I said.

"So it would seem." He crossed to the window and looked outside. Everything had returned to normal, except for the oppressive quiet. The usual patter of footsteps and carts on the street had stopped, and the faintest of noises hung too clearly in the absence of other sounds.

"Do you think they caught him?"

Jackaby raised an eyebrow. "It's possible. It would account for the rapid shift in our fates."

"I thought for sure the whole lot of us were dead," I said, letting the idea warm up inside me. "But, no one died at all! We're safe! Everyone's safe!" I smiled at my employer, who allowed himself a hint of a grin in response.

And then a distant scream cut across the silence. It was a woman's voice–not the banshee's, but a very human cry, full of shock and sadness and distress. It sounded very small and alone as it echoed across the quiet streets.

I swallowed hard, the elation of our survival draining out

of me. "Who do you think . . . ?" I left the question hanging in the air.

"I haven't a clue." Jackaby's voice took a hard edge, and he scowled out the little window for several silent moments. "I need to get out of this cell. This has gone on long enough." He began to pace.

"And how do you intend to go about that?" I asked him. The constant stresses that seemed to be riling my employer had the opposite effect on me. No longer in immediate danger, I felt my adrenaline rapidly wane, and the exhaustion of a day full of heady emotions weighed heavily on my eyes. I slid down to sit on the cool ground against the wall, and rested my head on my knees.

"I'll have to employ delicate and deliberate elocution. I'm sure our jailer can be persuaded to see reason."

"You're going to try to talk your way out?"

"Don't sound so skeptical. Just you watch, Miss Rook. We'll be back out and on the trail in minutes. I'm very good with people."

Many hours later, I was roused from near sleep by the loud rattle of my cell door opening. Jackaby was restlessly waiting by his own door, his persistent but fruitless efforts to negotiate our release having apparently abated some time earlier. A glance showed me that my release had come at the hands of Junior Detective Cane. He gave me a reassuring smile, and opened Jackaby's cell while I shook myself fully awake and rose. Charlie's posture was alert and professional, as usual, but I doubted very much if he had slept at all in the last two days. His hair was mussed, dark stubble was coming in thick across his jaw, and his eyes still looked bloodshot.

"So," I said, "we're free now?"

"We're being released on our own recognizance, Miss Rook," Jackaby announced, dusting off his sleeves and stretching.

Charlie nodded. "Marlowe's still not happy with you about hiding evidence, but he agreed that being in police custody during the murder is a fairly convincing alibi." His voice was hoarse and a little gravelly, and even his accent was slipping slightly, more Slavic syllables inserting themselves in his words.

"So there has been another murder?"

Charlie nodded. "Yes. We were nearly on the scene when it happened. That Irish woman, Miss O'Connor, was there when we found the body. It was just the same as the others, sir." His voice was solemn. "Mrs. Morrigan is dead."

Chapter Twenty-Three

Charlie nodded to the duty officer as we left the cell, and the portly man slid the door closed behind us. "The banshee," I said as we walked. "She was singing her own last song, then. That poor thing. We listened to her die, and we didn't even know it!"

Charlie led us down the same hallway we had taken to reach the interrogation chamber. This time we took an early turn, and he rapped on the barred window of a desk set into an alcove. Beyond a panel of glass and thin bars stood long shelves of wire baskets. Peeking out of the tops were items ranging from gentlemen's hats and gloves to a bullwhip and what appeared to be the top of a bowling pin. A few items, obviously too large to fit into the baskets, were arranged along the walls. While we waited, Jackaby chuckled to himself and pointed at an oversized Mexican sombrero with fine beadwork along the brim and a massive hole on one side. It looked as though some great beast had sampled it like a dainty chocolate, then returned it to the box. "That was a memorable afternoon," he said.

The clerk arrived at last, rolling his eyes as soon as he caught sight of Jackaby. Charlie began to state our names officially, but the man waved him off. He handed Charlie a clipboard through the big slot at the bottom of the window and then trudged back out of sight. When he reappeared, he had a large metal tray and a sheet of paper. He slid the tray onto the desk and read from the paper.

"A. Rook. One coat. One handkerchief. Please sign that all personal effects are accounted for, miss."

I pulled on the coat Jenny had lent me and tucked the handkerchief back in my pocket. Charlie handed me the clipboard, and I jotted my name on the line where he indicated. The clerk vanished again momentarily, and then returned, hefting three very full trays onto the desk with a loud clank. He sighed and stuffed Jackaby's empty coat through the slot first. Thick though the material was, with all its pockets emptied, the thing looked like a deflated balloon.

"I hate it when you spend the night," grumbled the clerk. "I only barely got finished cataloguing this stuff. Always takes me forever just to find all the damned pockets." He coughed and returned to a flat, professional drone as he slid the first tray out and read from the paper. "R. Jackaby. One coat—brown; one hat—various colors; one rabbit's foot on chain; one vial, unidentified liquid—blue; one vial, unidentified liquid—amber; one matchbox containing dried beetle; one . . ."

I had nearly nodded off again when Jackaby, once more loaded to nearly twice his body weight with paraphernalia, took the clipboard from Charlie and scrawled his mark. "Always a pleasure, Thomas. See you next time!"

The clerk took the clipboard with a grunt, then waved us away, trudging back to the recesses of his office.

I was surprised by how late it had gotten when we exited the police station. The sun was already approaching the horizon, and the innocuous shadows of the daytime were stretching to form a foreboding carpet of dusk. Lights had begun to sprout in a few city windows, reflected in broken patterns on the damp streets. They served only to darken and add menace to the shadows around them—although, admittedly, my perception was tinted by the knowledge that a serial murderer, one with motive to deliver us to our own horrific deaths, was lurking free in the city. My only consolation was that we were, at least, traveling with an escort. In spite of my earlier doubts about Charlie, I found I was once again grateful for his company.

"I think I had best excuse myself." Charlie's words drew us to a stop at the first intersection. "It has been a very long day. I'll be no good to anyone until I have had some rest."

It was no use arguing. The bags under Charlie's eyes had collected bags of their own. His face was wan and badly in need of a shave, and the sweat and rain had plastered short, dark curls of hair to his temples. Weather and weariness had done nothing to diminish his strong jawline or the luster of his deep brown eyes, however, and I found myself doubly relieved that he was neither our villain nor the latest victim.

"Certainly," Jackaby answered. "Do see that you are safe and secure before retiring, of course."

"Of course. You, as well," Charlie replied. "I have seen more bodies this week than I ever care to see again. I should not like to wake tomorrow to find yours."

With a nod, he turned down the street and quickly plunged into the shadows. Jackaby continued on straight, and I double-stepped to keep close. It was hard to ignore the eeriness of the deserted roads and encroaching chilly dark. While I doubted very much that one more companion would cause our dastardly villain anything but the slightest delay in dispatching us, I still lamented Charlie's absence, and mentioned as much to Jackaby.

"Really?" My employer zigzagged up the cobbles in his usual rush. "You seem to have a renewed faith in the man."

"Well, it is certainly a relief to know he's an ally, after all."

Jackaby slowed his pace and faced me, an eyebrow raised in my direction.

"What?" I asked. "You can't still suspect him! You saw

him at the station, same as I did. He's as much at risk as we are."

My employer pursed his lips and looked as one might while deciding whether or not to reveal the truth about the tooth fairy to a child who has failed to receive a coin beneath her pillow. He spoke in a measured tone. "Miss Rook, I've not decided on Mr. Cane's guilt by any means. He did say that his life is complicated, and I believe he was telling the truth about that. Do consider, however, the circumstances by which you found him innocent. During his visit to the cell, it became clear he could hear the banshee's wail—which suggested that he, too, was going to be a victim. As it turns out, though, *everyone* heard the wail, so we must assume that the murderer heard it, as well. The incident proved nothing."

I let the idea sink in. The shadows to every side darkened, and terrible fangs and bloodshot eyes inserted themselves behind every tree trunk. Something rustled in the foliage beside us, and—I'm not proud to admit it—I squeaked and leapt backward. A pigeon burst from the leaves and settled itself into the eaves of a building half a block down the lane.

"Then again, it may have proven slightly more than nothing," Jackaby amended, oblivious to my outburst. I hoped that he would be more aware of my distress if I were ever ambushed by a real nefarious fiend, but for the sake of my dignity I chose not to mention it. He went on, burrowing into his thoughts. "It reveals that the murderer was aware of Mrs. Morrigan—aware of who and what she was. With the banshee still living, each victim was alerted before the kill. So long as Mrs. Morrigan remained alive and keening, we had at least a clue as to where our killer was going next. He slaughtered her to eliminate our advantage."

We crossed the street, and I recognized where Jackaby was leading us. Half a block ahead stood the Emerald Arch. "Think we'll find any new clues?" I asked.

Jackaby shrugged. "Possibly. But I'm not here for that."

"Then, why . . . ?"

"This time, I am here to pay my respects."

Marlowe was at the front door, giving instructions to a few of the uniforms when we arrived. He spotted our approach and held up a finger for us to wait while he wrapped up with the officers. Once he had sent them on their way, he turned and fixed us with a stare for several long seconds.

"I told that boy to go get some rest, and we'd release you two in the morning. I swear, before you got involved, Cane was one of my best detectives. Reliable. Loyal to a fault. He would never ignore a direct order. You're a bad influence."

"I do what I can."

"Well, try not to ruin him, would you? He still has a sense about these things. He was first on the scene again, did he tell you?"

Jackaby shook his head.

"Got a funny look on his face just as we neared the building. He yelled something about the fourth floor and bounded up the stairs three at a time. By the time we caught up with him, he was at their door, and that O'Connor woman was answering. She didn't even know. She said she felt something was very wrong . . . but so did we all, I guess. She had been in the next room, and she didn't even know what had happened until Cane pushed open that bedroom door. Hell of a sight. She let out a scream and just fell to pieces. Can't say I blame her. Like I said, this sort of thing is not for the female temperament." He directed that last sentiment at me, making eye contact for the first time.

"I dare say you're right, sir," I conceded, meeting his gaze. "Out of curiosity, though, is there someone whose temperament you do find suited to this sort of thing? I think I would be most unnerved to meet a man who found it pleasant."

I wondered if Marlowe was going to tell me off for my forwardness, but he only grunted and shook his head. "Nothing pleasant about any of this." He fell silent again for several seconds. Finally, he sighed, and his eyes cast upward for a moment before turning back to the door.

"Come on, then." He trudged inside the building without any further explanation or invitation. Jackaby, not needing any to begin with, was right behind him, and I jogged through before the door swung closed.

I was alarmed to find Mona O'Connor still in her apartment. Someone had draped a thick quilt over her shoulders, probably the officer standing stiffly behind her, and she sat on the well-stuffed sofa, staring blankly into space. Her hair was disheveled, and several curly red locks hung across her face. She had the dull expression of one who has been scooped out entirely, and does not know what to do with the emptiness. No, not emptiness, exactly. Somewhere, through her eyes and deep inside the hollow, there was an ember of something just beginning to glow. It reminded me of Jackaby's oblivious intensity, but with a far more dangerous edge about it.

"Should she be here?" I asked Marlowe in a whisper. "Wouldn't it be kinder to take her away from . . . from the scene?"

The chief inspector nodded. "We tried." His eyes darted to the officer, who, I noticed, had a bit of gauze wedged up each nostril, and a bluish bruise blossoming across the bridge of his crooked nose.

Marlowe stepped toward the bedroom door and waited. Jackaby did not follow immediately, but went first to the sofa and knelt beside Mona. He spoke so quietly I could not hear a word, and he pulled from his pocket something that clinked gently in his palm. Some lucidity eased into her eyes for a moment, and she met his gaze and nodded, almost imperceptibly. He stood and crossed to the bedroom door. Marlowe opened it to admit the detective.

I did not follow. From the doorway, I could just see the woman's silvery hair, and I watched as Jackaby placed two coins gently over her eyes. I was grateful Marlowe had once again positioned himself to block the scene as much as he could. The smell of blood was cloying, even from a distance, and I did not wish to see the state of the poor old woman's body.

Jackaby murmured something that sounded like Latin, and then stepped out of the room. The chief inspector closed the door behind him. As both men made for the exit, Mona reached out and brushed Jackaby's arm. He turned, and she fixed him with a solemn stare.

"Kill him," was all she said.

My employer swallowed hard and met Mona's eyes, but he gave no reply.

We descended the stairs and reached the lobby in silence. Marlowe was the first to speak. "They're getting worse," he said. "The bastard's rushing, getting sloppy."

"He wouldn't have bothered to soak up Mrs. Morrigan's blood, anyway," said Jackaby, quietly. "Not the sort he needs, but you're right. He knows we're closing in."

"I must admit, Jackaby, I was hoping for a little more."

"Inspector?"

"That was a kindness, back there. I think you did right by the old lady, don't get me wrong. But the first time I actually invite you into a case, you barely glance at the scene at all."

"Marlowe, do you mean to say you are you finally enlisting my services?"

The chief inspector shuddered involuntarily at the question, clenched his fists, and cracked his neck. "Something happened this afternoon that I can't explain. People are dying. I don't believe in you, or your ridiculous claims about magic and monsters, but you have a way of making things turn up, things like that map. I can't ignore that just because you're a lunatic and I don't like you."

"Oh, Marlowe, you're being too kind."

"Stuff it," Marlowe growled. "And let me make this unmistakably clear. If you're on this case, you report back to me. You do not withhold information. You do not conceal evidence. I know where you are and what you know at all times. You will respect the chain of command, and you will not question it. I am in charge. Is that understood?"

Jackaby smiled, and his eyes glinted. Somewhere beneath the atrocious knit hat and that unkempt hair, cogs began to whir into motion.

"Is that understood?" Marlowe repeated.

"How quickly can you assemble every member of the police force at the town square?" Jackaby asked suddenly.

"What?"

"Every member. Every link in the chain. Highest to the lowest. If we're going to capture him tonight, we're sure to need every one of them."

"What?"

"You're right, that isn't quite enough. I'll need a few

books, as well! Just call them, all of them. Miss Rook and I will meet you at the town square in—shall we say—half an hour?"

"What?"

"I daresay, Marlowe, we should work together more often. This is brilliant!" With a manic grin, Jackaby flung the door open wide and vaulted the steps. "We shall have him this very night!" he cried, his scarf and coat whipping behind him as he flew into the evening.

Marlowe stood, speechless, in the lobby. I shrugged my bewilderment to him before chasing my employer down the street.

Chapter Twenty-Four

I could barely keep Jackaby in sight as we sped through the city streets. The wet cobblestones had chilled to glittering patches of ice, and my feet slid out from under me on more than one occasion as I tried to round sharp corners. By the time I reached the red door with its horseshoe knocker, I was sore and winded, and as baffled as ever. Jenny was hovering by the open door to the office as I came through the hallway. She looked to me for an explanation.

"Your guess is as good as mine," I said, and peeked inside.

The massive map had been stuffed to one side, and I noticed a few pins had managed to cling to their positions, dangling limply from the ruffled map, while the others must have been scattered across the floor. A book flew from behind the desk to land on the small pile beginning to collect in the leather armchair. Jackaby popped up, hurriedly flipping through the pages of another, and quietly cursing the lack of useful information he seemed to be finding.

"What are you doing?" I asked.

"Looking," he managed, without glancing up. He tucked two of the tomes under his arm and leafed through a third as he brushed past me, back into the hall. Jenny scowled as he passed right through her shoulder before she had time to pull away.

"Haven't you already been through all these?"

"Yes, but now I know what I'm looking for!" He zipped down the crooked corridor.

"And what, precisely, is that?" I was yelling after Jackaby, as he dashed out of sight. He either didn't hear me or couldn't be bothered to respond. I gave the still-scowling Jenny a quick apology. As I hurried out, I noticed that the frying pan had been removed from the wall. The rough hole it had carved still remained, and orange light from the sunset was trickling through it into the hallway. I found myself thinking that, all things considered, the poor ghost really was a remarkably patient roommate.

I caught up with Jackaby again halfway down the block. He was so buried in one of his books, I was surprised he was able to notice my arrival, let alone navigate the walk, but as I drew near, he pitched the other two books into my hands. His lips moved silently and rapidly as his eyes zipped over the pages.

"Jackaby—what are we looking for?" I demanded.

He pried his eyes slowly up from the page and caught my gaze. "Lead."

"Lead? What—as in the metal?"

He dropped the last book into my arms atop the others. "That might help, at least. And some decent kindling."

He picked up the pace again and hastened toward the center of town. It was all I could do not to drop his books or crack my tailbone on the icy roads as I struggled to keep up.

The sun was melting into a reddish haze behind the buildings and treetops, and I turned my collar to the biting cold. Here and there, stars were beginning to peek through the gaps in the dark sky, but the moon was nothing but a diffused glow behind the shifting curtain of clouds. It did little to illuminate the shadowy streets. Terraced with well-kept brickwork, a broad stretch of sidewalk opened ahead of us, forming a semicircle around a statue of an important-looking soldier on a rampant horse. A few large flower boxes had been erected at some point to lend color to the block, but the frost had long since finished off the blooms. Across the street sat the city hall, regal, white columns dominating its façade and leaving the recessed entrance a sheet of inscrutable black.

Around the rampant statue, a crowd of a dozen or so uniformed officers had begun to collect. They milled about, some attempting to look alert and attentive, others unabashedly sitting on the edges of flower boxes and puffing away on cigarettes.

Curtains in the surrounding buildings darted open here and there, revealing the curious faces of residents taking notice of the gathering. A few passing workmen stopped to lean against the fence, passing a silver flask around while they waited for something interesting to happen. By the evening's end, they would not be disappointed. I caught sight of a pair of ladies whispering and casting severe and condescending looks in my direction. One wore a bonnet overloaded with flowers, and the other was in a canary yellow dress.

"Yes, exactly," came flower-bonnet's nasal drone over the dull murmur of the square, "she's *that* sort."

"Shameful," intoned yellow-dress.

I had no intention of playing their repentant lost lamb, withering at their glances. Instead, I threw them a cheeky wink as I jogged up the steps into the square. They looked mortified and bustled away, noses raised, in the opposite direction. I drew up to my employer's side as he halted at last, my heavy breaths puffing out in pillowy, white clouds ahead of me. He was scanning the assembled officers, and those still trickling in from Mason Street, when his eyes narrowed slightly and his posture straightened.

I tried to slow my labored breathing and spot the target of his interest. "What is it?" I whispered.

Jackaby nodded in the direction of a slender alley through

which a figure was approaching, wearing a dark cloak and stiff top hat. The drainage grates billowed steam across the alleyway, shrouding the figure in a pale silhouette at first. As he neared, his features grew slowly more distinct, until he reached the street and came out of the fog and shadows, revealing a bushy-bearded face with rosy cheeks. Jackaby relaxed. "No one. Never mind."

"Wait, I've met him," I realized. "Let me see . . . Mr. Stapleton, I think. He tried to buy a tin of Old Bart's from me." He spotted me as we passed, and gave a polite nod of recognition, which I returned before he continued out of sight down the lane.

Jackaby looked at me. "Why were you selling tins of—wait, Stapleton?"

"Yes, I think so."

"As in Stapleton Foundry? As in Stapleton Metalworks?"

"Maybe? I don't know. He was nice. He told me to keep my chin up." Jackaby was already hurrying off after the man.

"Wait here!" he called over his shoulder. "I'm going to see a man about some lead!"

I stood, alone, clutching Jackaby's old books to my chest and stamping my feet to keep out the cold while I watched the police officers collect.

"Hello again, Abigail Rook," called a familiar female voice behind me, and I turned to see who had spoken. All around were men in uniform, and none of them appeared remotely interested in me.

"Something different about you," she continued. She was only a few feet away when I finally spotted her.

"Oh, hello, Hatun! I'm sorry, I didn't notice you at first."

The old woman smiled knowingly. "Findin' a place in the world, I see," she said, and brushed her shawl casually with one mittened hand. "And how are the new lodgings? Comfortable?"

"What's that? Oh, yes, I suppose. Jackaby has lent me the use of a room. Speaking of which, did you happen to see where—"

"That isn't it, though," she cut me off, subjecting me to the same suspicious, narrow-eyed examination as she had during our first encounter. "Somethin' else . . ."

"Right, well," I said. "I would love to talk, but I really must be . . ."

"Oh dear." Hatun shook her head and blinked several times, as if trying to clear from her eyes the drifting spots that come of looking at bright lights for too long. "Oh dear, oh dear, indeed. You oughtn't go looking for him. No, not a wise idea. Really for the best you stay clear of him tonight. Keep away from Jackaby." Her eyes squinted at me. "That's what's different about you, I think."

I hesitated. "There's something different about me, and it has to do with Jackaby?"

"I'm afraid so, dear. You must not follow him. It's simply dreadful."

"What is, exactly?"

She shook her head again, and her whole face tightened as though she had chomped down on a lemon. She looked up suddenly, and patted my cheek in a surprisingly sweet, grandmotherly gesture. "The—what's the word? Immense, innocence, imminence, yes—that's it. The imminence of it," she said, "your demise."

"The imminence of my demise?" I stared at the woman, with her tender eyes and layers of wrinkles, and let her words sink in.

I believed her, I realized, but I had already come to terms with my death so many times in the span of a day, I found it difficult to be frightened by the announcement. I had crested that emotional hill already, and the view was becoming familiar. "Thank you, earnestly," I said, all the same. "Your concern is touching."

Her omen delivered, Hatun seemed to, as Jackaby phrased it, "oscillate" instantly back to normalcy. She nodded and wished me well, as if we had just met at a casual luncheon, then shuffled away, melting into the milling crowd.

Soon the ranks of police had crept to nearly a hundred men, and they continued shuffling in from the streets and alleys. Some wore full uniforms; others had hastily pulled their navy blue jackets over evening clothes, clearly roused from their homes while off duty. One chilly-looking young fellow wore a pair of spotted pajamas, with only his stiff blue hat and black baton to identify him as a man of the law. I was impressed that Marlowe had agreed to Jackaby's wild request at all, let alone that he had managed to summon so many men so quickly, and at this hour of the night.

The chief inspector himself strode through the crowd at the far end of the square. The officers most familiar with him turned at the sound of the handcuffs, jangling at his side, and they were at attention the moment they caught sight of the imposing figure. Even those who must have been from different departments made at least a token effort to sit up straighter on their flower boxes. The inspector made a beeline to stand beside me, surveying the men as he spoke.

"Where is he?"

"He'll be right back," I assured the inspector, wishing all the more that I had kept a line of sight on my employer. I shifted my grip on Jackaby's books, feeling small and awkward beside the chief inspector. The last time we had been this close without Jackaby, he had been accusing me of murder. At least this time he was on our side. "You've certainly assembled an impressive crowd, sir. Is this every policeman in New Fiddleham?"

"Of course not," Marlowe grunted. "Most of the on-duty officers will stay right where they're assigned. It would be irresponsible to leave New Fiddleham unprotected. There are, however, runners rousing available men from every district in the city. I hope you understand, Miss Rook"—the chief inspector turned his head in my direction, looking down his arrow-straight nose at me—"that I have used the very last of my pull with Commissioner Swift to draw this much manpower. I have taken responsibility for what is becoming a remarkably public spectacle. It is of the utmost importance to me that this not become a colossal waste of time and resources. So where, I will ask you again, is Jackaby?"

"He's . . . about." I scanned the square frantically for any sign of that silly knit cap. I recognized a few faces in the crowd. O'Doyle, the barrel-chested brute I had first encountered at the Emerald Arch, was there, along with the two guards who had been given the unfortunate task of searching Jackaby's building. It appeared those two had at least had enough time to change into fresh uniforms. The portly officer with the walrus mustache was huddled with a few of his colleagues, chatting and rubbing his arms to stay warm.

Toward the back of the crowd, to my surprise, I even spotted Charlie Cane. The poor, tired detective had pulled his uniform back on—if he'd even had time to remove it—but he was clearly in bad shape. His well-polished buttons and pointed shoes still glistened, but his uniform was no longer crisp, and his posture sagged. He kept to the rear, not socializing with his comrades, and kept glancing back down the street, as if longing to return to his bed. I tried to catch his eye to offer a sympathetic smile, but the detective's head hung low and his gaze was downcast.

I finally spotted Jackaby on the far side of the statue, working his way inward through the field of uniforms, when there erupted a hubbub to my left. I turned and watched as idle chatter rapidly died away, and the wall of blue coats parted to allow through the commissioner himself. The officers' reactions to Marlowe's entrance now seemed lackadaisical compared to their instant metamorphosis in Swift's presence. Guts were sucked in, lit cigarettes vanished, and orderly ranks miraculously formed from the chaos. Charlie, uncharacteristically, seemed the exception to the spreading current of professionalism. He stayed to the back of the crowd and continued to glance from side to side, as if thinking of slinking away at any moment. Something else seemed odd about him. It took a moment to really see it across the square, but in spite of the icy chill, I realized Charlie was glistening with sweat. He was nearly obscured by the crowd's foggy breath and fading cigarette smoke, but I now noticed the steaming heat rising off him like a furnace. He was breathing hard, and I worried that his overexertions had made him terribly ill. Something in me ached to rush to his aid. My attention, however, was dragged back to the commissioner as he crossed into my line of sight.

Swift had taken the time to pull on his long, dark coat with the deep red trim and matching crimson derby, but below the charcoal hem of the coat, a pair of silk pajama legs was visible. His leg braces had been strapped over these with haste, leaving the material creased and folded. He marched with his usual determined, steady stride, sheer force of will driving him past pain and into general malice. Whether from cold or because he had not had time to oil them, the braces punctuated each step with a louder-than-usual squeak and clink.

"This had better be good," he snarled to the chief inspector, drawing to a stop beside him. The commissioner's voice was deep and ragged, and although he stood half a foot shorter than Marlowe, the chief inspector still straightened, looking like a boy called to the front of the class. Like Marlowe, Commissioner Swift now stood, surveying the crowd of men, scowling darkly as he did.

Shuffling through the crowd in the commissioner's wake came the scrawny fellow in the straw boater I had seen at the station. He drew up beside Swift and whispered something in his ear. I caught the word "constituents." Swift's eyes darted up to the faces in the windows and to the pedestrians beginning to gather on either side of the square. He met an eye here and there and attempted to turn his scowl into a congenial and reassuring political smile. The expression failed to extend to his eyes, and the result was an even more unpleasant grimace.

His eyes caught mine and lingered; then he turned his gaze to Marlowe. "Didn't I tell you to leave that one locked up until this was over?" he growled through a forced smile.

"Yes, sir." Marlowe gave me an annoyed glance, as if my

existence were a regrettable irritation. "There have been some substantial developments in the case."

Jackaby had made his way to the center of the square when I spotted him, at last. He was not carrying any metal that I could see, lead or otherwise, but seemed to have collected a few small, broken branches. Amid such a gathering of stoic, uniformed officers, he looked especially ridiculous as he grasped one of the horse's marble hind legs and scrabbled to climb atop the statue's base. At one point he hung nearly upside down, with his coat dangling beneath him.

Swift, of course, took notice. "Who the hell is that idiot?"

Before Marlowe could answer, Jackaby addressed the crowd.

"Excuse me! May I have your attention, please!" he called out, completely unnecessarily. Every eye was already on the mad detective, who was hunching slightly under the rearing hooves of the marble horse. "Yes, hello, everyone. Many of you know me, but if you have never had occasion to work with me—or to arrest me—my name is R. F. Jackaby. I would like to thank all of you for coming out tonight. I'd have liked a slightly larger showing, but I suppose you will have to do. And thank you, Inspector Marlowe, for pulling this together on my behalf."

Swift's head turned very, very slowly to Marlowe. "*This* is your informant?"

Marlowe, in turn, deflected the attention to me. "What is that lunatic doing?"

"I'm afraid I really can't tell you, sir," I said.

Jackaby continued from atop the pedestal. "Now then, I would like to assure you all that we will have our man tonight if we all work together. We shall need to prepare a few things first, so pay attention. First of all, it would be helpful if one of you toward the front could get a small fire going. It needn't be overly large, no bonfire, just a little campfire should do. Yes, you, there, with the turquoise aura and the cigarette tucked up in your ear—have you got a matchbox? Yes? Splendid. I've already collected up a bit of kindling that isn't entirely damp—here you are."

A soft ripple of subdued laughter and hushed voices was sneaking through the crowd, and the man Jackaby indicated was pushed forward. Jackaby reached down and dropped the branches into his hands.

Commissioner Swift's face was reddening to nearly the same tone as his hat. "Marlowe . . ."

"His methods are . . . unconventional." Marlowe stared at the detective as if the strength of his glare could will Jackaby to be less, well, Jackaby. "But, strange as it sounds, his meddling has managed to push investigations to their turning point on more than one occasion."

A voice from the ranks called out, "Come on, then! Make him a fire, Danny! He can't cast his magic spells without a good fire!" This was quickly followed by a round of barely muffled chortling.

Jackaby straightened and called out, "I assure you, I am

a consummate professional. I do not cast spells!" Which might have done a better job of quieting the crowd had he not clocked his head on the horse's rampant hoof as he said it. That would have been enough, but he insisted on defending himself further. "And, for your information, seldom has an open flame been requisite in the successful spells I have observed, and it appears to be a negligible factor in spell casting on the whole." He said it with such earnestness that the crowd paused for a moment, holding its collective breath before launching into another round of jeering and laughter.

Jackaby looked mildly hurt. Swift looked homicidal. "This is on your head, Marlowe. If your crackpot imbecile makes a laughingstock of my police force–a laughingstock of *me* right in the damned center of town, so help me . . ."

"Understood, sir." Marlowe was still staring daggers at the detective. "If he can point us to our killer, though, even if he is making an ass of himself publicly, then there's no harm done to the department's reputation."

"Gentlemen," Jackaby said, resuming his announcement, "this will not be easy news to bear, but the villain we're after is hiding behind a badge. I mean to say, he is here among us, even now, hidden in plain sight–a terrible creature in the guise of not just any man, but a policeman."

As he spoke, the clouds drifted apart, washing the square with moonlight and illuminating the faces of a hundred policemen–suddenly uncertain whether to be amused, offended, or afraid. The onlookers lost their smiles, and still more faces appeared in the surrounding windows.

Swift was practically vibrating. His eye twitched, and a dark vein had popped out on his temple. "You're through, Marlowe," he said through gritted teeth, and then took a step toward Jackaby and pronounced loudly, "That's enough!"

The commissioner's booming, furious command was all but lost in the sound of everything, which had already been going all wrong, suddenly going terribly worse.

Chapter Twenty-Five

One cry of alarm, and then another burst forth from the back of the crowd. The wall of uniforms surged, not parting fluidly as it had for the commissioner, but stumbling and shoving itself away from something on the far side. Even Swift, not accustomed to being ignored, looked more startled than angry as he attempted to identify the source of the disturbance. I stepped up onto a flower box to see what was happening just as a woman in a second-story window erupted into a sustained, throaty scream.

The officers had fallen back, leaving a wide radius around Junior Detective Charlie Cane. He was doubled over, clutching his sides as a spasm shook his body. Something was terribly strange about his arms. They looked dark, and the texture was all wrong; then his leg buckled and he dropped to the ground. His head shot up, and I saw his face in the unforgiving clarity of the moonlight—only it was not the same gentle face I had come to recognize over the past two days on the streets of New Fiddleham. It was not the face of a man at all, but the feral grimace of a beast.

I stood, transfixed, as my heart and stomach raced each other into my throat. Charlie's legs looked broken, bending in places a man should not have joints, but still he rose, pivoted, and launched himself into a run down the cobbled streets away from the stunned officers. He stumbled and caught his fall with his hands, throwing himself back into his run so quickly he scarcely broke stride. He tore off his uniform shirt, and tossed it behind him, revealing stiff, dark hair now covering his torso. His whole body shook with another spasm, and again he stumbled, and again, until he was on his hands nearly as much as his feet. As he ran, those polished shoes clattered, empty, to the pavement behind him, the moon highlighting the sharp point of the toe. By the time the figure that had been Charlie Cane vanished into the billowing steam of an alleyway, it was not a fleeing man, but the form of a massive hound, bounding away on four great paws.

The square was tensed in silence as the sound of the beast's footfalls receded into the distance. First to break the stunned hush was the commissioner. The flush of anger had left his cheeks completely, and he was now as pale as a ghost, but he puffed himself up nonetheless and yelled,

"Stop him!" His voice cracked just a little and he coughed. Then he found his voice and bellowed, "After him! All of you! I want that monster dead!"

The crowd of uniforms hummed with building energy for a moment, like a pot about to boil, and then burst suddenly into frantic motion. Jackaby snapped out of his own surprise at last and hollered, "Wait! Stop!" It had all happened so quickly, I couldn't tell if he was trying to keep the police from rushing into disaster, or if he was screaming after the creature . . . after Charlie Cane.

I tried to move toward Jackaby, fighting not to be carried away by the tide of uniforms. I had to plant my feet firmly on the brickwork just to keep from losing ground as they sped after Charlie. The books were nearly knocked from my hands, but I hugged them to my chest as I weathered the storm. I glanced around, lost in the human current. The commissioner and Marlowe had vanished into the thick of the surge, but Jackaby was suddenly off his pedestal and beside me.

"Quickly, Miss Rook!" he hollered, and pulled me into motion, the two of us sweeping along in the tail of the swarm.

"But . . . that was Officer Cane!" I stammered.

"Yes, and it is essential we catch up with him before this mob does. Everything's gone all wrong. If we don't move quickly, there will most certainly be more deaths tonight."

I swallowed hard. If people were going to die, then

reaching the beast before the police would simply increase the likelihood those deaths would be ours.

At the end of the street, the police force began to split. Someone up ahead was barking orders, urging the men to spread out the search and cover as much ground as possible. The pressing crowd of policemen thinned as I followed Jackaby, darting to the left and right down narrow New Fiddleham streets. A yell issued from an alleyway in the opposite direction, followed by the clattering of boxes and breaking wood. Two of the officers ahead of us turned and ran back toward the commotion, but Jackaby pressed forward. His hands moved about him while he ran, feeling the air as if tracing invisible lines of smoke.

"Do you see something?" I panted.

"He's been this way. It's fading too quickly—we need to hurry."

The chase took us out of the city center and toward the outskirts of town. We ran along the backside of several factory yards before the shrubs and bushes gave way to a grassy stretch spotted with birch trees. Away from the icy brickwork, my feet found purchase more reliably, and it was a little easier to keep pace with Jackaby as we cut across the sod. I even began to spot the telltale signs of the creature now. The moonlight sparkled on the tall, icy grasses, except in one long, dark path, cut like a scar down the center of the field. Something had carved a quick route through here, leaving a wake of bent and trampled plant life. As we hopped over a mud puddle, I spotted a giant, smeary paw print. I didn't need to be a seer or a master sleuth to know we were headed in the right direction.

The tracks took us along the edge of a stream, its banks lined with ice and slush, and ahead I spotted the familiar sight of Hammett's bridge. I hardly recognized it at first, though it had been scarcely a day since we had met Hatun on this very spot. How different it had seemed then, with the funny little woman hanging her fishing line over the ice in full daylight. Now, with water churning past chunks of ice and foreboding shadows bleeding into more ominous darkness, the old woman's superstitions about monsters lurking under the bridge seemed suddenly less benign.

I pushed the idea away as we hit the bridge, not wanting idle thoughts of trolls gnawing on my bones to get in the way of my genuine, reasonable fear of being ripped to shreds by–I allowed myself to think it–a werewolf. I noticed that even in his haste, Jackaby still absently pitched a couple of copper coins over the side of the bridge as he crossed it. I guess he, like Hatun with her token fishing efforts, felt it never hurt to cover all your bases. An idea flashed through my head.

"Jackaby, wait!" I skidded around the corner at the end of the bridge and stumbled down to the water's edge, to the spot where I had first seen Hatun. I laid the old books to the side and peered into the shadows under the bridge. It was pitch-black beneath the little arch, but my probing fingers quickly found what I was looking for. For the briefest of moments I could have sworn I felt clammy fingers on my wrist as I pulled it free. "I just have to borrow this for a bit," I assured the darkness. "I swear I'll bring you a whole halibut if we make it through this alive." My hand slid free, holding tight to the pole.

Jackaby skidded down the slope to stop beside me. "What on earth are you doing?" he demanded. "We don't have time to go fishing!"

I laid Hatun's fishing pole on the ground and fumbled with the knot, resolving after a few failed attempts to simply snap the line. I held out the pear-shaped metal sinker.

Jackaby looked unimpressed. He looked, in fact, only more annoyed.

"It's lead!" I exclaimed.

My employer's expression did not improve. "What are we supposed to do with a thimble's worth of lead?" he asked, his eyes darting back up to the path above us. "That little bauble could hardly coat his big toe! Tell me, Miss Rook." He looked back at me. "If you could outrun the fastest man in the world, how significantly do you think three or four grams of lead around your big toe would slow you down?"

"Not much," I admitted. "But you never said how you intended to use it! There are lots of ways people use lead."

Jackaby shook his head and began back up the path. I scooped up the old books and stuffed the sinker like a bulky bookmark into one of them as I scrambled up after him.

"All you said was that lead could kill it. Shouldn't it be silver, anyway? Isn't it usually silver in the stories?"

Jackaby pushed his way through the foliage ahead of me, pulling out a little collection of tinted lenses to hold up in the moonlight. He peered through a few of them before seeming to lock onto a path, which he followed with increased intensity.

"First of all," he responded on the move in a hushed voice, "I never said lead would kill him. It won't. I only said it would help slow him down. Second, silver appears in the lore as a weapon against werewolves, occasionally witches, and, in one brilliantly odd legend, a Bulgarian tailor–but not against . . ." Jackaby froze, his head cocked to one side, and I thundered into him, almost knocking us both to the ground.

"Not against *what*?" I whispered after we had stood still for several seconds. "If he isn't a werewolf, then what . . . ?"

"Hush!" Jackaby hushed me, clapping a hand over my mouth and listening intently.

After another long pause I heard the rustling of something moving very quickly through the trees. It seemed to be ahead of us at first, and then fading back in the direction of the bridge, moving impossibly quickly through the brush. I thought it must be gone, and was about to speak again when a sudden, strangled cry cut through the forest. A gunshot rang out, and Jackaby burst into a run, his gangly legs hurdling bushes and vaulting him toward the sound.

I leapt after him, catching a tree root with my foot and pitching forward. I had one arm loaded with books, and the other was too slow to catch my fall. My head thudded against a mossy stump and the forest flashed before me, bright and colorful. When I picked myself up again, I had lost sight of Jackaby. I tried to follow the sound of crunching branches for a few long strides, but it was useless. I was lost in the woods, totally and entirely.

The clouds were thinning, at least, and through the thick cover of the trees, I could see sparkling patches of stars. The moon hung full and bright almost directly overhead, flooding the woods with light, but offering little help navigating. I crept forward, not knowing what else to do. Should I call for Jackaby? Would that only make me a bigger target? Should I hide?

A flurry of motion nearby set my heart racing, and I flattened against a tree trunk as a uniformed officer careened through the bushes, slapping leaves from his face in a panic. It was O'Doyle, the brute of a policeman with the hawk nose, only he looked far less intimidating now. He was pale, dripping with sweat, and wheezing. He was running with his gun drawn, looking backward over his shoulder every other step. I called out, but he only fired his weapon in my general direction and kept moving.

I ducked instinctively, though the shots were wild and high. I stayed frozen until he had disappeared into the woods, but I wasn't going to stay to find out what had frightened him.

I pushed through the brush as quickly and quietly as I could, following O'Doyle's noisy flight. I was squeezing through a small copse of trees when those sounds abruptly stopped. Crouched in the shadows, I strained to hear anything. More gunshots sounded in the distance. I peered around the trees into a small mossy clearing and saw O'Doyle's feet first. He was lying on his back in a pool of crimson that was spreading across the moonlit grass, but he was not alone. A dark figure crouched beside him, its back to me. Once more, my heart raced and thudded against my ribs . . . until I made sense of what I was seeing. The figure was not the creature—not Charlie. The beast was nowhere in sight.

It was Commissioner Swift. He had slid down to one knee with his legs splayed stiffly, the iron braces only barely accommodating the position. His charcoal gray coat wrinkled as its hem brushed the ground. He had removed his hat, and from behind him I could see his graying hair and small bald spot as he bowed his head reverently over the body of the fallen officer. Contrary to his public bluster and bravado, his reaction to the grisly tragedy was heartbreakingly human. There came a shuffling of leaves in the nearby bushes, and I was jolted back to the reality of the situation. This was not the time to mourn. I crept toward Swift, doing my best to stay to the shadows, scanning the dark branches and creeping vines around us for any sign of the beast. "Commissioner!" I called in an urgent whisper. "Please, sir. It isn't safe. The monster is close and still on the hunt."

The commissioner slowly slid his hat back on to his head. "You're right. Of course, young lady." His voice was quiet and very low. The red velvet of the derby was a grim echo of the pool spreading at his feet. Swift steadied himself on his cane and began to turn and rise, but with agonizing slowness. His leg braces squealed and clinked in objection to the motion. And then an alarm sounded in the deep recesses of my brain. The sole of the man's shoe, to which the brace attached by little screws, was not stiff leather. It bounced the moonlight across my eyes like a polished mirror, and I saw that it looked like the flat of an iron, pointed at the toe and made entirely of metal. As he stood, the shoes sank heavily into the mossy sod, and the braces straightened with a soft *clink-clink*.

The derby glistened and its brim dripped crimson as he straightened it, gradually raising his eyes to me. The hat cast a shadowy mask across the top half of his face, but his eyes cut through, bloodshot and full of venom and fire. A spray of dark red had splashed across his chin and up his cheek, and his lips parted in a wide, wicked, sharp-toothed grin. "Yes, right you are," he said. "The hunt is still very much on."

Chapter Twenty-Six

I stumbled backward, the forest spinning around me. I turned to flee, but the commissioner was already beside me. I threw myself into a staggering run in the opposite direction, but he was there at once, moving with inhuman speed. Only the clank and squeak of his metal braces revealed that he was moving at all, and not simply appearing in each new location by magic.

I nearly tumbled straight into him, but caught myself and froze, mere inches away. As I looked into the commissioner's face, the glamour melted away. He looked as he had always looked, but my mind finally allowed me to see the features I had been forcefully ignoring until now. Above a grotesquely wide mouth full of too many sharp teeth, the bridge of his nose curved upward into a severe brow. His ears, which bent slightly under the brim of the hat, were pointed, and his skin was blotched and leathery. Hard, crooked cheekbones skewed the whole of his face in a disturbing angle. Most frightening of all was that horrible mouth and the jagged, bloodstained teeth—teeth that called to mind broken bottles and razor blades. He laughed, and his breath reeked with the coppery stench of the blood. He was a cat, toying with his prey before the kill.

There could be no escape, but my feet pulled me backward anyway. I tripped, landing at the base of an old tree. Jackaby's books fell from my hands to the muddy roots. Swift's lip twisted up in a final, wicked smirk, and vicious, bloodstained claws extended from his fingertips. Done playing with me, the cat pounced.

And so did the dog.

Swift was in the air, his horrible fangs and claws arcing toward me, when the massive hound hammered into him from the side. The two slammed into the ground and rolled. Swift's cane bounced away, his dark coat whipping and tangling around the shaggy brown fur of the beast. They ground to a stop, the enormous dog pinning the commissioner's shoulders under two heavy paws. It growled and snapped at the commissioner, who snarled back and ducked away from the hound's jaws. Swift's legs squeaked once beneath the hairy creature, and then the massive hound flew backward, the heavy iron boots cracking hard off its ribs. The beast collided with a broad tree and thudded to the ground, letting out a very human groan.

His handsome face had warped and vanished beneath the fur, but those warm brown eyes were still unmistakable. They were full of fear and pain and humanity as he shook off the impact and tried to reorient himself. Swift was up and behind him in seconds, claws out and teeth gnashing before the shaggy hound had even pushed itself to its feet. The dog was moving far too slowly. Someone screamed, "Charlie!" and I realized it was me.

The commissioner shot me a poisonous glance before lunging toward his target, but it was just enough of a pause for the hound to whip around, so that the attack glanced off his flank instead of striking his jugular. Three lines of red blossomed across Charlie's shoulder. A few inches closer and Swift surely would have opened the hound's throat.

The two circled each other. Charlie moved stiffly, as though the first kick had bruised or even broken his ribs. He waited for Swift to launch the next attack.

It came in a blur. The commissioner feigned a wide swipe with his wicked claws, but as Charlie ducked to avoid it, Swift kicked hard, catching his opponent solidly across the jaw. Charlie yelped in pain, and Swift cackled. He easily quickstepped around Charlie's retaliatory bite, and came at the hound from the other side with another feigned slice and a brutal kick. This time, Charlie predicted the move, and he caught the commissioner's ankle in his massive jaws and shook.

The commissioner hit the ground on his back, flailing with one hand and holding his bloody hat on with the other. Charlie did not release him, growling through clamped jaws as he continued dragging his opponent back and forth across the ground like a human paintbrush. He had scrubbed the moss from a six-foot swath of earth when a loud *ping* rang the hound's teeth like a dinner bell, and his head shot back. Swift hopped to his feet, bits of metal and leather straps hanging loosely at odd angles around his knee. He ripped the mangled remnants of the brace from his leg and glared at the great hound.

His iron shoes dug into the freshly churned dirt and he waited, like a sprinter listening for the starting pistol. Charlie lowered himself, and his lips peeled back in a vicious growl. In a blur, Swift was behind him, and the dog's teeth snapped at the empty air. Swift had carved a chunk out of the hound's ear, and it bled dark ribbons through his shaggy coat. Again and again Swift darted around Charlie, piercing gashes and pounding kicks into his shaggy hide from every direction. Charlie spun and snarled and bit. He was keeping himself low, and protected from any serious wounds, but for all his ferocity, he was no match for Swift. It would only be a matter of time.

At last, the barrage of fast attacks paused. Swift taunted his opponent arrogantly, tipping his hat in mock cordiality and smiling wickedly, and then he turned his back to the hound and stepped away. "You're good," he said, amused.

Though panting heavily and covered in patches of deep red, Charlie held his stance, watching the commissioner's movements.

"Monsters like us shouldn't be brawling with one another, though, should we?" the commissioner continued, still facing away and sauntering to the center of the clearing. "We have so much more in common, after all. And a pup like you, so far from your pack–you could use a strong master. I tell you what, when I'm through with this one"– he waved a nonchalant hand in my general direction– "you're welcome to finish off the scraps."

Swift's casual steps had brought him to the spot where his cane had landed. He stooped to pick it up, not presenting even the slightest defense, his back still wide-open. I caught the treacherous glint in his eye as he leaned down slowly, wrapping his fingers around the metal rod. Charlie took the bait and threw himself toward the commissioner in one powerful bound.

In a flash, Swift had pulled the broad hand grip from the cane and thrown it aside, revealing a long, flat blade on the end of the shaft. The metal cane was braced and waiting for its target before Charlie could stop his own momentum. It lodged itself in the hound's right side, piercing clean through and out his back, just below his shoulder blade. Charlie bellowed in pain and sank onto the iron pike.

Swift stood and sauntered around the beast's head, tutting softly to his victim. Without warning, he grimaced and kicked the glistening metal with a sharp clank where it protruded from Charlie's hide. "Bad dog!" he yelled.

Charlie whimpered and shuddered. His whole body was shivering, his paws twitching.

"A few inches to the left and you'd be finished, you mangy mutt. Now I have to put you down myself."

And there they were, not twenty feet from my stunned stupor. The horrible, grotesque form of Commissioner Swift knelt over Charlie's soft, bloody head. He was drawing his claws down Charlie's cheek in a sickening caress, savoring the kill, and Charlie had abandoned resistance. I wanted to scream or run or . . . or anything, but I was just a foolish girl, lost in the woods, and this was not one of the adventures in my books.

Books. Jackaby's books still lay where they had fallen on the muddy roots. My shaking fingers found the closest leather spine, and they let fly before my mind had even considered the decision. The hefty volume turned slowly through the air, the pages whipping slightly as it spun like a wounded bird toward the commissioner's grisly face. I was twenty feet away from my target. The book landed at fifteen. The commissioner paused to raise an unimpressed eyebrow in my direction.

I scrambled until I had found another, and heaved harder. Swift did not bother to flinch as it sailed wide over his shoulder, but he raised his head to fix me with an arrogant, somewhat scornful look. "Do you mind?"

The last volume was dead-on, and I thought, for a fraction of a second, that it might connect. I'm not sure what I expected a bit of leather-bound paper to do to the horrifying commissioner when a two-hundred-pound hound could hardly leave a mark. As the projectile neared, though, Swift's hand left his victim's throat and caught the book with a snap. Carried by momentum, the little sinker from Hatun's line sailed free of the pages in his grasp and caught the commissioner squarely in the forehead. We both glanced down as it rolled to a stop in the dirt a few feet away, then looked back to meet each other's eyes.

Swift's face flushed with anger, his eyes narrowed to menacing slits, but his voice remained icy cold. "I was right in the middle of this, but if you absolutely insist"—he dropped the hound's head and stood—"I suppose I can make time for you. Ladies first, and all that."

He stepped over Charlie's limp, bleeding body and strode toward me, not bothering to rush. Like his asymmetric face, the rhythm of his gait was now distinctly uneven. His left leg, still strapped in the brace, swung stiffly, creaking and clinking with each bend. His right swung free, but those iron shoes still clanked their own beat, muffled by the soft earth. As he drew near, that smell, the sickly sweet coppery smell, came with him. He was dripping with blood, and none of it his own.

Hatun's premonition had come true. Just as she had warned me not to, I had followed Jackaby into the forest and to my demise. My heart hammered against my ribs, I shook, and my whole body felt clammy. My breath was ragged and too fast. Above me, Swift seemed to be enjoying my frantic last moments, sneering his crooked, broken-glass smile as he drew to a stop before me. Jackaby would not give the bastard this satisfaction, I thought. *What would he do?* Keep his calm. Keep control. I willed my heartbeat to slow and took a long, deep breath.

"It's a lucky thing for you, Commissioner," I managed with great effort, "that politics are not a lady's domain, because you have lost my vote."

The sound that came out of the ghoulish figure may have been a throaty laugh or a wet growl, but I did not have time to decide before his wicked claws buried themselves in my chest. The wave of pain hit me with a . . .

BANG!

For the second time that night, Swift was knocked back, spinning to the earth and away from me. As the terrible talons pulled away, my chest felt as though it had caught fire. Through a haze of intense pain and adrenaline, I half imagined Charlie had once more risen to my aid—but, no. The commissioner was alone, struggling to his feet, and the great hound lay where he had been skewered, barely breathing.

BANG!

Swift hit the ground again, and my eyes traced their way to the figure marching across the clearing, a pistol fixed steadily on the commissioner. My vision swam, but there was the bulging coat, the draping scarf, and that ridiculous knit cap.

"You were right, Miss Rook," called Jackaby. "There are a lot of ways that people use lead."

My chest throbbed with hot pain, and my vision was darkening, but I smiled up at the detective.

"I would still prefer to have done the thing properly, with a solid coat of the stuff," he continued, his voice so casual he might have been discussing afternoon tea, "but given the circumstances, a few bullets should slow him down long enough to see the job done." He stood directly over the commissioner, who was writhing on the ground, and pulled a small leather volume from his coat. He fixed the weapon on Swift's chest as he read aloud.

"'The life of a creature is in the blood . . . It is the blood that maketh atonement for the soul.' Leviticus, seventeen."

Swift snarled. The pistol rang out a third time, and then the forest went quiet as a warm blanket of blackness swept over me.

Chapter Twenty-Seven

Flickering light and the aroma of smoke dragged me by slow inches back into wakefulness. I attempted to sit up, wincing against the pain in my chest. My long coat, which had been draped across me like a blanket, slid away, and the cold air snapped me back to reality. I was still in the forest. I looked down to find Jenny's warm shirtwaist had been removed, and Jackaby's scarf had been wrapped around my torso like a long, clumsy bandage. Startled, I instinctively reached up to cover myself, and my chest seized with the pain of the sudden motion. I caught my breath and very slowly brushed my fingers over the scarf, tenderly exploring the wound on my chest.

"It's superficial," Jackaby said. I glanced up to see him adding kindling to a little campfire. "You'll be fine, I'm sure, but have it looked at in the morning, if you like. You've lost some blood, but I imagine it was exertion, not injury, which ultimately did you in. You should try to exercise more often." He propped another branch across the flames. "You've been out for a couple of hours. It took longer than I anticipated to get the fire going, and, of course, I've had to attend to both of you myself. I'm afraid our friend's condition is rather more bleak."

I looked around. Beyond the campfire, Charlie, still in the figure of a hound, lay in an immobile heap. The blade had been removed, and in its place a crude compress made of torn strips of fabric had been applied. I recognized amid them the hem of Jenny's formerly beautiful shirtwaist. His breath was so shallow that the movement was almost imperceptible in the flickering firelight.

On the opposite side of the fire lay a pile of darkness that could only be the commissioner, draped in his charcoal gray coat with hints of its crimson lining visible amid the shadows. Jackaby tossed a few final twigs onto the flames and walked over to the body.

I shivered and gingerly pulled the coat back over myself, pushing the aching sting to the back of my mind. "Is he . . . ?" I began.

"Dead? Not yet. He won't be dashing about any time soon with those lead rounds in his chest, but until this thing is neatly burned, the creature will live." He knelt beside the commissioner's head.

I looked at Jackaby's meager campfire. It was not a bad job, downright impressive given the wet, frozen landscape, but it was no funeral pyre. Tossing a body onto that would only smother the thing. Swift's coat, alone, would probably choke it out. "We're going to need a lot more wood if we're going to—" I swallowed my last words. Swift was not a good man, not a man at all, but my mind still recoiled at the thought of burning someone alive.

"Not at all." Jackaby stood. He held the commissioner's crimson derby in front of him by a finger and thumb, as one might carry a gift left on the doorstep by an overzealous cat. "We may not reduce it entirely to ashes, but I think we've more than enough to render it charred to a crisp and bone dry."

"His hat?" I asked.

"Well of course his hat! What else?" Jackaby shook his head in exasperation and gave a curt nod toward one of his leather volumes that lay in the wet moss. "Maybe if you would bother *reading* a book once in a while instead of hurling them about every chance you get, you would have put the pieces together yourself by now." He sighed. "What we have been battling is a creature called a redcap," he explained at last.

"The redcap is a horrible goblin who usually haunts the ruins of old castles, especially in Scotland and England. They're antisocial beasts. It is unheard of to find one in a bustling metropolis, but as times change, so must we all, I guess. I was right about my first instinct as well. His magic is ancient. Redcaps are old creatures, nearly immortal if they tend to their namesakes properly." He waggled the glistening hat as if in explanation, and a thick, sticky drip fell to the earth.

"I should have caught on much sooner–stupid of me. All of it fits with your descriptions, but I'd never met the man, myself, not until tonight. Those silly drawings of him in the newspaper don't look a thing like him, of course. The polio braces were a nice bit of misdirection, I must admit. Covered the sound of his shoes and drew attention, while his fairy glamour helped him hide in plain sight. That's classic, old magic, glamour. He kept the telltale signs, though–clearly not ready to give up his traditions. Redcaps stand apart from most of their fairy brethren in their immunity to iron, which, historically, they flaunt by wearing heavy iron shoes and wielding an iron spear or pike. He kept his hidden as a cane, but Swift had the lot, the arrogant bastard, and I missed it all."

"Don't feel bad," I offered. "I met him face-to-face, and I missed it, too."

"Yes, but no one expected you to be clever, Miss Rook."

"Thanks for that," I said.

"We got him in the end, at least. That's something."

"So, how do we finish this?" I asked. "You said it's his hat that's keeping him alive?"

"The blood," answered Jackaby. "So long as the cap is

kept wet with fresh human blood, he will not die. That's why he had to keep finding new victims."

"What are you waiting for, then? Burn the horrible thing!"

"Not so fast!" A new voice thundered out of the darkness of the forest. Jackaby froze with the bloody derby poised over the fire. A heavy drip sizzled on the burning embers. We both turned to watch as Chief Inspector Marlowe pushed past the underbrush and into the clearing, his pistol trained on Jackaby. His eyes passed over the scene as he moved, pausing on the fallen form of Officer O'Doyle, then Swift's prone body, and widening as they took in Charlie. "I don't know what happened here, Jackaby, but I'll thank you not to destroy the evidence."

"Oh, put it down, Marlowe," Jackaby replied. "We've done your job for you. It's over. All that's left is to finish him off before he kills again"–he nodded toward the commissioner–"and then get some medical attention for that one as soon as possible." He gestured over his shoulder at Charlie.

Marlowe lowered his weapon and eyed Charlie. "You're right about that," he grunted. "The city will sleep safely tonight with that thing dead and buried."

"What, Charlie? Don't be an ass. You said yourself that boy was one of your best detectives."

At the sound of his name, Charlie stirred, one deep breath sending a ripple of shudders through his body. He remained prostrate, but his heavy, felted eyelids flickered open a crack.

Marlowe started at the sudden motion, and his gun flashed back out, fixed on Charlie. Jackaby was almost as fast, stepping between the inspector and his mark. "Come now, Marlowe, let's not do anything rash."

"Have you gone completely and totally insane?" Marlowe demanded. His weapon, now pointed squarely at Jackaby's chest, did not waver.

I heard a quiet clink and my eyes shot to Swift. The commissioner still lay on the damp earth, but now the shadowy form was beginning to awaken. The silky gray coat rose and fell in slow breaths, and the moonlight glinted off his heel as the iron shoe twitched.

"Jackaby!" I cried in a hoarse whisper, but the detective was occupied with Marlowe.

"As usual, Inspector, you have entirely failed to see things for what they truly are."

"What is wrong with you, Jackaby? For the first time ever, there really *is* an impossible monster behind everything, and now you're the one who *doesn't* believe it?"

"Marlowe!" I called out as the commissioner's leg brace creaked again ever so slightly.

"You saw what that thing did to O'Doyle and Swift," the chief inspector was busy barking. "Move aside!"

"I did not personally see how Officer O'Doyle was dispatched, as it happens, but I doubt Officer Cane was involved," said Jackaby, "and he definitely did not put those bullet holes in the commissioner. I did."

Marlowe actually stepped back a little. "You are alarmingly bad at making yourself sound sane, do you know that?"

A faint wheeze escaped the commissioner, and his dark coat shifted as signs of life crept back into the body.

"Men! Please!" I cried.

"You think I'm crazy?" Jackaby continued. "Then let me burn the hat."

"Yes, because that doesn't sound crazy at all."

"If I'm crazy, it's just a hat. It burns. Nothing changes. Then you kill the poor beast. If I'm right, then burning the hat will destroy Swift, the monster behind all of this, and you'll see what magic has been at work here. Either way, you get your murderer."

Marlowe thought about this for a long moment, and my heart thudded as I considered leaping up and throwing the bloody thing into the flame myself. Pushing off from the tree trunk, I immediately realized that leaping was not an option. The smallest exertion sent pain hammering through my chest and left me reeling. My vision swam and I sank back to the dirt.

"We're too late," intoned Jackaby with sudden sobriety. I struggled to focus my eyes in the direction of his voice. "See for yourself, Marlowe. Swift is on the move . . . God help us all."

I choked, whipping my gaze back to the spot where the villain had lain, willing my blurry vision to crystallize. Marlowe spun around as well, that much I could see, and then he swiveled slowly back to Jackaby.

"No," Marlowe said evenly, with the forcibly patient tone one uses with a small child. "He's right there." My eyes found the gray shape in the dark at last. Swift had not moved.

"My mistake!" chirped the detective. "Oh dear, in my excitement I seem to have dropped the fellow's hat."

The ruby red derby perched atop the tower of sticks, tongues of flames licking the brim. For a moment the hat seemed immune, the fire even dimming a little beneath it, and then it began to crackle. The feather fizzled to nothing in one rapid puff, and the ribbon was suddenly alight. The thing popped and cracked violently as syrupy drips fell into the heart of the fire, which sizzled and spat. The derby smoldered, and thick, black, greasy coils of smoke rolled off it in a plume that darkened the stars. At last it burst into flame. Swift screamed.

The commissioner's body spasmed and twisted upright until Swift was on his knees. His grotesque face contorted in agony, and his eyes went mad with confusion and rage. Smoke seeped from his charcoal gray coat, and he lurched forward. Whether because of the brace still lashed to his left leg or whatever internal hell was boiling inside him, he stumbled, clanking and crumpling to the dirt before he could take a full step. Swift's sharp, leathery fingers clawed at the mossy earth, pulling him forward a few more feet before his arms, too, gave out and he shrank into himself, writhing in misery. The air grew thick with acrid clouds of smoke, and the commissioner's clothing crumbled into soot, the skin beneath crackling and flaking away like ash. All the while, the man screamed in wretched fury, his voice losing all humanity and deteriorating into the guttural howls of an animal in pain.

And then it was over. The screams ceased and the air was thick with inky, pungent smoke. The hat's stiff brim, the only skeletal remains of the wretched item, shifted and slid into the heart of the little fire beside us.

No one spoke as the smoke gradually cleared. There, at the edge of the flickering firelight, lay a scorched patch of moss, a few hinged rods with burnt leather straps, and two thick, iron shoes.

Chapter Twenty-Eight

Time passed in uneven flashes as I drifted in and out of consciousness. In one moment I was on the cold forest floor, and in the next I was lying atop the desk in Jackaby's front room. Jenny was hovering over me, looking gentle and reassuring. The same ghostly face that had sent me tumbling backward over my chair two days before now filled me with a sense of relief and normalcy.

In a blink, Jenny was gone. Jackaby and someone else—old Hatun, I realized—were setting Charlie onto the broad wooden bench on the opposite wall. Somewhere between the darkness of the forest and the paving stones of Augur Lane, he had returned to a human shape. He was naked except for the blood-caked strips of fabric that had once been a blouse. His face was nearly as white as

Jenny's, and he was drenched with sweat. My head swam and I stared, unable to look away from the terrible damage. Without fur to hide them, the deep red gashes from Swift's claws were visible all over him. Worst of all was his shoulder. In his human state, it appeared Charlie had been stabbed just under his right clavicle, barely above his lung. I winced and closed my eyes, fighting back tears as I realized he would be lucky to survive the night.

I was surprised to awaken to the early-morning rays of sunlight cutting across the room. My head rested on a pillow, and a soft blanket lay over me. Charlie, still looking harmless and human, slept on the bench. Douglas perched over him like a feathered sentinel. A pillow had been tucked under Charlie's head as well, and a quilt had been draped over his lower half. A little color had returned to his cheeks, and a proper bandage of white gauze was wrapped expertly around his chest and back, though beads of sweat still glistened on his brow and his skin looked clammy.

I watched his chest rise and fall with shallow breaths. A bruise was beginning to blossom along his side in yellows and blues, and the cuts were everywhere, red and angry. As my eyes passed over each mark, the blows replayed in my memory. My breath caught in my throat, and I felt my chest throb in a dull ache.

My own small scar was tender as I reached a hand to the injury, but the sensation was something deeper. The thought of Charlie, as either man or beast, falling victim to that horrible monster on my behalf was a dreadful barb, caught beneath my ribs. Now, as he lay barely breathing beside me, I had to add guilt to the already confusing emotions I felt for the man. Hushed voices from the hallway drew my mind back into the room. I craned my neck and listened.

"You really shouldn't have moved him in that condition," a woman whispered. It was not Hatun or Jenny, but the cadence and Irish accent were familiar.

Jackaby answered her. "I realized the risk, but Inspector Marlowe made it quite clear that after last night, leaving him where the police force would be responsible for him would be far more hazardous to the poor fellow's health. Thank you for coming so quickly. This has been a rather bizarre situation, and not an easy one for you to be thrust into."

"If what you said last night truly happened, then I owe him at least this much for the part he played in all this."

"How soon do you think it would be safe to move him again?"

"Let him rest as long as you can, but all things considered, he's healing remarkably well."

"I'm sure the lunar cycle has had a little to do with that. We can only hope his convalescence continues so well from here on. Thank you again, Miss O'Connor."

Light poured in as the hallway door slid open. Mona O'Connor, the nurse from the Emerald Arch, came through first. She looked exhausted, with curly strands of red hair escaping from where they had been pushed behind her ears, and dark, rust red stains smattered across her apron. She gave me a nod.

"I see you're awake, dear. Good," she said. "Drink plenty of liquids in the next few days, and try to rest while you heal up, understand?"

I nodded.

"Lovely. You'll be fine. A nice, soft bed would do you more good than this slab, if you feel up to stairs."

She collected her coat and hat, and Jackaby saw her out. He turned back to me after he had closed the door.

"She really is quite talented," Jackaby said casually. "She has competent hands, although I found her bedside manner somewhat rough. Then again, I imagine most of her patients don't unconsciously metamorphose into animals and then back in the middle of her care. She had to be a little creative with her use of force."

"He'll be all right, then?" I asked. My chest felt tight and sore as I spoke, but the pain had dulled considerably. I propped myself up on my pillow carefully, keeping the soft blanket wrapped around my shoulders for both warmth and dignity.

"He will heal, but the real question is whether we can get him safely away from here before Marlowe decides to come looking for him."

"Marlowe?"

"The man's prejudice is infuriating. After the fine service the good detective rendered, the self-sacrifice and personal injury he sustained, that stubborn oaf still wants to call Mr. Cane a werewolf and a public enemy and have him trussed up in chains!"

"Well, can you entirely blame him? If Charlie isn't a werewolf, then what . . . ?"

"'Caini,' they call themselves. 'The Dogs.' In Romania they are sometimes called the 'Om-Caini,' or the 'Caine Barbati.' They are a nomadic tribe—therianthropic, yes, but not lycanthropic—and not malevolent, although much maligned."

I blinked. "Come again?"

My employer sighed heavily and dragged his hand across his face. "Charlie is a member of a very old, very reclusive family of shape-shifters. The House of Caine has no permanent home, rarely settling anywhere for long, and you can see why. They are gypsies, feared and misunderstood, and constantly on the move. The Caini are less fiercely powerful than werewolves, but more fiercely loyal.

"I saw him at once for what he was, of course, and was immediately impressed to find he had made a life here in New Fiddleham. I did my best not to expose the fellow, but I suppose it's too late for that, now. The Caini's powers wax and wane with the cycles of the moon, but a full grown Dog like Charlie should have been able to maintain either form at will at any time of the month. It was his own stubborn loyalty that pushed him into overexertion after the banshee was killed, and you saw what came of that. I knew he was losing control, the fool. Now, thanks to his devotion to this ignorant town and its superstitious people, it seems Charlie Cane must follow in his ancestors' footsteps and flee."

I watched as Charlie shifted fitfully in his sleep. The quilt over his legs wiggled as his feet twitched unconsciously. He reminded me of a puppy, pawing softly at the floor as he dreamt.

"So . . . he isn't really a monster, after all," I said, weakly. "Good. That's good."

Jackaby regarded me for several long moments. "Do you see those paintings by the door?" he asked.

I followed his gesture and nodded. On the left hung the knight slaying a dragon, and on the right was the ship being towed through stormy seas by a massive, golden fish. I had seen them on my first day exploring the house.

"Do you know the stories?" Jackaby asked.

"I recognize Saint George, but no—not really."

"Saint George. The Golden Legend," said Jackaby, walking under the image of the knight. "A city besieged by plagues brought on by a terrible dragon. Livestock and then human children were sacrificed to appease the beast. When the king's own daughter was offered up, Saint George intervened, saving the girl's life. He wounded the creature and bound it, bringing it back to the city to slay before the eyes of the townsfolk."

Jackaby stepped over to the other painting. "What about this one?"

When I shook my head, he went on.

"This is the story of Manu and the Fish, from Hindu tradition. As the legend goes, a small fish came to Manu for protection. Manu took pity, and kept the thing safe in a jar until it could grow large enough to fend for itself. The fish grew larger and larger, and was enormous when Manu finally released it back into the river. Because of Manu's kindness, the fish warned him that a great flood was coming, and told Manu to prepare. The fish returned in the midst of the flood to help tow Manu to a safe place to wait for the waters to recede."

At this point, Jackaby returned to stand beside me. "Saint George's legend tells of the dangers of mythical creatures, and the value of man asserting dominance over them. Manu's tale, quite conversely, stresses the value of mercy, coexistence, and peaceful symbiosis."

He paused, watching Charlie breathing slowly in and out for a few moments. "Were it not for the assistance of our young 'monster,' here, you almost certainly would not have survived Swift's attack. Marlowe is a good man," Jackaby added, thoughtfully, "but he only knows how to slay dragons. This world is full of dragon-slayers. What we need are a few more people who aren't too proud to listen to a fish."

I felt my chest tighten. I had failed to listen. "Jackaby," I said, "I think Hatun knew what was going to happen."

He raised an eyebrow at me.

"I think she knew I was going to be attacked. Although she made it sound as though I was going to die."

"She said you were going to die?"

"Basically," I answered. "She said that my demise would be imminent if I followed you. I guess you were right about her being unreliable. A lucky thing, too—I much prefer damaged to dead. She was trying to warn me to stay away, but I didn't listen."

Jackaby did not respond. He was surveying me with a brooding, sober expression. I was just starting to grow uncomfortable when he broke out of the moment with a wave. "Yes, well, anyway," he said, the storm clouds vanishing instantly from his eyes. "Nice to have the whole affair behind us. I'll be whipping up a bit of breakfast. Toddle on over to the laboratory when you're ready."

Douglas, from his perch atop the bench, shook his feathery head in a silent caution. I nodded as Jackaby bustled off down the hall. In the distance I could hear him calling, "Jenny! Have you seen that saucepan? The one from that set your grandmother left you?"

"You mean the one you riddled with buckshot dents last month?" came the spirit's muffled reply. "Or the one you melted last summer with that alchemy nonsense?"

"The first one!"

I eased up to a seated position. The motion was difficult, but not overwhelming, and I found myself smiling as I took in my outrageous surroundings again. It was good to be home.

Chapter Twenty-Nine

By midday, Charlie had regained his color, and many of the nasty red scratches had somehow already faded to pale scars. I watched his chest rise and fall again until Jenny came to help me into a fresh, loose blouse. I found it in me to finish a cup of tea and a bit of toast, but still Charlie slept.

Now that I was awake, Douglas had relieved himself of his post and flapped off into the house somewhere, leaving me alone with the injured man. I stepped gingerly to the bench where he lay. He looked every bit as sweet and unassuming as he always had, perhaps even a little more so when his brow crinkled ever so slightly and his muscles tensed in his sleep. I hated to think he might be reliving his savage battle, and dearly wished there was something I could do to ease his turmoil. I reached out a hand to brush a curl of dark hair from his forehead, and then hesitated.

My heart thumped, beating hot against my scar. In the storybooks, a beautiful princess would revive him with a kiss, and the pair would live happily every after–but I was not a beautiful princess. I was a girl from Hampshire who liked to play in the dirt.

A cold breeze brushed my elbow, and a moment later Jenny's soft voice came from over my shoulder. "How are you feeling, Abigail?"

"Helpless," I answered, honestly. "I don't like feeling helpless."

She stood beside me, looking over Charlie. "He's doing quite well, all things considered."

I nodded. He was improving impossibly quickly, it was true. In a peculiar way, that was a part of my frustration. I wanted to balance the scales, but I had no special gifts to lend to his recovery–he had to manage that all on his own, and he was. I was surrounded by the spectacular. Charlie, Jackaby, Jenny–they could all do such astounding things, and I was just Abigail Rook, assistant.

"He saved my life," I said, "and all I could do was watch while he was sliced to ribbons."

"That isn't how Jackaby tells it," Jenny said. "As I understand, you were pretty heroic yourself last night. I think he was downright impressed."

"Jackaby said that?"

"Well, he might have focused a bit more on the hurling about of antiques . . . and I believe the term he used most was 'foolhardy,' but you learn to tell with Jackaby. Did you really fight off a redcap with a handful of books?"

"Something like that," I mumbled.

"Sounds like you did the saving, then."

"I suppose we took turns." I returned to the sleeping junior detective and brushed back the loose lock of dark hair. He stirred ever so slightly at my touch, breathing in deeply. His tense brow relaxed and he softened into a more peaceful slumber.

It was well into the afternoon before Charlie was fully awoken by the sound of Jackaby banging in through the front door. "You're awake! Good. About time. How are you feeling, young man?"

"I have been better. Swift . . . is he . . . ?" Charlie began.

"Dead? Yes. It's over."

Charlie stiffly eased himself to sitting and accepted a cup of tea. "There is much I still don't understand," Charlie said. "Why now? Why them? And if you could see me for what I am, why did you not recognize Swift right away?"

Jackaby nodded and looked out the window as he gave his reply. "The last question is the easiest. Swift had repeatedly avoided meeting with me, and I with him. I never actually saw the man, or *creature,* until last night—possibly a coincidence, but it is likely he had heard of my reputation as a seer and did not want to risk the rumors being true. For my own part, I don't make a habit of engaging police bureaucracy if I can avoid it. I find those nearer the bottom of the chain are more inclined to collaboration—and are also less likely to expel me from matters of interest.

"Regarding the scoundrel's victims, they fell as follows: Mr. Bragg, the journalist, clearly stumbled upon the pattern of Swift's killings, and must have made the unfortunate mistake of mentioning the discovery to the commissioner, probably during an interview for some silly political piece. Swift couldn't have the newsman alerting the public to his villainy, so he dispatched the fellow, then followed centuries of instinct and practice by soaking up the blood in his grisly red cap. Having murdered Bragg, Swift had to make his escape. He hastened first to the window, but Hatun was in the alley below, so he retreated down the stairwell instead. In his hurry, he allowed his iron shoes to leave their impressions in the wood.

"That might have been the end of the bloodshed in New Fiddleham, but it was you, Mr. Cane, who unwittingly sealed the next target's fate. To avoid mentioning our visit with the banshee, you fed Marlowe a convenient lie about Mr. Henderson having had some information regarding the killer. This proved truly inconvenient for Henderson, because the commissioner was close at hand, privy to every word. Swift could not risk his identity being exposed by a victim's nosy neighbor. Thus, even though the poor man knew nothing to endanger Swift, Henderson became victim number two."

Charlie swallowed hard and looked to the bottom of his teacup. Jackaby continued. "Henderson's demise was far more rushed than Bragg's. Your standing guard in the hallway forced Swift to make his entrance and exit through the window. Either because of your presence, or possibly because Swift's hat was still freshly damp from the night before, this time the commissioner barely brushed the corpse before hurrying away. He left the telltale smear, but he abandoned most of the blood to pool on the floorboards. If it weren't for Marlowe's bullheadedness, you might have tracked him then.

"Swift's third victim, alas, is on our hands. Miss Rook and I both testified openly about the identity of Mrs. Morrigan, the banshee, and it was shortly after Swift looked over our statements that she began her own final lament."

"But why kill the old woman?" he asked. "She didn't even know about the redcap."

"It wasn't for her blood, not that time—she wasn't human, after all. I believe Swift perceived her as a warning system, an alarm before each kill—too great a liability for him to leave in peace. Bragg, Henderson, Morrigan—one by one Swift snuffed out the threats to his secret, but the whole thing was unraveling too quickly."

"I see." Charlie looked up again. "And . . . last night? I'm afraid it's rather a blur."

"After we left you, Marlowe helped me put the last piece in the puzzle. His nonsense about not questioning the chain of command told me precisely where a brazen monster would hide: the top. I recalled Miss Rook's detailed descriptions of the commissioner, and the answer plowed into me. Now I knew what I was up against, I looked for a means to stop the fiend. The most infamous of their brood, one Robin Redcap, was coated in lead and then burned along with his malevolent master—but in the end we did not have time for that. The surest, fastest way to destroy the creature was to destroy its red cap. The cap and the beast are one. I employed a more modern use of lead and a few Bible verses for good measure, but burning the hat was the real deed."

Charlie nodded and opened his mouth to speak again just as the horseshoe knocker sounded out three loud clacks.

Jackaby peeked through the curtains and scowled. "Marlowe. I was hoping for a little more time, but I suppose this was to be expected."

I offered to help Charlie down the hall, but he refused to run from his chief inspector. Jackaby grumbled something about stubborn loyalty, and opened the door. Pleasantries were brief, and not particularly pleasant. Marlowe took up a position just inside, maintaining his distance from Charlie.

"Well then," said Jackaby cynically. "I suppose you're

ready to cart the young man off? Tell me, will it be chains and cement walls, or straight to the firing squad?"

"Neither," responded the inspector. His voice was rough and tired. "That's not why I'm here."

"Oh, don't pretend you're going to let the man be, Marlowe. We both know that's not in the cards."

There was a pregnant silence as Marlowe took a deep breath. "No," he said at last. "No, that's not possible. Too many people saw his . . . transformation, and that's not something they will quickly forget. Even if I did let Officer Cane stay, his life here is over."

Jackaby nodded grimly. "Exile, then? How charitable."

"Something like that," the inspector grunted. "Mayor Spade has asked me to assume the interim position as police commissioner until a proper election can be held. Getting trapped behind a desk is about the last thing I want, but I told him I would accept it . . . for the time being."

"This is what you came to talk about? Your promotion?"

Marlowe continued, ignoring the detective. "It will give me a chance to push for greater communication between neighboring districts. My boys tell me Bragg had been swapping telegrams for weeks, looking into this thing. Pretty sharp detective work, actually, though it's a sad state of affairs when my people need a journalist to find their criminal. If we had been comparing notes with Crowley and Brahannasburg, Swift's spree should never have gone on this long. I've even got them talking about extending the telephone lines out to the more rural towns."

He stepped a little farther into the room. "Speaking of which, I've sent a telegram to Commander Bell in Gadston, just this afternoon," he continued. "Have you ever been to Gadston? It's small—much smaller than New Fiddleham—but I'm told it's very pleasant. A lot of open countryside down in Gad's Valley, too. Excellent for wildlife." For the first time since his arrival, he made eye contact with Charlie. "One of the benefits of becoming a commissioner, even just 'acting commissioner,' is that the job holds a lot of sway. My recommendation for the transfer of an upstanding young officer can hardly be ignored. You will need a new name, of course, but I think the paperwork can be arranged."

All of us took a moment to let the comment sink in. "Thank you, sir," said Charlie softly.

"I won't take any more of your time. Gentlemen. Miss." He nodded a good-bye and put a hand on the door. "Oh, and in case you haven't heard, the memorial will be this Sunday at noon. All five victims are to be honored in the same ceremony. Mayor Spade felt it would help everyone in town put this whole unpleasant business behind them."

"Thank you, Inspector," said Jackaby.

"Five?" I asked, before Marlowe could close the door.

He nodded. "Caught that, did you? This one's sharp. Yes, young lady, five. Three at the Emerald Arch Apartments, then Officer O'Doyle in the forest last night . . . and finally the tragic loss of the town's own Commissioner Swift."

"What?" I blurted.

Jackaby scowled darkly at the inspector. "Sounds about right."

Marlowe sighed. "People have a hard enough time believing in this sort of thing at all. When Swift was in charge, he forbade our giving credence to anything even remotely supernatural—said it hurt our public image for the official record to look like backwoods superstition. He was just using his position to hide, of course, but he wasn't entirely wrong, either. One monster in the newspaper is more than enough, and by this point, half the town will swear to you they saw a werewolf—even the ones who didn't see anything at all. It will be easier for everyone to accept if Swift is simply laid to rest as one more victim."

"Yes," Jackaby said with a sneer. "The truth can be so detrimental to one's credibility."

"Good day, Jackaby." Marlowe took his leave.

The weather warmed somewhat over the next few days, though the winter chill still hung about, crouching in shady corners to surprise passersby with the occasion sudden gust. The world had brightened. On the second morning after the incident, Jackaby arranged a carriage to Gad's Valley. He had wired an old acquaintance with a cottage where

Charlie could rest and recover under a new name. Then he could decide if he would resume his efforts to take root and build a life for himself, or return to traveling with his family.

Marlowe had sent a case with Charlie's effects, and he looked much more like himself in a clean pair of properly fitting clothes.

"Are you sure you'll be able to put New Fiddleham behind you?" Jackaby asked once we'd helped Charlie manage the walk to the cab. "You have an aura of unshakable allegiance. Don't try to deny it, it's downright sickening. Marlowe won't be there for you to tether your loyalties to him . . . nor will I."

Charlie smiled. "I guess I am . . . rather devoted," he told the detective, "but not to you. Nor to the chief inspector, although it was an honor to work with you both."

"Then who . . . ?" Jackaby's eyes darted to me, and I felt my cheeks flush at the notion.

Charlie looked away shyly. He leaned on Jackaby's shoulder for support and fumbled in the pocket of his coat. He held up his polished badge, standing up a little straighter as he did. "I took an oath, Detective."

Jackaby chuckled. "Ah. Of course. Lady Justice could not ask for a more stalwart watchdog."

The men shook hands, and Jackaby held open the carriage door. Charlie gave me a courteous nod. "Miss Rook. It has been a pleasure."

"You must write once you're settled in," I said.

His expression clouded. "I don't know if that would be wise. You have both been exceptionally kind, but not everyone is so understanding. I would hate to bring more trouble to your door because of . . . what I am. After everything that happened—everything the townspeople saw—well, some things are very hard to explain."

My heart sank. I stood mute, suddenly aware that this was a last good-bye.

"How auspicious," Jackaby chimed from the carriage door. "Unexplained phenomena just happen to be our specialty. No excuses. You know where to reach us."

Charlie allowed himself a smile and nodded his assent. I could have kissed them both.

I spent the remainder of the week mostly in the serenity of the third floor for my own recuperation. Although my chest felt better with each passing day, I would occasionally catch myself painfully on a deep breath or sudden turn. I wondered if the little pink scar would eventually vanish, or if my skin had been branded forever. I'm not entirely sure I would have wanted it gone—it was a private badge of my first real adventure.

I lay on the soft grass often, watching the reflections of the pond dance across the ceiling and enjoying the good company of Jenny and even Douglas. Jackaby, however, had made himself scarce as we approached the day of the memorial. Once, while I had nodded off on a carpet of wildflowers near the water's edge, I was awoken by Jenny's soft voice.

"She's doing very well," she was saying. "She'll have the scar to remember it by, but it's healing cleanly. Poor girl. She's still so young."

I kept my eyes closed and breathed evenly as Jackaby responded. "She's older than her years," he said.

"I think that might be sadder, somehow," Jenny breathed.

"Anyway, it's not her chest I'm concerned about—it's her head."

"Still deciding whether she's fit for the job?" asked the ghost.

"Oh, she'll do," answered Jackaby. "The question is, is this job fit for her?"

In the evening, I found myself back in the waiting room. The piles of paperwork and books, which had once occupied the desk, were still lying in a heap on the floor, having been shoved aside while the room served as an impromptu medical ward. Otherwise, the chamber looked much as it had on my first visit. I glanced around, remembering not to linger on the terrarium.

Poking out of a bin in the far corner, alongside two umbrellas and a croquet mallet, stood a polished iron cane, fitted with what I knew now to be a false grip. Swift's deadly pike was housed innocuously among the bric-a-brac, but it was a subtle memorial to his victims—and to my own blundering, which had nearly made me one of them.

Jackaby's eclectic home began to make a little more sense to me, then. The man had no portraits or photographs, but he had slowly surrounded himself with mementos of a fantastic past. Each little item, by the sheer nature of its being, told a story. Looking around was a little like being back on the dig, or like deciphering an ancient text, and I wondered what stories they would tell me if I only knew how to read them. How many carried fond memories? How many, like the redcap's polished weapon, were silent reminders of mistakes made or even lives lost?

Chapter Thirty

The memorial was a regal affair, and half the town seemed to have come out to mourn or to take in the spectacle. Heartfelt condolences and eager gossip were circulating through the gathering crowd as Jackaby and I arrived. The event was originally to be held within the small church adjacent to Rosemary's Green, but the sheer number of attendees had moved the service outdoors. A light layer of snow dusted the ground and the air held a chill, but the day itself was cloudless and clear.

Jenny had convinced Jackaby to forgo his usual bulky, ragged coat in favor of a more respectful black one she had found in the attic. In lieu of his myriad pockets, he insisted on strapping across it a faded brown knapsack. I hefted the thing to hand it to him before we left, and, small though it may have been, it felt like a sack of bricks.

"It's a memorial," I said. "What have you got in there that you could you possibly need at a memorial?"

"That sort of thinking is why you, young lady, have a scar on your sternum, and why my priceless copy of the *Apotropaicon* has a broken spine. I prefer preparedness to a last-moment scramble, thank you."

We found a position toward the back of the assembly and waited for the ceremony to begin. Still fuming about the decision to cover up the truth about Swift, Jackaby stared daggers at Marlowe and Mayor Spade, seated at the front of the crowd. Because two of the deceased were respected members of the police, at least according to public record, the whole matter was being conducted with great pomp and sobriety. All five coffins were hewn of matching oak, probably far more expensive models than most of the families could have afforded on their own. I wondered what, if anything, they had put inside Swift's to weigh it down.

Over the susurrus of the crowd, I noticed the faintest of gentle melodies slowly growing, rising and falling like a building wave. The melancholy tune reminded me of the late Mrs. Morrigan. Focused as I was on the sound, I barely recognized that Jackaby had been speaking.

"Sorry, what was that?"

"I said that I have come to a decision, Miss Rook. I have

given this a great deal of thought, and I've decided not to utilize you in the field any further."

"What?"

"Oh, don't worry, I'm not giving you the proverbial boot. You will still be tasked with cataloguing old files and tending to the house and accounts. I believe Douglas also had a collection of notes that he had not yet properly filed–I should certainly like you to look into that when you get a chance . . ."

"You don't want me along? But why?"

"Because the last thing I need is another ghost hanging over my head–or worse, another damned duck. I would feel more comfortable knowing you were safe in the house. Although, come to think of it, it really is best if you avoid the Dangerous Documents section of the library . . . and don't fiddle with any of the containers in the laboratory . . . and generally steer clear of the whole north wing of the second floor."

I felt my ears grow hot and my heart dip, but wasn't entirely certain why. I squared my shoulders to my employer and took a deep breath. "Mr. Jackaby, I am not a child. I can make my own choices, even the bad ones. I have spent my entire life preparing for adventure, and then watching from the front step while it left without me. Since I picked up my first book, I have been reading about amazing discoveries, intrepid explorers, and fantastic creatures, all while scarcely setting foot outside my own house. My father used to tell me I had read more than most of his graduate students. Yet, for all my preparation, the only thing remotely daring I'd ever done before meeting you was running away from university to hunt for dinosaurs–which amounted to nothing more than four months of mud and rocks." I stopped to breathe.

"I didn't know you hunted dinosaurs, Miss Rook."

"You never asked."

"No, I didn't. I suppose I don't tend to focus on that sort of thing. That is what impressed me about you on your first day–your attention to the banal and negligible."

"Once again, not the most flattering way to put it, but thanks, I'll take it all the same. As for your decision, my answer is no."

"There wasn't a question. My decision is still final."

I wanted to protest, but the priest had wound his way up to the makeshift podium at the head of the crowd, and the crowd was settling. I bit my tongue as the ceremony began, but I would not be content to let the matter lie.

With the congregation quieted, I found the source of the lilting music. Four women with long, silvery hair and pale gowns stood just to the left of the podium. As various speakers took the stand to deliver sentimental eulogies, the gray women quietly wept and hummed, their cries carrying tender chords across the assembly. As the proceedings drew to a close, the women began to sing the most beautiful, mournful dirge. It was unmistakably akin to

Mrs. Morrigan's final song, but magnified in intensity and complexity. Their voices harmonized, elegant melodies and countermelodies weaving a tapestry of sound that drew tears from every listener, but with it grew an overwhelming sense of peace as well.

When they had finished, the ladies knelt before Mrs. Morrigan's coffin before stepping away to the churchyard gates. I caught sight of Mona O'Connor, who embraced each tenderly as they passed. The last of them brushed Mona's curls of red hair back behind her ear, and kissed her on the forehead, like a kindly aunt. Mona held her hand a moment longer, and then the woman stepped out of the churchyard gates, vanishing into the bright daylight.

All through the crowd handkerchiefs appeared, and tears were wiped away as the people began to disperse. Before withdrawing, the young woman with blond ringlets I had seen outside the Emerald Arch stepped timidly forward and set a white carnation on Arthur Bragg's coffin. A few more came up to offer similar tokens: flowers, silver coins, and even a box of cigars on the late Mr. Henderson's casket. Only one coffin remained bare.

"Shall we resume our discussion over lunch?" I suggested to my employer, but Jackaby's gaze was fixed on the front of the crowd. "I'd like to swing by Chandler's Market on the way if you don't mind," I persisted. "I do still owe a troll a fish." My employer made no indication he had heard me, instead taking sudden, deliberate strides toward the head of the assembly. I followed, squeezing past the exodus of mourners like a trout swimming upstream.

As I reached the front, Jackaby stood before Swift's coffin. "Let's not have a scene, Jackaby," Marlowe was saying. "Just let it go."

"It's an insult," Jackaby said. He gestured to the coffin. "It's a dishonor to the dead!"

"Jackaby . . ." Marlowe growled. His muscles tensed, and I could see he didn't want to have to forcibly remove the detective from a quiet memorial service. "These nice families just want to say their good-byes in peace."

"But it isn't right," continued my employer, opening his little brown satchel, "that our dear, honorable commissioner should be the only friendless corpse without so much as a lily at his head. Let me see, I'm sure I have some appropriate token in here."

Marlowe looked dubious, but he stood down as Jackaby made a show of rummaging. "Ah, here we are. He was so fond of these." It took a swing of his arms to get them up onto the box, but the echoing clank of the redcap's impossibly heavy iron shoes as they crunched into the wood was satisfying. A bent and charred piece of the leg brace still clung to one, fastened by a rivet at the ankle. Jackaby left the explaining to Marlowe and marched away.

I caught up just outside the gates. "I know, I know . . . ," he said before I could comment. "I don't need to make things difficult for Marlowe."

"You don't need to make them easy, either," I said. My employer raised an eyebrow at me as we walked. "Swift tries to kill me and gets to be a public hero. Charlie saves my life, and now he's a public enemy. You don't owe me any explanations."

Jackaby nodded contentedly as we headed back to 926 Augur Lane.

Chapter Thirty-One

The following morning, I planted myself at the front desk and began sorting the mound of bills, case notes, and receipts that lay before me. Jackaby had conveniently disappeared before we could return to discussing my future duties, so I resolved to just make the best of the task. After several hours of stacking and shuffling, I was finally drawn out from behind the mess by my employer's return. He hung his scarf and hat on the hook without apparently noticing me.

"Good morning, sir. I didn't know you had gone out."

"The postman's come," he said, riffling through a handful of mail. He paused on a small brown parcel, pursing his lips.

"What's that, then? Something you ordered?"

"No." He tucked it hastily beneath the rest of the mail. "Or yes, actually, but I'm not sure I should . . ." He trailed off. "This one's addressed to you. Here." Still without making eye contact, he dropped an envelope into the empty space I had cleared on the desk, and continued on his way down the crooked hallway.

The letter was from Mr. Barker of Gadston, Charlie's new identity. Gad's Valley, he wrote, was as lovely as Marlowe had suggested. Commander Bell had offered him a quiet post on the police force there as soon as his injuries healed, and Charlie was strongly inclined to accept. He was feeling better every day, and took frequent opportunities to slip out to enjoy the countryside now that he was walking again. The detective and I, he insisted in his postscript, must come and visit when next we had the chance. Since Charlie's departure, I had tried to put my feelings for him to rest, but butterflies rose in my stomach at the thought of seeing him again.

Jackaby burst energetically back into the room just as I finished reading the note. "We've gotten word from Charlie," I informed him.

"No time for that now, I'm afraid. I've urgent business in town."

"Is something wrong?"

"I should say so, fantastically wrong!" He brandished a letter of his own, waving the page with enthusiasm. "A woman with a lamentably forgettable name has asked me to look into a matter of her ailing cat. The cat, I believe, is called Mrs. Wiggles."

"Bit of a step down, isn't it? From catching a serial killer to a sick pet?"

"Ah, but the details are delightful." Jackaby tossed his scarf around his neck and pulled on his knit hat. "It seems Mrs. Wiggles has recently shrunk in stature, begun to molt, and started lounging in her water bowl for hours at a stretch. Most perplexingly, she has begun growing scales from tip to tail as well. The veterinarian just made useless jokes about it being 'rather fishy,' and then prescribed some skin ointment, the tit. The whole thing is marvelously odd."

"And you do love odd," I said. "Let me just get my coat. Where are we going, anyway?"

"You are going nowhere," Jackaby said flatly. "As for me, I am tracking this post back to its origin. There are distinct traces of the supernatural saturating the paper—no doubt remnants of the lady's curious pet. The document will have left an aura along its path, one that I can navigate as long as I make haste before it fades."

"Alternately," I said, tilting my head to peek at the back of the torn envelope in my employer's hand, "we could try 1206 Campbell Street."

Jackaby glanced at the return address and then back to me. "I suppose your approach might complement my own in the field—but no!" He shook his head, the ends of his ridiculous cap flapping as he attempted to steel himself in his resolution. "Just think how it would look to your parents," he said, "if they found out you left your civilized books and classrooms to go running all over town after supernatural nonsense. Not to mention how you must look to the townsfolk right here in New Fiddleham. They'll think you're as bad as I am."

I considered this for a moment before responding. "I have ceased concerning myself with how things look to others," I said. "As someone told me recently, others are generally wrong."

His eyes glinted for just a moment, but he fought against the suggestion. "No, it's for your own good, Miss Rook. You're staying here. Marlowe was right. This business is not fit for an impressionable young lady."

"I hate to break it to you, Mr. Jackaby," I said, "but the damage is done. The impression is made. I don't want to wait at the doorstep any longer. I want to go dashing off after giants and pixies and dragons. I want to meet with mysterious strangers at crossroads and turn widdershins in the moonlight. I want to listen to the fish, Jackaby. Come to think of it, I am already keeping correspondence with a dog, with whom, I must admit, I find myself rather smitten. Also, I'm secretly hoping Mrs. Wiggles ends up a full halibut when this is through, because that would save me a trip to the market . . . although if Hatun's troll keeps company with a tabby, perhaps he wouldn't much appreciate a meal that used to be a cat."

Jackaby stared. "I've already ruined you, haven't I?"

"Looks that way."

"And I suppose there's nothing to be done about it?"

"Not a thing."

"Well then, perhaps you should have this, after all." Jackaby reached into a pocket and produced the brown paper package, turning it over in his hands. He tapped the little parcel against his palm and seemed to consider for a long moment, then extended his arm and handed it to me. "It isn't anything, really," he muttered. "Empty symbolism."

Curious, I unwrapped the package. The paper fell away and I smiled. The notebook's cover was smooth and black, cut from expensive leather. I flipped it open, top-wise. The pages were pristinely white, and a handy loop toward the top held a small, sharp pencil. It fit comfortably in my palm and would slide easily into a pocket. On the back cover had been inscribed the initials "A.R." beneath a relief of a blackbird in flight—a rook.

"Standard police books are just flimsy cardstock, but you mentioned something about leather, I believe. I had that little stationery store on Market Street do it up as a custom job. Oh yes, and this." Jackaby rummaged through his pockets and produced a magnifying glass, about five inches in diameter with a simple wooden handle. "I have others, if that one won't do. Also, while we're on the subject, I have given the issue some thought, and I wouldn't mind if you called yourself a detective." He handed me the glass.

"Really?" I laughed. "I would be a proper investigator instead of an assistant?"

"Certainly not," he said with a dismissive wave of his hand. "The nature of your job would remain the same. Titles, like appearances, are of very little interest to me. It seems to make you happy, though, so call yourself what you like. You've dropped some paper on the floor. Do see that you attend to it."

I thought it over for a moment and decided I was still going to enjoy it, meaningless or not. "Thank you, Jackaby."

"You're very welcome. It's good to have you on the team." The hint of a grin peeked up from beneath his long scarf. "Well, what are we waiting for, then? Get your coat, Miss Rook. There's adventure to be had!"

Supplemental Material:
The History of the Three Forks

During the events of the Case of the Silent Scream, an item belonging to my employer was confiscated by the police as evidence. Following the whole ordeal, Jackaby was quite vocal with his indignation at their failure to return it promptly. A "miscarriage of justice," he called it. "Unprofessional. Downright disreputable. I fear I may be forced to declare 'shenanigans'!"

After some time, I was able to convince him that it was most likely a normal bureaucratic delay, and that a polite letter requesting the item's return would likely do the trick. What follows is the letter Jackaby dictated, with just a little of my own editorial revision:

To the attention of the New Fiddleham Police Department: You've got my middle-C, and I would like it back. To convey the importance of its swift return, I will share with you its unique history.

There was once an old church. It sat in the center of town, as was often the case in those days, and it was in every way the heart of the little community. Neighbors came to meet for celebrations, babies were baptized, lovers were married, and funeral processions commenced at that humble church. The heartbeat of the little town rang with the sound of church bells.

In the bell tower hung not one, but three masterfully crafted bells. On very special occasions, the vicar would ring all three together, and their notes would complement one another in a rich chord, but more often they rang alone, each bell serving a distinct purpose.

In 1861, a civil war shook the country. Men and boys who had grown up to the tolling of the church bells were called away, and those left behind did all they could to support the war effort. The vicar at that time felt it was his duty to contribute as well, and so he offered up the beautiful bells to be melted down and reduced to cannons or blades.

The very day the bells were removed, the vicar developed a terrible fever and a sharp ringing in his ears. Relics of the church had been reduced to weapons, fated to help brothers slaughter brothers. It was an unholy day, indeed. When his temperature finally broke, the vicar found he had lost his hearing entirely.

Meanwhile, the soldier responsible for their transport was overcome with an urge to preserve at least some memento of the magnificent bells. Against orders, and against his own better judgment, he saw that small scraps of each were set aside. These he brought back to his own hometown and presented to a master craftsman he knew capable of reforging the metal. A bell, once rung, wants to ring, and he asked the man if he could return to them their voices in some way.

The smith melted and cast the shards into three wholly unique tuning forks. There was never any question in his mind as to which tone each fork should possess, for the metal sang to him from the first pump of the bellows. When he had finished, they each hummed the very same notes they had rung in the bell tower.

There was something stranger still about the forks. Each had become a pure and concentrated version of its former self, and carried with it the emotional power of its past incarnation.

The lowest, its toll accustomed to sounding the slow announcement of funerals, was imbued with a tone of somber tragedy. Those who heard it could not help but shed a tear. Not so powerful as a banshee's keen, the note was like a single moment stolen from her complex melody of sorrow. Still, the sensation would wash instantly over any who now heard it chime.

The second fork, forged from the middle bell, had faithfully rung every hour for nearly six centuries. It had been a comfort to the townsfolk, and a beacon to guide them home when the mist and fog had turned them about in the hills. The middle fork, when sounded, issued a sense of normalcy and calm. It cut through the fog of fear and turmoil to reassure any in earshot.

The last fork, the highest, came from the bell used to announce the most joyous occasions: the births of children, baptisms, marriages, and all manner of celebrations. The fork forged from this bell could elate listeners with a single sound. While its tone held out, it became possible to forget the everyday stresses of life and be overcome with happiness.

These artifacts played a small role in the recent unpleasantness, which my assistant, against my advisement, has given the ridiculous title of "The Case of the Silent Scream." During our investigation, I carefully selected the second fork, a middle-C, to instill in the doomed Mr. Henderson a sense of calm. This was a careful and deliberate choice. Had I rung the low tone, his misery would only have intensified. The highest note would have sent him into a state of madness from two supernatural sources pulling his mind toward opposite emotional extremes. The implementation of this invaluable resource proved an integral step in unlocking the mystery and putting a stop to the murders.

I hope, now, that you can appreciate the value of the complete set in my line of work. Miss Rook has suggested that a written reminder might aid in expediting the return to me of the aforementioned middle-C, still being held in evidence in spite of the closing question.

When Jackaby had finished dictating and left the room, I wrote a second letter. It read: *Please return Jackaby's tuning fork. He's getting even more obnoxious than usual.* This I sent out with the morning's post.

The courier arrived that evening.

Jackaby was pleasantly surprised to find that the letter had prevailed. "At least someone in that station house has some sense," he remarked. "I scarcely believed the dunderheads would bother to read it at all, but look."

He passed me the note as he exhumed his property from the wrapping. The processing officer had written just three words. I smiled as I read them. *I completely understand.*